C.E.
X

Lincoln's Ransom

A Western Story

Also by Tim Champlin in Large Print:

The Last Campaign
The Survivor
Deadly Season
Swift Thunder
King of the Highbinders
Colt Lightning
Dakota Gold

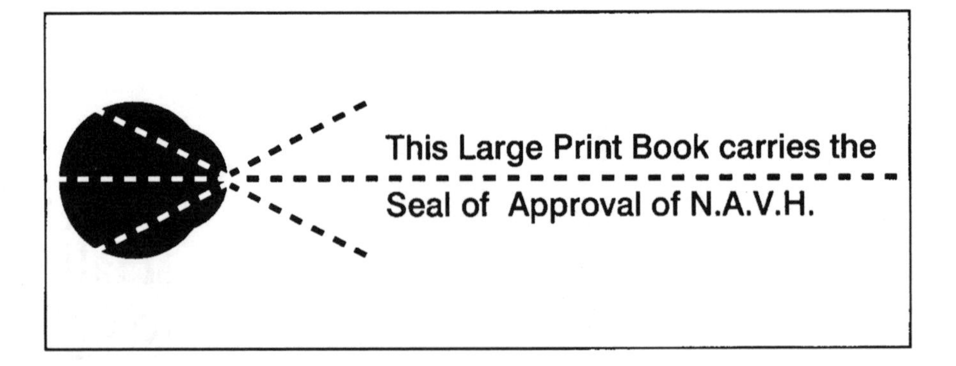

Lincoln's Ransom

A Western Story

TIM CHAMPLIN

G.K. Hall & Co. • Thorndike, Maine

Published in 2000 by arrangement with
Golden West Literary Agency.

G.K. Hall Large Print Western Series.

The text of this Large Print edition is unabridged.
Other aspects of the book may vary from the original edition.

Set in 16 pt. Plantin by Al Chase.

Printed in the United States on permanent paper.

Library of Congress Cataloging-in-Publication Data

Champlin, Tim, 1937–
Lincoln's ransom : a western story / Tim Champlin.
p. cm.
ISBN 0-7838-0313-3 (lg. print : hc : alk. paper)
1. Lincoln, Abraham, 1809–1865 — Tomb — Fiction.
2. Body snatching — Illinois — History — 19th century —
Fiction. 3. Large type books. I. Title.
PS3553.H265 L5 2000
813′.54—dc21 00-024242

For my granddaughter,
Abigail,
on whose day of birth this novel was begun

Author's Note

This book is a work of fiction, but the theft of Lincoln's body is based on an actual event. A special thanks to Mrs. Nanette Holbrook for graciously allowing her charming personality and appearance to be borrowed and twisted by the author into the fictional character of Janice Kinealy.

Prologue

September 18, 1863
North Georgia

"Double quick! Close up in the rear!"

Sterling Packard scrambled into line with the other men, fumbling to fix the bayonet to his musket. Scattered banging of small-arms fire increased.

"Guide center!" The sergeant swung his arm. "Forward at a. . . ." The boom of artillery blotted out the rest of his words as he pointed toward the federal line some three hundred yards away through the woods and across a meadow.

Packard glanced to his left at the pale face of a recent conscript from Mount Pleasant. His own stomach was in a knot, but he tried to smile and nod reassuringly as the skirmish line started forward among the trees. Packard gripped his musket and broke into a trot, part of a ragged line abreast. A yell burst from his lips as taut nerves gave way. The shout was taken up by other men to his left and right. A few paused to shoot and reload, but the range was not yet effective, and experience told him to hold his fire and ignore the spent leaden hail falling all around. Thirty yards. Sixty yards. A hundred jogging steps sweeping them toward the line of cannon that bucked and thundered, belching great clouds of white smoke. The earth quaked and trembled with the concussion, and grapeshot screamed overhead, showering them with shredded leaves and twigs. Balls whistled around their ears like the escape valves of ten thousand steam engines. Bullets were thwacking against tree trunks with that peculiar thudding sound he had come to know so well.

General Forrest's cavalry had opened the battle and now needed support, but infantry stood no chance across an open meadow into the maws of six-pounders and Parrott guns. The terrible cacophony numbed his senses, and he felt as if all the fires of hell had been turned loose in one mighty roar to devour the opposing forces of men.

Just ahead of him a man dropped his musket and pitched forward. Packard knew he shouldn't stop but, on impulse, crouched to aid the stricken man. He rolled his fallen comrade onto his back and instantly saw it was too late. Shrapnel had disemboweled the man. Packard had no time to be appalled or sickened by the bloody sight. Just as he started to rise, a bullet struck his left side like a red-hot hornet.

"Aaaahhh!" The shock spun him half around, and he sat down hard, dropping his musket. Surprise, as much as pain, jarred his mind for a few seconds, so that he was unable to grasp what had happened. After many weeks and many battles without a scratch, he'd almost begun to feel he

was immune from injury. But then his mind started to function again, and his imagination leapt suddenly out of control with wild forebodings, even as his hand sought his side. Warm blood was already soaking his cotton shirt under the threadbare woolen jacket. Yanking the shirt-tail out, he twisted around to squint at the wound in the uncertain, pale-green light filtering through the canopy of trees. There was so much blood he couldn't see the hole, but his probing fingers told him there was no exit wound.

Packard hoped the slug had missed his kidney as he pressed the soggy shirt back against the wound and looked around for someone to help. But the line of skirmishers had swept on ahead into the meadow and were too far away to hear him shout above the roar. The booming artillery barrage slackened, and he could hear the ripping sound of musketry, as if someone had touched off a string of Chinese firecrackers. The clashing armies moved away, leaving only the smell of burnt gunpowder drifting on the light breeze. No one was left behind to assist him, he realized as he looked around. Bodies of the slain lay here and there in his field of vision, their clothing clawed and rumpled, as if someone had littered the woods with sacks of dirty laundry.

He got to his knees, then carefully to his feet, feeling the warm wetness flowing down inside his belt. Leaning against a tree, he came to the hard, clear realization that he might be joining his dead comrades shortly as life continued to drain out of the hole in his side. The thought made him suddenly queasy, and, in spite of the September heat, a cold sweat burst from the pores all over his body. He began to feel faint, and slid to a sitting position. Taking deep, slow breaths to calm himself, he leaned back against the rough bark of an oak and closed his eyes. He had to stop the bleeding before he got too weak to move, or passed out. Packard stirred himself to action and struggled to a big tree a few feet away, ripped a handful of moss from its north side, and pressed it to the wound. The cool moss felt good, and he didn't care how many bugs might be in it. He forced himself to sit quietly for a minute, then added another handful of moss, as the process seemed to be working. He fervently hoped the bullet hadn't clipped a blood vessel.

Finally, he felt the blood returning to his face as the pain and shock began subsiding to a deep, dull ache. *What now?* He carefully eased out of his jacket and shirt and tied the shirt around his waist tightly to hold the moss in place. He slipped the jacket back on over his bare torso and, removing the bayonet so he could use his musket as a walking stick, made his way slowly back toward the Confederate lines. But there were no Confederate lines. This battle, opening that morning a few miles south of Chattanooga, was just a series of disconnected clashes with units surging back and forth through the thick timber, now and then bursting out into sunny meadows. In this wild disarray, litter-bearers were few and scattered, and field hospitals were usually some tent or commandeered cabin with a table where a surgeon could practice his bloody trade.

But the fortunes of war did not concern Packard at the moment. It was personal survival. Everything in his being wanted to live, to keep from sinking down and rotting away into the earth like the hundreds of other men he'd seen die around him in the past few months. His natural instinct made toward life. His intellect accepted the fact that he would eventually cease to be. Yet his fear of pain and the unknown made him shudder at the empty eyes and cold breath of the grinning death's head that dogged his halting steps.

Leaning on the musket cane, he scuffed on through the dead leaves, tripping over creepers and fallen branches, detouring around massive rotting logs and clumps of blackberry vines. Gradually, the noise of battle faded until it only fringed his consciousness.

The early afternoon sun was still high, screened by thick foliage, and gave him no hint of direction. He tried to backtrack but was confused as the featureless forest stretched away on every side. He felt light-headed, and his mind began to drift. He ceased to be an injured refugee from a war and became, instead, the last man on earth, wandering, lost and alone, through a never-ending forest. Like hovering giants, pines and cottonwoods and oaks towered more than a hundred feet over his head. No birds cheered the day. No squirrels or rabbits scampered through the decaying humus on the forest floor. He was totally alone.

Suddenly a deer came crashing through the dry leaves and bounded past, not twenty yards away, fleeing the terrible human commotion. Packard's heart pounded in sudden alarm, causing the wound to throb and jarring him back to reality. His clothes were damp with terrified sweating. Excessive perspiration and loss of blood had brought on a terrible thirst. But he'd dropped his canteen along with his blanket roll when he was shot. The wound was burning and aching fearfully as he steadied himself against a tree and slowly straightened up. If he could find Chickamauga Creek, he could not only slake his thirst but could possibly follow the stream to find help, if the Yankees didn't have control of the creek.

A thin, high-pitched screaming drew his eyes upward. Through a break in the elms and tall pines overhead, a hawk wheeled away from a closely pursuing black crow that was cawing raucously. Then the two birds disappeared, and he could still hear them for several more seconds. Even nature was at war, he reflected, but probably for a better reason than the armies of men.

Packard remembered wanting to serve under General Patrick Cleburne, the dashing, Irish-born leader who was so popular with his soldiers. But a man could be killed whether he was following one commander or another, on horse or afoot, in the Army of Tennessee or Virginia. He'd seen thousands fall, or die of mortified wounds in "hospitals" during the past few months, and he wondered idly if there would be anybody left alive when this war was over. It was a war of attrition, more than of conquest. His befuddled mind saw the dispossessed Cherokees and Creeks once more filtering back onto the depopulated land, wondering at these insane white men who had killed each other off. For some reason, this image struck him as hilarious, and he laughed aloud. He was so light-headed he began to lose his balance and stumbled onto a clear, well-defined trail curving away through the silent woods. The dead leaves and pine needles of the path had been torn up here and there by the sharp hoofs of horses. But the spider webs he clawed from his mouth and eyes every few yards told him no one had been down this trail for at least a couple of hours, and probably longer, so the chances of encountering another soldier of either side were slim.

Once more Packard's mind slipped a cog in time. He saw himself standing in front of the small classroom of students, chalk dust on his hands, explaining, cajoling, encouraging. Over time, he had brought forth reading and writing skills, and even an appreciation of literature to a few of the older students. Teaching was often more frustration than satisfaction, but now it seemed a peaceful haven. Too soon the hands of the clock had spun off the busy hours and days to be followed by the fiery tornado of war that had swept everything away. Maybe it was his fate to end his life now, at the age of twenty-five, in this hellish green wood that was so hot and dry, and where he couldn't seem to get enough air, where crazed men rained fire and brimstone and screeching canister on one another.

The sun was farther down the sky. A breeze sprang up, combing dead leaves from the limbs of the forest giants and sending down a cascade of red and brown and gold. He welcomed the cooling wind on his feverish face. He didn't remember sitting down, but found himself resting against a tree. His mouth and throat were parched as he struggled to his feet, body aching, head reeling. When his vision steadied, he started down the trail once more.

After what seemed an interminable time, the trail curved and Chickamauga Creek appeared, shining in the dappled sunshine. The sight gave him a surge of energy, and he staggered off the path toward the water, half rolling down the foot-high bank into a clear, shallow pool. Splashing the cool water over his face and head gave blessed relief. Then he put his lips to the surface and drank deeply, coughing and sputtering in his haste.

Finally he was sated and crawled up to lie, face down, in the shade on a gravel bar, his legs still in the creek. He would just rest a minute to calm the queasiness in his too-full stomach, then he would see about cleaning his wound. One minute became five, then ten. His limbs were heavy, the wet gravel cool to his cheek.

Long, fearful nightmares tortured Packard before he opened his eyes again. It took several seconds for him to realize he was lying on his back, staring at a board ceiling about eight feet above him. His boots had been removed.

"Ah, you're finally back with us," a cheery female voice said. A woman moved into his view, and a cool, smooth hand covered his forehead. "Good. Your fever's gone." She leaned over, and he got his first view of a young woman with flowing brown hair. The slight pain and physical heaviness when he moved told him he wasn't dead.

"Where am I?" he asked weakly.

Briefly she told him that she had gone to the creek for water less than a half mile from this log house, had found him on the gravel bar, and determined he was still alive. She had left her water kegs, wrestled him across the back of her mule, and brought him here.

"Who are you?"

"Janice Kinealy," she said, regarding him with concerned brown eyes.

"Oh," he replied, as if this explained everything. He tried to focus his thoughts. "My name's Sterling Packard."

She took his hand, and he tried to converse with her. But his eyes were heavy. The breaking fever had left him very weary, and shortly he fell into a restful sleep.

When he awoke again, it was dark outside, and she was dozing in a chair by his bed with a lamp turned low on the table. When he stirred, she awoke, and they began to talk in low tones. He asked her about the severity of his wound.

"Looked like it was probably a spent ball that hit you in the side," she said, "because it went through and lodged just under the skin of your back. Only had to slit the skin and pop it out." She brushed back his hair and felt his forehead. "Still cool. Good. It wasn't the bullet that almost did you in. It was the fever and the infection."

"I'm thirsty."

She took a canteen from the table and helped him drink. "Take it easy, now. Not too much."

"How long have I been out?" he asked when she pulled the canteen away.

"The better part of two days. You missed the second day of the battle. The Yankees have retreated toward Chattanooga."

The running fight, the din of battle, the shock of the wound — it all seemed unreal and distant, until he moved and felt the catch in his side.

"I'm still tired." He lay back and closed his eyes.

"That's good. Get some rest. I'll be in the next room, sleeping, if you need anything."

He wasn't even aware when she left.

Packard was awake but a little groggy, when Janice entered the room. The sun was up, and a warm breeze blew fitfully across the bed from the window.

"Well, you've got some color back," she greeted him. "Ready to have that bandage changed?"

Without waiting for an answer, she got briskly to work, easing him over on his side. The pain was now more of a sore-muscle ache, when he moved. She loosened the cotton bandage that was tied around his body and, very gently, pulled the wide bandage away from his left flank. She examined it closely, then sniffed the bloody stain on the white cotton. A slight smile stretched her full lips. "So far, so good," she said, straightening up. "No putrefaction. If we can keep it clean, you should heal up fine. Here, want to take a look?" she asked. Her shoulder-length chestnut hair brushed his face as she slid an arm behind his back and raised him just enough so he could get a look at his left side. The wound was still raw but had been cleaned, and there was no sign of infection.

"Did you clean it with carbolic?" he asked.

"No. Didn't have any. Just washed it off with some lye soap as best I could, then sprinkled some black powder in the wound, and lit it."

"What?"

"Sure. Cauterized and sterilized it at the same time."

"I'm glad I wasn't awake for that," he said with a wan smile.

"So am I. But it usually works when you have nothing else. By the way," she added, admonishing him with a mock frown, "next time you're shot, don't be stuffing that dirty moss in the wound."

"I hope there isn't a next time. And it was the only thing I could find at the moment."

"Best thing to stop the bleeding is spider webs. There are lots of them in the woods this time of year."

"Ugh. Spider spit." He grimaced.

She smiled at him while testing the dryness of some strips of white cloth fluttering lazily in the breeze on a makeshift cord clothesline at the open window. Apparently satisfied, she took them down and proceeded to re-bandage his side. Some remaining edges of lace told Packard the dressings had probably been torn from her petticoat. When she finished, the wrappings felt snug and comfortable around his bare torso.

"Now, for some food," she said, walking out of the room. She returned a minute later with a bowl of soup, and Packard recognized the delicious aroma he had been smelling since he had awakened.

She put the bowl on the side table and propped him in a sitting position at the head of the bunk. Then she pulled a chair close and began spooning the soup into his mouth.

"I can do it . . . my hands aren't hurt," he protested, feeling well enough to be embarrassed at having to be fed.

She handed over the spoon, but held the bowl where he could reach it.

He could feel her critical gaze on him as he ate.

"Where are you from?" she asked.

"Nashville," he replied. "What about you?"

"Bardstown, Kentucky."

"Not far away," he murmured, looking at her, trying to guess her age.

They talked as he ate, and he told her about having been a schoolteacher in a west Tennessee village.

"Did you like it?" she asked, more to make polite conversation than for information, he thought.

He nodded, chewing some barley in the soup. "It was barely a livelihood. But more satisfying than clerking in a store, and a lot easier than farming."

"What will you do when this is over?" she asked softly, looking at him as if he were the last soldier in Confederate gray.

"Don't know." He shook his head. "Haven't thought that far ahead. Surviving is my main object right now."

"Well, if I'm any judge, you'll survive this." She nodded at his wound.

"Is your husband farming this land, or is he a soldier?" Packard asked, noting her wedding ring as he placed the spoon back in the bowl, indicating he was finished.

"Neither. We're just passing through."

It seemed a rather evasive answer, but he was too tired to care. With a weary sigh, he laid his head back on the folded blanket at the head of the bunk. For the first time since he'd been shot, he felt as if he were actually going to live. And he had this woman — a total stranger — to thank for it. He rested his eyes on her classic features — the straight nose, the arching brows, the slightly prominent cheekbones above the smooth planes of her face. He found himself wondering if Helen of Troy might have looked like this. " 'The face that launched a thousand ships and burned the topless towers of Ilium . . . ,' " he murmured.

"What?"

"Nothing." He felt a slight twinge of regret that she was married. "Why did you rescue me?" he asked after a short silence, thinking she was probably in sympathy with the Southern cause.

She shrugged. "I couldn't just leave you there to die," she said simply.

"Well, ma'am, I'm mighty grateful to you."

"The name is Janice."

It could have been the sultry heat, but he thought her complexion seemed to glow a little more at his expression of gratitude.

She got up quickly, her long dress rustling. "You need to sleep. I'll look in on you a little later."

"There are hundreds of men dying all around

us in these woods. Why in hell did you drag this one back here to die? And in our bedroom at that!" James Kinealy glowered at his wife.

Janice turned away so he couldn't see the hurt in her face. She busied herself stirring the pot of soup on the cookstove, feeling the familiar stab of denigration in her stomach.

"No, he won't die," she replied firmly, her back still to him. "At least, he won't die from this wound."

She ladled out a bowl of the steaming soup and set it on the table for him. But the stocky man was carefully placing stoppered bottles of various chemicals in a wooden box and stuffing rags in around them.

"What are you doing?" she asked.

"As soon as Rafferty gets back from fetching the water you didn't get, we'll load the press into the wagon and be ready to move out of here by dark."

"Do we have to leave?" she asked. "The soldiers have moved off to the north. They won't find us."

"Can't take the chance," he grunted, shutting the lid on the box and slipping a padlock through the hasp. "Military officers are no respecters of property. There's a command post near Lee and Gordon's Mill, not two miles away. They're liable to bust in here any time and appropriate this house. We can't be caught printing phony money. We'll go deeper into the mountains for a few days until it's safe to move again."

"What about him?" she asked, nodding across the dogtrot at the other room of the two-room cabin.

"He's a Southern boy. We'll leave word with the first Rebel troops we see."

She realized it was probably too risky to remain here, and any further protest would draw her husband's quick wrath. But the thought of leaving the wounded man pained her.

The expression on her face must have revealed her feelings, because he paused in his packing and looked closely at her. "I guess you always were soft about bringing home injured animals," he said in a milder tone. "Go see to him while you can. . . ."

Packard came out of a doze at the tag end of the day to the sound of a man's voice somewhere outside the door. "We'll move out as soon as it's dark. Everything's packed."

A burly man with thick hair and mustache looked around the door frame, as if to confirm that Packard was still alive and well.

A minute later, Janice came in and stood by his bed. The late afternoon sun, pouring through the open window, was lighting her dark hair and brown eyes with a luminous glow. She squeezed his hand and looked at him. "You'll be all right now. We have to leave, but we'll send someone for you." She set a full canteen on the bed, then bent and kissed his forehead.

How do you thank someone for your life? He

opened his mouth to try, but she put her fingers on his lips. "Get well and stay well," she said. "Or you've put me to a lot of trouble for nothing." Then, with one last, lingering look, she was gone.

The next morning he was found and taken into one of the units of Breckenridge's command until he was well enough to be returned to his own outfit. After two months of recovery, he was given the job of orderly for General Thomas Wood and managed to serve in various clerical positions until he was mustered out three days after Appomattox.

Chapter One

October 26, 1876
Springfield, Illinois

It was the craziest idea he'd ever heard — stealing Abraham Lincoln's body from the tomb for ransom. If this gang of counterfeiters had spent years cudgeling their brains, they couldn't have come up with a scheme that would rile up the citizenry quicker than desecrating the final resting place of their late, beloved President. But Sterling Packard was into the plot up to his fake identity, and dared not back out now. He leaned back in his chair and glanced at the four other men who slouched around the vacant tables in Kinealy's saloon. He hoped his half-bored expression gave no clue to the icy fingers of suppressed fear and excitement that were clutching at his stomach. His life wouldn't be worth a three-cent piece if they knew he was actually a Secret Service operative, posing as a professional grave-robber.

James "Big Jim" Kinealy had closed his saloon two hours before midnight to hold this secret strategy session. But only a few minutes into the meeting an argument was breaking out over who was to blame for the aborted plot four months earlier.

"Let's get this straight." Kinealy said, setting his beer glass on the bar and turning to face the four men. "I'm in charge of this operation, and what I say goes. No questions. Got that?"

There was a murmur of assent as the others nodded their allegiance. In the few moments of silence that followed, a hard gust of wind from the late October storm rattled the shuttered windows.

"If there's another incident of drinking and blabbing to whores, I'm gone for good," Kinealy went on, raking the fingers of one big hand through his thick, graying hair, obscuring the center part. "We'd all be in jail right now if the Lincoln Memorial Association hadn't thought my plan was too incredible to be true." The lines in his broad, rugged face were deepened by the overhead light of the coal-oil chandelier.

"They can't arrest nobody for rumors and talk," Stan Mullins pouted, a defensive look in his blue eyes. His unkempt, dirty-blond hair reminded Packard of a stray dog. "They didn't give that story no credence a-tall."

Mullins appeared to be the weak link in the operation, Packard thought — a young man, long on looks and short on brains.

"Hell, no!" Kinealy turned on Mullins. "But, thanks to you, they could've caught us in the act. That prostitute believed your brag and went straight to Police Chief Wilkinson."

"It wasn't just because the story was too wild to be believed," Rip Hughes ventured, flicking ash from his cigar into a brass cuspidor by his foot. "Chief Wilkinson was planning to run for mayor. Word got out that he'd invented the whole tale so his department could arrest a couple of fall guys as the plotters and make himself look like a hero just before the election."

As Hughes relit his slim cigar, Packard noted the carefully manicured fingernails and the smooth cheeks that had a sallow look, as if there were no blood beneath the skin. His black hair was neatly parted and slicked back, completing the somewhat oily but rakishly handsome appearance. Adding this to his debonair habit of dress, Packard could see how some women might find him attractive.

"It was pure luck that the news got into the paper, or we wouldn't have known they were on to the plan," Kinealy declared, taking a long draught of his beer. "And we can't go around, depending on luck." He swept the foam from his mustache with the back of his hand.

"They'll be mighty surprised in a few days when they find out the story is true!" Jack McGuinn grinned, showing tobacco-stained teeth under his brown mustache. A bent nose, white scars in the heavy eyebrows, along with the bulging shoulders of his wool jacket hinted at his former occupation of pugilist.

As the outside professional, Packard took no part in this fence-mending among thieves. They were like a pack of strange dogs, walking stiff-legged around one another and sniffing, but with tails cautiously wagging, not quite sure if the others could be trusted.

In late June the story of a plot to steal Lincoln's body had hit the newspapers. Packard, hoping the gang would not abandon the scheme permanently, saw a chance to get inside this ring of counterfeiters by selling his services as an expert grave-robber. Through a "roper" — a criminal informant — Packard had put out feelers in the half light of the Chicago underworld. Big Jim Kinealy had taken the bait and, through an intermediary, had arranged a rendezvous. When the two finally came face to face in a Chicago saloon known as The Hub, Packard reminded Kinealy of their brief meeting during the war. This tenuous connection from the past was enough, along with Packard's fabricated reputation, to secure him a place with the plotters, and Kinealy had proceeded to confide the tomb-robbing plan to him.

Kinealy had come south from Chicago to lead this small group of "coney men," as counterfeiters were commonly known, in the theft of Lincoln's body from its massive mausoleum outside Springfield. His primary goal in doing so was to force the release of his chief engraver, Ben Boyd, from prison. Boyd was probably the best engraver in the country who wasn't employed by the U.S. Treasury Department. He was so good, in fact, that bills and notes printed from his plates could only be distinguished from the real thing by the slightly inferior quality of their paper. The fancy, intricate pictures, interwoven geometric patterns, state seals on national bank notes, portraits and designs on the U.S. currency denoted an artist of exceptional ability. But Boyd had been tracked through several Midwestern states by two of Packard's fellow agents who had finally surprised and arrested Boyd in Fulton, Illinois a year ago. He'd been caught in the act of engraving a plate for a twenty-dollar bill on the First National Bank of Dayton, Ohio. After a trial and conviction, he was sentenced to ten years in Joliet prison.

Kinealy usually confined himself to arranging the sale of hundreds of thousands of dollars of counterfeit money to other gangs — a spreading economic cancer that was affecting a wide area of the country. But, since he never actually touched a dollar of phony money himself, the Secret Service could not secure enough hard evidence against him to stand up in court. If the government couldn't nab the elusive Kinealy for counterfeiting, perhaps they could catch him in the act of breaking into the tomb, Packard reasoned.

The deed was to have been done on the country's centennial, July 4, 1876. With the country's patriotic fervor at its height, Kinealy had thought to collect a sizable reward for the return of the body. But the secret had been leaked and the plot abandoned. When Kinealy saw their plans printed in the Springfield newspaper, he was dumbfounded. When he found out Mullins was responsible, he was furious. He'd immediately called the whole thing off and left for Chicago on the train. But now he was back in

Springfield and the bizarre scheme was about to become reality. Big Jim had rented a building and set up this saloon with his living quarters upstairs. The saloon was only a front for selling bogus money, and now for working out the details of the plot.

"I'm willing to forget all those foul-ups. They're past history," Kinealy said. "Let's get down to business. It's getting late."

He leaned back against the bar and appeared to collect his thoughts. Rain was slashing down outside, and a few drops sizzled as the wind whipped them down the hot stove pipe. Packard automatically shifted his chair a little closer to the warmth of the Franklin stove in the middle of the room.

"Where to hide the body, once we've got it . . . ," Kinealy began. "The original plan was to take it to the Sangamon River about two miles north and bury it in a gravel bar under a bridge. That's out. Too close. We'll have to take it farther away."

"There's some caves up in the bluffs along the river about thirty miles north," McGuinn volunteered. "Nobody would find it there."

Kinealy appeared to consider this briefly. "No . . . too difficult to get the body up there without removing it from the coffin. We don't want to have to touch it."

"That lead-lined casket's going to be mighty damned heavy," Hughes growled, "wherever we tote it."

"I've thought about this a good deal," Kinealy continued. "And I think we should haul it as far away as possible . . . as quickly as possible."

"We'll think we've whupped into a hornets' nest for sure when daylight comes and they find out it's been stole!" Mullins glanced around at the others with a grin that was not returned.

"Every place in the immediate area of Springfield will be searched. You can bet the law won't leave a stone unturned," Kinealy continued. "The nights are long this time of year. We can haul it a good distance in a light spring wagon before daylight."

Hughes shook his head. "Too many people on the roads to be packin' old Abe around in a wagon," he objected.

"Why do you think I picked November Seventh as the date?" Kinealy answered, giving him a condescending look. "Everybody and his mule will be in town near the telegraph and newspaper offices, trying to get early news of the election returns. Hell, with Rutherford B. Hayes and Sam Tilden running, this promises to be one of the closest contests in United States history. There won't be anybody on the roads that night."

"I've got an idea," Packard said, putting in his two cents' worth just to show he was really one of them.

"OK, let's have it."

"I've got a friend, Dan Clark, who's in the same cadaver-procurement business as I am," Packard said, nervous energy forcing him out of his chair. He paced up and down, his boots clumping on the wooden floor. "He owns a piece of land six miles northeast of Mount Pulaski in the bottomlands of Salt Creek, near the Isaac DeHaven grist mill." He gestured as if they could see what he was describing. "There's a big hollow log in some pawpaw bushes near the bridge. We could easily get there before daylight and hide the body in the hollow log. But here's the main part of my idea. . . ." He paused for dramatic effect, until all eyes were on him. "Since Clark can't be connected to us in any way, why not hire him to accidentally discover the body after a reward has been posted for it. Then he collects the reward and shares it with us. That way, we avoid all the danger of demanding a ransom."

Kinealy was silent for only a few seconds. "That's OK as far as it goes," he said slowly. "But it won't do . . . for a couple of reasons. I don't want any more people let in on this. And it's not only the ransom. We have to force Ben Boyd's release from prison."

Kinealy apparently still had some of Boyd's plates that had not been confiscated and had been able to continue overseeing the printing and selling of bogus bills as long as there were no design changes in the currency or no new series issued. But continued operation of the coney men was totally dependent on the services of a highly skilled engraver. Boyd was the key. His freedom was indispensable.

Packard nodded. "You're right. If Ben Boyd is to be sprung, then we have to go with a straight-up ransom demand of the governor."

"That's why we have to get the body far away . . . fast," Kinealy continued. "We'll put the coffin on a train headed west. By daylight, the coffin, with one of us riding coach, will be across the river into Missouri."

"What?"

"That's crazy!"

"We can't go fooling around any trains. We'll be caught for sure," came the immediate chorus of protest from the other three, as they all tried to talk at once.

"There are a hundred good places we could hide it around close," Hughes said thoughtfully, removing the cigar from between thin lips.

"I don't want no part of this," Mullins whined. "Too dangerous. We'll be arrested before we get out of the dépôt."

Kinealy held up his hand until they all had stopped talking, and then a few seconds longer to be sure he had the floor. "OK, now. If you trusted me before, then give a listen to me now. Don't you think I've planned all this out? We won't be at the dépôt. There's a westbound express from Toledo that highballs through Springfield at ten minutes to midnight. Thirty miles west of town, in some rolling farm country, it stops to take on water. We can reach the spot with the body in a wagon just before the train gets there, close to one o'clock. There's only a little freight station there. We'll have the coffin in a wooden crate labeled 'harrows' to be shipped to Saint Joe, Missouri. I've already got the papers made up for it. Marking the crate as farm implements made of iron will account for the weight of it in case anybody's curious. While the locomotive's taking on water, the Wells Fargo messenger routinely loads up any odds and ends of freight that have been left there by folks from the surrounding towns or farms."

"There's no freight agent there?" Hughes interrupted.

"Only during the day. The Wells Fargo messenger has a key to the shed. We'll just set the crate on the platform, like the freight agent hauled it outside for quicker loading. By daylight our crate of harrows will be across the Mississippi River into Hannibal. Before the country wakes up to the news on the telegraph wires, the body will be well on its way across Missouri. One of us will go east of here about thirty miles, buy a ticket, board the train, and ride all the way to keep an eye on things."

"Where will it go from Saint Joe?" the stocky McGuinn wanted to know.

"Haven't quite decided yet," Kinealy said smoothly. Too smoothly, Packard thought. Anyone as meticulous as this man would have already figured out the final destination and hiding place of the body while ransom demands and negotiations were being made. He was probably keeping this last detail to himself as a hedge against any leaks or betrayal. But the others seemed to accept his answer.

"Whoever is riding the train will rent a rig in Saint Joe and claim the crate when it's offloaded," Kinealy continued.

"I don't know." Hughes frowned, black eyes narrowing to mere slits behind the curling cigar smoke. "With all that handling of the body and all those connections to be made, it seems like there are just too many things that could go wrong. I think we should keep it simpler and hide the coffin somewhere nearby." A very cautious man, Hughes liked to brag that he'd never been in jail. Packard had him pegged as the smartest one of the bunch, next to Kinealy.

"You can back out, if you want to," Kinealy replied. "We all knew this was not going to be a completely safe operation. But big rewards require big risks."

Hughes nodded grudgingly, although Packard could see he wasn't really satisfied. "I'm in."

The dull Mullins and the former boxer, McGuinn, raised no objections.

"As a matter of fact, Hughes, you can ride the train if you want to, and the rest of us will do the hard part," Kinealy said. "You and my wife can appear to be traveling together as an innocent married couple. Once you've claimed the crate and have it stashed safely in Saint Joe, or wherever I decide to take it, I'll wire the governor and open negotiations for its safe return. If anything goes wrong with the plan before you get to Saint

Joe, then the two of you can just go on your way as if you are completely ignorant of the whole thing. Couldn't ask for a simpler assignment than that."

A sly smile crept over Hughes's face at this prospect.

"And, speaking of my wife, here she is, right on cue," Kinealy said as they all turned toward the sound of footsteps on the stairway at the end of the room.

Chapter Two

If every man has his Achilles heel, Packard's was Janice Kinealy. As she gracefully descended the stairs, carrying a tray of sandwiches, he felt that old familiar twinge in his stomach as his heart began to beat faster. It was a completely involuntary reaction but one which, to his dismay, occurred every time he saw or spoke to her.

"With all this talk, I thought maybe you were getting hungry," she said, sliding the bottles and glasses aside to make room for the tray on the table. "Hello, Rip . . . Stan . . . ," she nodded as she spoke to each of them individually. "Jack. . . . How are you, Sterling?"

"Thanks, Janice. You think of everything," Kinealy said.

"I hope you've thought of everything," she returned, giving him a forthright look. "Once we start this business, there will be no turning back, you know."

She spoke matter-of-factly since she would be as fully involved as the rest of them. Packard thought this was one of the things that he found so alluring about her — she could be coy and flirtatious, or she could, as now, look a man in the eye and speak simply, but with a confidence that somehow never crossed the line to bossiness or nagging. There was no formality among them, and she was completely at ease in the company of men. Moreover, she was a willing participant in the preparations and gladly took on any job, however menial.

As she moved toward the steaming coffee pot on the stove, Hughes hastened to find a cup behind the bar for her.

"Well, have you got it all sorted out?" she asked, taking the chair Mullins offered her.

"I believe so," Big Jim replied. "Let me fill you in."

Still standing, Packard was munching on one of the ham sandwiches and wondering why his mouth was so dry as he stared at her. It wasn't as if her beauty were striking him for the first time. It had been thirteen years since he had first met her and Kinealy during the war, but he hadn't seen her again until about four months ago when Kinealy, on the recommendation of that underworld contact, had commissioned Packard's services as an alleged grave-robber. Both of the Kinealys remembered him, which helped in gaining their confidence. They assumed he had also followed a road outside the law in the years since the war.

Working off some nervous energy, Packard went behind the bar and drew himself a beer to wash down the sandwich. Janice Kinealy had lost none of her charm. Time had traced some very fine lines in the skin of her neck and face, and a few silver threads now shone in the brown wavy hair. She wore her thick hair touching her collar instead of the sweeping chestnut tresses he remembered so well from their first meeting years ago. While no longer the stunningly gorgeous young woman who could turn any man's head, she still retained the graceful, classic beauty and personal charm that tugged irresistibly at him. Janice was probably in her late thirties, Packard guessed — close to his own age and several years younger than Kinealy, whom he knew from Secret Service files to be forty-five. It was fortuitous the Kinealys were childless, considering their life style, he thought as he continued to stare at her. Suddenly, beer was foaming over the top of his glass and down his hand, and he hastened to shut off the tap, wiping his fingers on his pants leg.

When Kinealy told his wife he wanted her to accompany Rip Hughes on the train from Decatur, Illinois to St. Joseph, Missouri, she slowly nodded, looking at Hughes, and then turning her eyes to Packard with a glance that pierced to his core. It was a look that, as much as any words, said she would prefer that he accompany her. Pretending not to notice, he tipped up his beer and prayed that Kinealy had not seen and interpreted the look as well.

Packard heard nothing of the next few minutes of conversation while he tried to get his emotions under control and Kinealy briefed her on what had been discussed and decided.

The meeting finally broke up sometime after midnight. A few details still needed to be worked out, but Kinealy was feeling the strain of a long day and decided to call a halt.

McGuinn!" Kinealy called, the germ of an idea sprouting in his mind. "You and Hughes hold up a minute."

The two men paused from shrugging into their overcoats as the door slammed behind Mullins and Packard.

Kinealy looked toward his wife who was collecting the empty glasses and setting them on the bar. "Go on to bed, Janice. I'll finish cleaning up."

"Oh, I don't mind."

"I said . . . go upstairs!" he repeated more forcefully.

He saw her flash a defiant look at him, but then she glanced at McGuinn and Hughes, and started silently toward the stairs.

Kinealy waited until she had disappeared before turning to the waiting men. "You know what this operation means to us. If it succeeds, we're set up for years to come. If it fails, we might spend the next twenty years or more behind bars."

They nodded, somewhat impatiently he thought.

"I'm repeating this to you two because I don't want another foul-up like that thing with Mullins. Keep an eye on both of them. Packard was recommended to me by someone I trust, but I don't really know anything about the man. Don't say anything to him, but just report to me if he says or does anything unusual. Janice wanted to. . . ." He broke off. "Well, never mind. That's all." He decided not to mention the fact that he would not have taken Packard into the fold but for Janice's urging. He felt sure her interest stemmed from the fact that she had saved Packard's life during the war and probably found him an attractive diversion. And he usually let his wife have her way, if he could, just to keep her happy. For the same reason, he had reluctantly agreed to make her part of this mission which was outside the normal realm of his counterfeiting activities.

"I'm sure he's probably OK," Kinealy went on. "This is just a precaution. We've all got to pull together on this. Understand? I don't want any dissension in the ranks. Just keep your eyes and ears open."

"You bet, boss," McGuinn said.

Hughes merely nodded.

The two men disappeared into the darkness, and Kinealy turned the key in the lock behind them. For several long minutes he stood by the door, hearing the late autumn rain beating at the front of the building. But he wasn't listening to the storm. Thoughts of the upcoming burglary filled his mind, just as it had for the past several weeks. He had no misgivings about it. He was the type of man who, once he put his hand to the plow, did not look back. Mentally reviewing his own words at the meeting, he was satisfied his performance had been convincing. At least, it was good enough to deceive slow-witted Mullins and the plodding McGuinn into thinking they'd actually had some rôle in deciding the details of the plan. Hughes and Packard probably weren't fooled, but they were the smarter ones.

He knew he probably wouldn't sleep this night. The prospect of such an outrageous and dangerous scheme filled his mind and excited him like nothing had in twenty years. He felt his heart beating faster and, without thinking, began an agitated pacing. This was the stuff of life. Some men fought duels, others gambled their lives in battle, or risked death driving a schooner to windward around Cape Horn. A few of those who willingly dared such things felt truly alive only when their earthly existence was in imminent peril. He had never thought of himself as a thrill-seeking risk-taker. But when he took time to reflect on it, he recognized the attraction of the heightened sensation, the keener perception that came with danger. Long periods of selling counterfeit bills had become relatively safe and boring. So much so that he felt he was aging before his time and accomplishing little. He needed a change, something big to stretch his capabilities.

He turned to pick up the half-empty bottles and stash them behind the bar. He poured himself one last drink, hoping this would serve to calm him enough to sleep. He stared into the amber-colored liquid, and then sniffed its slightly sweet aroma. Although basically a man of action, he also fancied himself a gentleman of refinement, having acquired a taste for fine Kentucky bourbon and several kinds of imported champagne. He could even distinguish between a Mozart composition and one by Bach. True, this had come after numerous trips to the concert halls with a favorite mistress while he was in St. Louis on business. He smiled at the thrills and pleasures of the good life, as he toasted his reflection in the back-bar mirror before throwing down the shot. A small glow warmed his insides. He set the glass on the bar and cocked his head, listening for any movement upstairs. Perhaps Janice wasn't asleep yet. He hoped not.

When Sterling Packard took his leave and stepped out into the blustery night, he welcomed the cold wind that quickly cleared his head of the cigar smoke and whiskey fumes. As he walked along the dark Springfield street toward his boarding house several blocks away, the alluring presence of Janice Kinealy went with him, even as he berated himself for being emotionally drawn toward another man's wife. It was an unhealthy temptation that he could have resisted much easier had he thought the attraction was only one-sided. He'd tried various ways to shake the feeling as being morally wrong and also dangerous and unprofessional. Maybe his feeling for her was a result of the way they had met, he reflected, as he climbed the steps to the porch of his boarding house, shaking the rain and sleet from his hat and fumbling for his key. Chickamauga Creek, Georgia, 1863. The long-healed wound in his left side that was now beginning to ache with the advent of cold weather was an enduring reminder of that time and place.

He went quietly to his upstairs room, undressed to his long johns, and lighted the lamp beside the bed. Then he climbed in and pulled the covers up, vaguely aware of the wind moaning around the eaves of the dark house. He picked up a novel from the night stand and made a half-hearted attempt to read, but his mind's eye kept drifting away from the printed page to a scene much more vivid — a green Southern forest thirteen years earlier. Many a day after that miraculous rescue he had thought about and prayed for the woman who had saved his life.

After a few years, the classroom lost its appeal, and he'd left teaching in 1870 to take a job with the U.S. Secret Service. Through the newspapers and his agency's internal correspondence, he had followed the growing reputation of James Kinealy's counterfeiting activities. He had often wondered about Janice. Was she still with him? If so, what kind of a life did she have?

Last year he'd been transferred from St. Louis to Chicago to help trace the source of the phony currency that was flooding the country and playing havoc with an economy weakened by the financial panic of 1873. And four months ago, through a paid underworld intermediary, he'd been recommended to Kinealy as an expert, experienced grave-robber. Under the guise of a grave-robber who supplied illegal cadavers to medical schools, he had again met Janice and James Kinealy. It was then he knew he'd carried feelings for her all these years. It had to be only a patient's infatuation with his nurse, since he'd barely gotten to know her during those few days in Georgia. But that realization still didn't lessen the intensity of the sparks that seemed to arc between them at their re-acquaintance.

He tossed restlessly in his bed, knowing it had to be after one o'clock. He was tired from a strenuous day and from reliving the old battle in his imagination. There was an emptiness in the pit of his stomach, when he realized that the real battle lay ahead. His job would force him to betray the woman who had saved his life and see to it that she and her husband were sent to prison. The additional fact that he was attracted like a magnet to her was going to make his job supremely difficult.

Chapter Three

"You are all doomed to perdition! Look upon the never-ending fires of hell all you sinners!" the street preacher thundered. "You men who swear and blaspheme, you who are drunkards and whoremongers, you who seek to pile up earthly riches, you who cheat your fellow man . . . all of you will be damned to eternal punishment unless you repent! Repent and abandon your evil ways, or damnation will follow as night follows day!"

The bellowing of the fire and brimstone preacher could be heard nearly a block away. An amazingly powerful voice coming out of a man who was probably less than five and a half feet tall, Packard thought, as he sidled up to the back of the crowd of a hundred or more who had collected to listen. It was near the supper hour of a very mild October 30th in Springfield, and the man who was exhorting the passers-by was standing on a two-foot high stone retaining wall so he could be seen by everyone in the audience. The westering sun was dropping rapidly, but its late rays were illuminating the fiery orator as if with a halo of divine light.

"You who harbor secret lust in your hearts, you who covet your neighbor's wife, you who bear false witness. . . .”

At the mention of coveting his neighbor’s wife, Packard felt a twinge of conscience. This red-faced street preacher who wore his hair long and parted in the middle had struck a nerve. Packard squirmed inwardly, telling himself the feeling for Janice was only a temptation he was trying to resist.

“If your eye offend thee, pluck it out! If your hand scandalize thee, cut if off!” the preacher boomed, warming to his subject. “For it is better to enter the kingdom of heaven maimed than to be thrown into the pit of hell with all your parts,” he yelled, paraphrasing the New Testament’s sobering admonition.

“I hear he’s done that very thing.”

“What?” Packard was startled by a man standing at his elbow.

“Mutilated himself.”

He turned to face a man about his own height and age, dressed in a black topcoat and hat. He sported a black mustache and no-nonsense steel-rimmed spectacles.

“You know this man?”

He nodded.

“What do you mean . . . mutilated himself?” Packard continued, looking with renewed interest at the preacher. He seemed to be intact.

“The devil in your hearts must be driven out! Give glory to God!” the short, stocky preacher extolled all of them.

“He castrated himself,” the man beside

Packard stated matter-of-factly. "After a couple of whores approached him."

Packard cringed inwardly at the vision of such a thing.

"At least, he practiced what he preaches," the well-dressed man added.

"Who is he?" Packard asked, fumbling for something to say.

"Thomas Corbett. But the world knows him as Boston Corbett. He took the name of the city where he got religion."

The name rang a distant bell in Packard's memory. "Boston Corbett?" he repeated aloud.

"The sergeant who shot and killed John Wilkes Booth."

Then the name and the face merged in Packard's mind. "Ah, yes, I remember seeing his picture a few years back." He nodded, studying the head bobbing above the crowd. A scraggly mustache and forked goatee surrounded the mouth.

"He's mad as a hatter," the stranger said. "In fact, that's apparently how he became mad . . . working as a hat maker in various factories for years. Absorbed a solution of mercury through his skin."

"You seem to know a lot about him," Packard commented.

He nodded. "I've followed his wanderings since the war."

"May I ask why?"

"I have a personal interest."

"My name's Sterling Packard, by the way." He offered his hand.

The man gripped it. "Robert Lincoln."

"Not Robert Todd Lincoln, by any chance?" Packard asked, his eyes widening slightly. "The late President's son?"

"The same," he replied with what appeared to be a slight grimace.

"Sorry. I'm sure you get that all the time."

"No matter. I'm used to it. It comes with being the progeny of a famous man."

Packard knew that Robert Lincoln was now a successful Chicago attorney.

"The man who shot my father's assassin . . . ," he mused, his voice trailing off as he shook his head. "I just wish . . . well, no matter."

"What's that?"

Robert Lincoln continued to stare at the preacher as he replied thoughtfully: "I only wish he had not killed Booth. By putting the actor on trial, we probably could have learned much more about the conspiracy."

"Corbett disobeyed orders when he fired," Packard said. "I remember reading his testimony at the conspirators' trial that God Almighty had ordered him to shoot."

"That's right," Lincoln replied. "He justified it by saying that the Lord had directed his bullet in an uncommonly excellent shot through that crack in the barn and hit Booth in almost the same spot as the bullet hit my father. Edwin Stanton, the Secretary of War, saw to it he was made into a national hero, instead of being court-martialed for disobeying a direct order not to shoot. But I suppose none of that matters now," he added in a lower tone. "That man up there is pitiful. He should be put away in an insane asylum."

"Well, his religious fervor doesn't seem to be hurting anybody," Packard remarked, noting that a few of the casual listeners had begun to drift away.

"You painted street-walking Jezebels . . . repent!" Corbett thundered, pointing over the heads of the crowd toward a few women. Apparently embarrassed, the curious female onlookers hastily retreated.

"I'm not so sure of that," Lincoln said, nodding toward the women. "He's been run out of at least a dozen different churches for being too extreme." They were silent for a few seconds, before Lincoln continued: "But, I'll have to say, in spite of his strange delusions, the Glory to God man, as they called him, was one terrific soldier in battle. He always said he would pray for those Rebels' souls, then pop 'em off."

"Wasn't he a prisoner at Andersonville?" Packard asked, referring to the notorious Georgia prison stockade.

"Sure was. Mosby's raiders captured him after one hell of a fight. He was in Andersonville for several months. Tried to convert the whole camp, I hear. Even escaped through a tunnel once, but the dogs hunted him down."

"Amazing fella."

"I guess it takes all kinds," Lincoln said. "But the man makes my skin crawl. A fit subject for All Hallow's Eve tomorrow night. I'd like to know what goes on behind those wild eyes."

"What brings you to Springfield, Mister Lincoln?" Packard asked, abruptly shifting from an obviously painful topic.

"Oh . . . ," he paused and shook himself as if coming out of a dream. "I came down to bring some things to my mother. She lives with her sister here now."

"She's well, I hope," Packard said cheerfully.

"Actually, she's been quite ill for several years," he replied, and Packard could have bitten his tongue when he remembered that Robert Lincoln had had his mother committed to an insane asylum the year before. She had been released after only a few months when another doctor declared her sane. "I'm afraid the tragedy of my father and the deaths of my younger brothers have taken quite a toll on her."

"I'm sorry."

He gave a slight shrug as both of them began to move away from the crowd and leave the preacher still ranting and quoting scripture. "As Boston Corbett might say . . . it's the will of God," he finished in a resigned tone.

It was difficult for Packard to picture the former Mary Todd, whom he had read about as a society belle from a good Kentucky family, now living as an aging eccentric, going on buying binges and railing at various public officials.

Robert Lincoln looked at Packard. "This may be indelicate, but I believe I detect a trace of Southern dialect in your speech."

He nodded. "Yes, sir. Middle Tennessee, born and reared."

"Ah, a border state, like Kentucky where my folks were from."

"Yes, sir. I fought for the Confederate cause. Took a ball at Chickamauga. All for naught, I'm afraid."

"Not at all. The whole thing was a terrible tragedy for both sides. But I firmly believe this country has become the stronger for it. It was a national boil that had to burst before it could heal. But the world moves on. . . ."

It seemed strange having this conversation with the son of Abraham Lincoln, and all the while Packard was deep into a plot to foil the theft of his father's body.

"Well, Mister Packard, I must go to catch my train," he finally said, thrusting out his hand. "It was a pleasure making your acquaintance." His eyes were honest and appraising behind the clear lenses.

"The pleasure is mine, Mister Lincoln," Packard replied, returning his hearty handshake.

Then Robert Lincoln slipped away among the pedestrians toward the dépôt. A vague feeling of sadness for the past and unease about the future crept over Packard as he watched the late President's oldest son disappear into the gathering gloom.

Chapter Four

Janice Kinealy wrapped her cloak closely about her and edged away from Rip Hughes, keeping her small, black, leather grip between them as they stood on the platform of the Decatur, Illinois dépôt. She tried not to be obvious about it, but Hughes caught the movement and muttered under his breath: "We're supposed to be man and wife. This isn't going to work, if you keep acting like I've got the plague."

"We're not on our honeymoon," she retorted quietly, forcing a smile and turning her head away as he leaned close to her. Freshly bay-rummed and pomaded, his sweet scent was overpowering. His hair was neatly parted on one side and slicked back, giving off a dull, black sheen in the lantern light. "Just blend in and be anonymous," she added.

She hoped he would take the hint. She had an uneasy feeling about Hughes and his overt advances. It was partly her fault, she knew, since she had made the mistake of using her beauty to tease and tempt him for several weeks before Packard had come on the scene. Hughes was smart, and he wasn't bad-looking, but to her it was strictly a cruel form of entertainment she had indulged in since her teen years. She would never have let it go very far in any case, but this man had apparently taken her flirtations seriously, even though she was married — and to his boss, at that. But it was like teasing a wolf with a piece of steak — one didn't break off the game, leaving him snarling and hungry.

She should have insisted that Sterling Packard accompany her on this trip. It was much more pleasant to think of him, than of the man beside her. But Packard was needed to help rob the tomb. It was going to be a long trip of a night and a day and another night before they reached St. Joe. Since the midnight express from Toledo didn't stop in Springfield, she and Hughes had ridden the train east thirty-five miles to Decatur that morning to board the westbound express in the evening. Hughes would have plenty of time and opportunity to be alone with her, even though they would be sitting up in day coaches all the way, as no Pullmans were available. And this man was one who mistook "no" for coyness. Rejection would be a blow to his self-declared reputation as a womanizer, she thought. He wouldn't dare try to rape her in public, but she would have to be constantly on the alert to ward off his hands during the long, dark hours of the night when she couldn't readily get away from him.

Hughes picked up both their bags and preceded her up the steps of the last coach. He selected a seat near the back on the left-hand side, and she slid in next to the window while he wrestled the two grips into the overhead rack before sitting down next to her. He patted her hand affectionately, but her thoughts were already far away as she stared out the window into the darkness.

Sterling Packard. He was pleasant to look at—lean and handsome in a rugged sort of way. More her own age than her husband. When they had met again, some four months ago, she had felt as giddy as a schoolgirl. It was almost as if she had rediscovered an old flame. A strange feeling, since she had known him for only a few days thirteen years earlier, and he had been unconscious most of that time. She had learned to trust her own instincts and rarely tried to reason things out, but this attraction bothered her. She sensed an innate decency in Packard that was lacking in most of the other men she'd met in recent years. It was strange how his reappearance had triggered thoughts and memories that hadn't come to mind in a long time. And many of these thoughts brought twinges of loss for times past.

She had met Jim Kinealy, a dashing twenty-four-year-old, at her graduation from St. Vincent's Academy at Nazareth, Kentucky in the spring of 1855. Even though he was not a Catholic himself, he had come down from Illinois to see a cousin graduate from the boarding school run by the Sisters of Charity. A classmate had introduced Janice to her cousin, Jim. Their attraction was mutual and immediate. She blushed even now to think how she'd considered herself, at age seventeen, to be worldly and sophisticated. In truth, she knew very little about anything beyond the limited experiences of her life at her parents' home, and then at the girls' school. But she felt a nostalgic pang for those simpler, pleasanter days.

After a whirlwind courtship of picnics and socials, they became engaged. And, before the leaves were gone from the trees that fall, they were married. He took her off to Chicago where he was a partner in a printing business. Even then, without her knowledge, he was being drawn into a small circle of men who were making and circulating phony paper money. Several months later, when she had first discovered what he was doing, she was appalled. This had led to harsh words and the beginning of the rift between them. But there was no changing his mind. In order to keep the marriage intact, she had tried to ignore his activities. Then, as the money began to flow in, she gradually acquiesced to the point of spending it and looking the other way. Although dishonest and illegal, counterfeiting was relatively safe in those pre-war years. It was as common as distilling untaxed whiskey in the Kentucky hills. For one thing, there was no government agency whose sole job was to track down and arrest counterfeiters. For another, there was such a vast number of widely varying bills and notes produced by both the federal government and the many state banks that hardly anyone could tell real currency from the fake. It was a hodgepodge of hundreds of different kinds of bills, made even more numerous by Confederate currency after the war began. That was how she and Kinealy had come to be in the Georgia farmhouse when the battle of Chickamauga had swept in around them. With the drop of the Southern merchants' confidence in the value of the Confederate "shinplasters," U.S. currency had become even more sought after. And Kinealy was there to supply that demand.

When she had found the seriously wounded Packard, she herself was barely a year past the one and only pregnancy of her marriage that had ended in a miscarriage after four months. She had very nearly bled to death and was never able to conceive after that. The experience still seared her memory. It had left a terrible void in her life — an emptiness which she had tried to fill over the last dozen years with beautiful clothes, diamonds, and gold jewelry, a personal masseuse, a phaëton drawn by a pair of matched grays and driven by a coachman, a passion for gambling, plays, anything to take her mind off a life that seemed devoid of love. Her female friends were many and brief — more like passing acquaintances because of Kinealy's frequent moves to elude and confuse the law. From city to town, from state to state, they never spent more than a few weeks or months in the same place. Only once had they settled into a small house in Chicago where they'd lived for two years before the great fire drove them out.

During most of her married life, she had remained in the background, letting her husband handle the delicate and dangerous business of counterfeiting, while she entertained herself. But, mainly due to Packard's presence, she had wheedled Kinealy into letting her take part in this risky caper. He had acted surprised, as well he might, since their relationship had long since deteriorated into what one of her women friends had termed benign neglect.

Her thoughts were interrupted as the train jerked into motion and her leg brushed against Hughes. Almost immediately, she felt his hand sliding along her upper thigh. She gasped in sudden surprise and looked to see if anyone in the coach was watching, but the few passengers had settled down for the night. Just as she started to react, the portly conductor came in from the far door and swayed along the aisle. Hughes removed his hand.

"Do that again, and I'll shoot you," she said quietly, sliding a nickel-plated Derringer out of the pocket of her cloak just far enough for him to see it.

"Well, aren't we getting high and mighty all of a sudden!" he snorted. "You were a lot friendlier a few weeks ago before that damned Packard showed up."

She didn't reply, knowing he spoke the truth.

But the laugh in his throat choked down to a cough, and he seemed suddenly to lose interest in her, reaching across the aisle for a magazine someone had left on the seat.

She kept her hand on the gun in her pocket, thinking that it was going to be a long trip. At least, her part would be easier than that of her husband's, Packard's, and the other two who should be breaking into the massive Lincoln tomb just about now. She swallowed to relieve the dryness in her throat, wondering if the perilous burglary was going well. She would have prayed for them, but it had been years since she'd uttered a prayer of any kind. Besides, how does one ask God to bless a crime?

Chapter Five

"Let me take a turn at that," Packard said, nudging Stan Mullins aside. "Here . . . hold this so I can see." He shoved the bull's-eye lantern at him and took the file from his hand. Mullins willingly stepped back so Packard could move up to the chain and lock that secured the wrought-iron gate to the mausoleum. Placing the edge of the file in the groove that had been worn in one of the heavy links, he filed quickly for a couple of minutes as the tiny metal shavings glittered in the lamplight. They'd already broken a hacksaw blade trying to cut through it.

"Whew!" Packard paused to rest a moment, flexing his hand. "Should have a triangular file for a job like this."

"Well, you're the expert grave-robber. You should have brought one," Kinealy said from the darkness.

"Most of the graves I've robbed are not as well secured as this one. Usually a crowbar, a pick, and a shovel will get the job done." Packard grunted as he filed rapidly.

"Well, you cased the place a couple of times," Kinealy persisted, sounding irritated. "You should have known."

"You're right," Packard said evenly, to keep from riling him. "But as long as we use the edge of this flat file, I think it'll do just as well. There . . . we're over halfway through already."

"Let McGuinn have a go at it," Kinealy said.

Packard stepped back and handed the file to the ex-boxer, glad that Kinealy couldn't see him in the darkness or he might have suspected something was amiss. Packard had more than an average case of nerves, as evidenced by the perspiration pouring off him in spite of the cold November night.

They were all armed with revolvers, but Packard's stomach was in turmoil because no more than sixty feet away on a straight line from this spot were six men — three Secret Service operatives, two Pinkerton detectives, and the caretaker of this monument. They were waiting for Packard's signal to grab these grave-robbers in the act.

The monument, in the cemetery two miles outside Springfield, was set on the summit of a low hill. Built mostly of marble, it was composed of a huge square base, about seventy feet on a side, and some fifteen feet high, the top surrounded by a stone railing. This base supported a sixty-foot high stone obelisk. At the north end, where they were, was a semi-circular room containing the remains of Lincoln, while a circular room on the opposite south end housed a museum known as Memorial Hall. It was in this museum that the six men were hiding, waiting for his signal.

He was vainly trying to keep a grip on his emotions and think of what he had to do. Because of a maze of corridors and stone walls between the two rooms, the men on the south end could neither hear nor see the burglars. They were depending on Packard to relay a password to them when the time was right for their ambush. The word they had agreed on that morning at a meeting in the St. Nicholas Hotel was — "Wash." — as part of the name of Elmer Washburn, Midwestern chief of the Secret Service, who was one of the six waiting men. Robert Lincoln had been informed of the plot and had approved of the plans to foil it, but it was doubtful he knew that he had been talking to a Secret Service undercover agent on a Springfield street only the week before.

It was Tuesday, November 7th, a Presidential election day that had generated plenty of excitement around Springfield. Men and women had been flocking into town from the surrounding countryside all day by horseback and wagon so the men could vote, and there was a festive atmosphere in the restaurants and hotels. But, for Packard, the day had been one of unrelieved anxiety that this whole secret operation would go off properly and the trap would be sprung without anyone getting hurt or killed. The weather had been heavily overcast and gloomy with a biting north wind swirling dead leaves in the streets and whipping American flags from at least a hundred balconies and windows. Although Packard hadn't seen them, the six lawmen were to have gathered one or two at a time in the museum shortly after five o'clock as soon as darkness had closed down this short winter day. He had to believe they were now in position and ready, even though Packard had made a pretext of checking the museum door with the lantern when they first arrived.

"There! Got it!" McGuinn's exclamation broke in on his thoughts as he heard the chain and padlock jangle to the cement sidewalk.

"Mullins, stay out here and keep a sharp lookout," Kinealy ordered in a low voice as he took the bull's-eye lantern from him, swung the iron gates open, and the three of them entered the catacomb. He flashed the beam of light around. They all jumped at a sudden echoing clatter as McGuinn dropped a heavy, single-bitted axe on the marble floor.

"Why don't you try to make a little more noise?" Kinealy grated sarcastically.

"Sorry, boss."

As the light panned around the back of the room, Packard saw the several panels that hid the burial chambers, both full and empty, of the Lincoln family. The room looked eerie by lantern light, totally different than it had earlier when they came to the shrine, posing as visitors.

"Sure glad they decided to bring Abe out of that hole a couple of years ago," Packard said, indicating the eight foot-deep empty crypt in the center of the back wall where the remains had once been laid. The marble sarcophagus now rested in the middle of the room.

"Huh!" Kinealy snorted. "You may not think so when you start trying to break into this thing. It must weigh a couple o' tons." He handed him the axe. "Go to it."

Packard put the axe down and took the lantern instead, focusing the beam under the edge of the overhanging marble lid. After examining both sides, he said: "This top is set down on four copper dowels. If we can lift it up, we can probably slide it off, or at least turn it sideways far enough to get the coffin out. Won't make near as much noise."

Kinealy immediately stepped to the door. "Mullins, get in here. We need your help."

Packard set the lantern on the floor, and each of them took a position at one of the corners.

"Ready? Heave!" The four squatted and strained upward in unison, their shoulders under the lip of the marble lid. There was no hint of movement. They might have been trying to lift the Taj Mahal. "Once more. Ready? Heave!" It didn't budge.

"So much for that idea," Kinealy grunted, straightening up.

"The pegs could be glued," Packard said. "I'll have to use the axe."

"No. Too noisy," Kinealy replied. "Maybe we can break into the end of it," he mused, taking the lantern and examining the sarcophagus. "Nope. It'd make just as much racket."

"So what?" Mullins asked. "There ain't nobody around to hear us."

Kinealy gave him a withering look, but didn't reply.

"I've got an idea," Packard said, shrugging out of his jacket. "Here. Hold this up under the edge as a pad and I'll see if I can tap it loose."

"Don't hit my fingers," McGuinn said, taking the folded coat and, holding it gingerly by the corners, pressed it up under the marble lip of the lid.

"Move it to the left a little . . . there." Packard took the axe and gave it a couple of tentative swings, thumping the blunt side of it up against the coat. The noise was almost completely muffled. "OK, here goes." He brought the back side of the axe up from the floor with all the speed and power he could muster. It was like hitting the base of the monument itself. The concussion jarred him to his collarbone. McGuinn was standing back as far as he could, holding the coat at arm's length, eyeing him dubiously. But on the second try Packard felt the lid give a fraction. "Ah! Got it!" he exclaimed, examining it with the lantern. "Now, just three more dowels and it'll be loose."

"Here, you hold the coat and let me do it," McGuinn said, taking the axe from his hand. "I'm more used to throwing punches."

In just a couple of minutes they had the rest of the dowels unstuck without even cracking the marble. Kinealy, McGuinn, and Mullins would have been thoroughly disgusted had they realized what a waste of time and effort all this was, Packard thought. As soon as they were caught in the act, the body would be immediately placed back in its resting place.

"OK, now all we have to do is lift it up, turn it sideways, and slide it back far enough to get the coffin out," Packard said, assuming his rôle as master grave-robber.

Kinealy set the lantern on the floor. "Good. Nothing's broken except that chain on the gate. We'll put it all back together before we leave, and maybe nobody will notice the body's missing until we're long gone."

The four of them again assumed positions at each corner, their shoulders under the lip of the massive stone lid. But they had underestimated the weight of the marble slab.

"On the count of three," Packard said. "One, two, three!"

They all stood up — except Mullins, who was about a half count late. The weight of the marble slab tilted toward him, and his knees buckled. For a second he was almost able to straighten his bent legs, but then, with a strangled cry of sheer terror, he scrambled out of the way, and the overbalanced lid went crashing to the floor, snuffing the bull's-eye lantern.

Had they been able to see, Packard was sure the air around them would seem to have turned blue from Kinealy's cursing. "Mullins!" he grated hoarsely while Packard's ears were still ringing from the clatter. "Where the hell are you?"

At that point Packard wouldn't have been surprised to see Abe Lincoln rise up out of the coffin and complain about all the noise they were making.

"You hurt?" McGuinn rumbled.

"No. No . . . I'm OK," came the quavering answer from somewhere in the back of the room.

"Where's the damn' light?" Kinealy growled.

The smell of coal oil smote Packard's nose in the velvety blackness. He could hear the others scuffling around in the dark, but stayed put. Finally, Kinealy struck a match and held it up. By the flaring light, Packard caught a glimpse of the marble slab, still unbroken, one end on the floor and the other tilted up against the sarcophagus. Mullins had barely escaped being crushed by the lid and was just now getting to his feet, trying to salvage some of his dignity in front of a very angry Kinealy.

"Ooww!" Kinealy dropped the burning match he'd held a fraction too long. There was a second or two of darkness, then light came up, brighter than ever, as the still-blazing match ignited the coal oil spilled on the marble floor.

"Shit!" Kinealy jumped back to avoid the spreading flames. But the blazing pool covered no more than a few square feet, engulfing the crushed remains of the bull's-eye lantern. As soon as they realized there was nothing else combustible nearby, Kinealy said: "That's it for the lantern. Let's use this light while we've got it."

From then on, they made no effort to be quiet. After knocking out the forward end of the sarcophagus that contained the name LINCOLN enclosed in a wreath, the four of them hastily slid the red cedar casket out and set it on the floor.

"That thing's still awful heavy for a wood box," Mullins panted.

"There's a lead liner inside," Packard reminded him.

"Are we gonna take him out of it?" McGuinn asked.

"No. The lead doesn't have carrying handles," Packard said, trying to sound experienced and knowledgeable about this sort of thing. Actually, he had no idea but knew he didn't want to open the box. He did know that if they tried removing the body to carry it only in the lighter cedar coffin, they'd need a plumber to cut the sealed lead container.

"Packard, go get the wagon and bring it up near the door. We have to get this thing out of here . . . quick!" Kinealy's voice was low and urgent. He wiped a sleeve across his brow and took a deep breath as if the stale, smoke-filled air in the room was getting to him. Maybe the sight of the late President's coffin was finally bringing him to the realization of what he was doing.

Packard knew there was no rush, because the three of them would be under arrest within minutes.

"Be right back," he said, slipping into his coat

and starting for the door.

"Make it fast," Kinealy said.

Once outside in the dark, all he had to do was walk a few steps down the slope, then circle around to Memorial Hall on the far side of the monument, tap on the glass door, give the password, and stand back out of the way to wait for the six hidden men to rush around the monument to the mausoleum and make their arrests. But as soon as he pushed past the wrought-iron gate, Jack McGuinn was at his side. "I'll go with ya," he said.

Packard's stomach tensed in sudden alarm. Kinealy suspected treachery and was sending along a bodyguard to be sure of him.

"Don't need any help," Packard replied, trying to keep his voice steady. "The horses are all hitched and tied to a tree just off the road at the bottom of the hill. I can handle it. Won't take but a few minutes."

"Think I'll come along, anyway," McGuinn said, not dissuaded. Then he added in a lower voice: "I gotta get outta here for a little air."

Packard glanced at the burly figure beside him in the darkness. The voice sounded a bit shaky.

"Bodies and tombs give me the willies," he said by way of apology.

Even so, Packard was in a panic to get away alone so he could alert the lawmen. McGuinn was now several steps ahead of him, and there was nothing he could do but catch up with him. He ground his teeth in frustration at this unexpected turn. The whole plan was thrown out of kilter because this ex-boxer was queasy about graves. All Packard could hope for was that Washburn, Tyrell, Power, and the three others would finally get tired of waiting for him and go to investigate.

The wagon and team were about two hundred yards down the hill, just off the main Valley Road, and Packard's mind was in such a whirl he didn't even remember getting there.

"I know you do this for a living," McGuinn was saying, "but I'm a coney man, and this seems like robbing the poor box in church. I think every man should stick to what he does best."

Packard mumbled some response, his mind hardly registering what McGuinn was saying. If the six hidden men suddenly burst out and attacked just as they were loading up, Packard could very likely get caught in the crossfire.

The night was still as black as the inside of a boot while he and McGuinn untied the horses and climbed onto the seat of the wagon. A cold north wind was whipping away the sound of jingling trace chains as he clucked to the team and guided them up the curving driveway toward the monument. He would be able to get the wagon to within a few yards of the door where the driveway circled the base of the stone structure.

Just as he reined the team to a halt, the scene around them suddenly became vaguely visible as the wind shredded the overcast, allowing a three-quarter moon to begin peeking in and out of the ragged clouds. The monument loomed even more massively above them, squatting dull gray and deserted in the dim light.

It was anything but deserted.

McGuinn jumped down and headed up the grassy knoll while Packard set the brake and looped the reins around the iron rod that formed the edge of the wooden seat. His heart was pounding when he saw the light from the door was dimming as the spilled coal oil burned away. McGuinn had gone on ahead. Maybe now Packard would have time to run around to the other end and give the signal, even though the moonlight had erased his cover of darkness.

But it was not to be. The desperate thought had hardly entered his mind when he saw McGuinn's rolling gait striding back toward him.

"The boss says to get a move on," he said in a low voice. "We need your help to tote this thing."

Packard was trapped. All he could do was go along and hope for some chance to betray them.

"Right. Let's go." The two of them jogged several yards up to the door. The lead-lined cedar coffin was a load, even for four good-size men, Packard discovered as he gripped one of the brass handles, and they staggered down the slope and slid their burden into the back of the wagon. Mullins shut and latched the tailgate while Packard unrolled a piece of white canvas to throw over it. He fumbled with the tie-down ropes in the dark, trying to appear that he was hurrying instead of stalling.

"Let's go," Kinealy said, stepping up onto the wheel hub and grabbing the reins as he settled into the seat to drive. McGuinn and Mullins scrambled into the back beside the load. With a last, despairing look at the silent monument, Packard climbed up beside Kinealy. Where were the agents and detectives? Still waiting for his password, he thought, as Kinealy pulled the horses around and started the wagon back down the way they had come.

Elmer Washburn struck a match and looked at his watch. The five men around him were illuminated in the flare briefly before he blew the match out.

"Damn. Where's Packard?" he fumed under his breath. "He should have given the signal by now."

No one responded to the rhetorical question.

The head of the Chicago Secret Service fidgeted in the dark, loosening his tie and sliding the double action Smith & Wesson in and out of his shoulder holster. He was sweating under the wool jacket in the close air of the small museum.

"How long has it been since he flashed the lantern through the glass door here?" asked John Power, custodian of the Lincoln monument.

"Almost thirty minutes."

"You reckon something's gone wrong?" came

the tense voice of Patrick Tyrell, a Secret Service operative.

"I don't know. But I'm only giving him a couple more minutes, then we're going in after them."

James Brooks, assistant to Washburn, Lewis Swegles and George Hay, Pinkerton detectives, made up the remaining six men in the darkened room. They had been there since shortly after dark, and the strain of waiting was beginning to tell, since they couldn't converse, smoke, or play cards to pass the time.

This must be what it's like being thrown into the hole in solitary confinement, Washburn thought. He would never again consider "solitary" a mild form of punishment. The four or five hours they had spent here seemed like an entire day. He was not by nature a patient man, more inclined to action than waiting. In fact, since his promotion to agent-in-charge of the Midwestern division, he had been a hands-on supervisor, preferring to accompany his agents into the field whenever he could instead of reading reports and dealing with personnel problems in the office. It was a tendency that his superiors in the Treasury Department unofficially disapproved of.

The silence was heavy, oppressive as Washburn leaned against the wooden side of a display cabinet. He strained his ears. Some fifteen minutes earlier he could have sworn he heard a faint clatter from the other side of the monument, but the maze of rooms and passageways in the stone building had effectively muffled any sounds that might have indicated what the burglars were up to. Now the only sounds were the faint breathing of the unseen men a few feet away and the scuffing of their shifting positions every minute or two.

Finally Washburn's patience reached the end of its tether. "That's it. Let's go." He moved toward the door, and the lock clicked as Power opened it for them. "I'll lead the way," Washburn said as the six men crept cautiously along the outside of the marble wall in the moonlight, guns drawn.

When they reached the opposite side of the monument, Washburn saw the wrought-iron gate standing open, and motioned the others to flank him as he entered the darkened room.

"Throw up your hands!" he yelled, sweeping the unseen quarry with his pistol. There was no sound, no stirring, no voices. He backed to one side, his heart hammering as he felt his men scuffling in behind him. When there was no response, he reached into his vest pocket for a match, striking it on the stone wall behind him. In the flare of light, he saw the wreck of the marble sarcophagus, one end of its lid on the floor, the still-smoking residue of the burned coal oil.

"They got away!"

Just then the flame reached his fingers, and he dropped it, plunging the room into darkness again. Suddenly, a shot exploded, with a flash and boom amplified by the confined space. Washburn felt a slug ricochet past his ear. He flung himself to the floor and fired toward the door.

"No! No! It's me!" a Pinkerton man yelled. "My thumb slipped off the hammer."

"Dammit!" Washburn bellowed in complete frustration. "Get outside and spread out. They've got to be close by."

The men raced outside and scattered. Washburn followed and swore again when he saw the blowing clouds had obscured the moon. "Sing out if you see anything!" he yelled as he jogged downhill toward a few trees and white marble markers that were barely visible.

"There goes one of 'em!" A pistol cracked. Three more shots blasted in quick succession and then two more, as wind-whipped shouts sounded from somewhere near the stone steps leading to the parapet of the monument. Darts of flame lanced out from different directions, and Washburn heard the slugs whine off the stone walls.

A shout of pain was heard and then protesting voices that Washburn recognized. "Stop firing!" he screamed. "Stop it, you fools! You're shooting at each other." The fusillade tapered off and halted.

"Get back down here!" he thundered. If the Secret Service chief had been prone to apoplexy, he probably would have dropped dead on the spot.

"Somebody was waiting for us!" Kinealy spat as he whipped up the team.

The pair of deep-chested Morgans broke into a trot. The noise of the hoofbeats and the iron-shod wheels grinding over crushed cinders was whipped away in the darkness by the stiff north wind, masking their getaway.

"There's one of 'em!" The faint shout came from at least a hundred yards behind. "Up by the balustrade!" This was immediately followed by three gunshots.

As Kinealy slowed the team to turn onto the Valley Road, Packard twisted in his seat to look back and could see flashes as gunfire was exchanged.

Kinealy took a quick glance and laughed out loud. "Silly bastards! Must be shooting at each other." He turned forward once more. *"Hyah!"* He snapped the reins, and the team lunged into a gallop. Through the scattered trees of Oak Ridge Cemetery flashing past, Packard saw several more yellow darts of flame as the cracking of pistol fire receded behind them.

Packard's heart sank, and he was forced to pay attention to staying on the pitching seat as the wagon bounced over some frozen ruts. The sturdy Studebaker wagon was nearly new and built to take the pounding of hard usage. He had picked it out himself in St. Louis, while Rip Hughes was selecting and buying the team of horses from a farmer some forty miles from here.

The moon was silvering the deserted road ahead. Packard glanced sideways at Kinealy, wondering why he was driving them toward town. But he held his tongue and squinted against the cold wind that was whipping tears from his eyes. Since he had never expected the theft to reach this point, Packard had paid little attention to the details of what was planned after the body-snatchers left the cemetery. Now he found himself spinning down the road with three gang members and the corpse of Abraham Lincoln while all six lawmen were yelling and bouncing slugs off the stone monument and probably ventilating each other back there in the night. It was enough to make a grown man cry.

Chapter Six

The plan had gone awry. Icy wind swept the fog from Packard's stunned mind, and it became clear that his only chance of survival now was to continue playing the rôle of grave-robber. He hugged the lightweight wool coat around himself, vaguely conscious of his freezing, gloveless fingers as the team thundered along, stretching the distance between them and Oak Ridge Cemetery.

About a mile farther, when they were halfway to town, Kinealy reined the team to a trot, and then to a walk. As the wagon rounded a bend in the deserted road, a square of yellow light appeared ahead, pouring out of an open barn door. The structure loomed up in the moonlight, slowly materializing into a large livery stable. Kinealy guided the team off the road and reined up behind the building.

"Stay here," Kinealy said to the two in the back of the wagon. He set the brake, looped the reins, and jumped down. Packard followed. He slid the big door open a crack on its rollers, and they went inside. A man who had apparently heard them drive up was looking out the open front door.

"We're back here," Kinealy said.

The man jumped and turned around. "Gawd! You scared me. What're you coming in the back way for?" He stretched and rubbed the back of his neck as if he'd been asleep.

"I need a load of hay," Big Jim said, ignoring the question. "We'll just fork it into my wagon," he added as the man started to say something.

"How much you gonna need?" the man asked, glancing at them. "I could throw down a few sheaves from the loft."

"Good. Make it enough to fill my wagon," Kinealy said. "How much?"

"That'd be about three dollars."

Big Jim didn't haggle about the price. He just handed over a five-dollar gold piece. "Don't bother about the change," he waved as the man fumbled in a pocket of his overalls. "Just get the hay. We're in a hurry."

The man took the lantern from its peg on a post and began carefully to ascend the wooden slats of a vertical ladder.

Just as they started toward the rear door, a figure rose up out of an empty stall. "What's all the noise?"

Kinealy jumped back, hand on his gun, and Packard felt a cold chill go up his back.

"Nothin'. Go on back to sleep," the liveryman said, pausing on the ladder and holding the lantern aloft.

The apparition moved closer. Straw was stuck to the matted hair and goatee, and his dark eyes glared at them in the light. Some drunk sleeping it off, Packard thought, recovering his composure.

The hairy, wild-eyed man, rising from the depths of the stall, stepped out to block their way to the door. "Why do you prowl the night?" his deep voice demanded. "Vice and corruption walk in darkness. Good deeds are done by the light of day."

"Boston Corbett!" Packard gasped.

"Who?" Kinealy asked, glancing between the two of them.

"Never mind," Packard said, brushing past the short preacher. "I'll tell you later."

"Hey, you, get away from that wagon!" Kinealy lunged at Corbett who had followed them out the door.

"Put on the armor of light!" Corbett croaked as he dodged away from Kinealy and snatched at the canvas in the back of the wagon.

Before McGuinn or Mullins could stop him, Corbett had yanked off the end of the cover.

"A coffin! Whose mortal clay is this that should be resting safely in the earth?" His fierce eyes glared at them in the light from the partially open door. "Fear him who can kill the soul as well as the body!" he cried.

"Get the hell out of here!" Kinealy yelled.

"Coming down!" the liveryman called from the open door of the loft above.

They jumped back as three bundles whumped onto the ground between them. He kicked out several more, then withdrew from sight.

"McGuinn! Mullins! Get those sheaves into the wagon and busted open. Make sure it looks like we're hauling nothing but a big load of hay," Kinealy said. "Packard, do something about that idiot!" He gestured at Corbett, who was still roaming around the wagon, rattling like a cup of dice.

"Death comes like a thief in the night!" the wild-eyed one intoned. "But no man is buried at night." His face bore a crafty look as if he had just discovered some secret.

McGuinn and Mullins ignored him as they tore at the hay, throwing it in piles over and around the coffin.

"Ah, ha!" Corbett rasped, waving his arms and pointing an accusing finger. "You're not burying this body. You're hiding it. You stole it! You're going to sell it for filthy lucre. Spawn of evil! Grave-robbers! Desecrating the temple of the Holy Spirit!"

"I said, get rid of him!" Kinealy grated.

"Don't mind him. He's crazy," Packard said, not really knowing what to do.

Kinealy looked across the wagon at the short, stocky evangelizer who was staying out of reach.

"Ghouls! Sons of Satan! Judases!" he raved. Then in an eerie, almost wailing, tone that sent a chill up Packard's back: "Whooose body is this? Whooose flesh and bones will not be allowed to return to dust as the Lord intended?" He skipped nimbly away as McGuinn jumped out of the wagon and went after him. "Almighty God, in His Gargantuan wrath, will smite you like the Philistines!"

"What's a Gargantuan wrath?" Mullins wanted to know.

Packard finished sliding the barn door shut so the liveryman would not hear this tirade and guess what they were about. Even though Corbett was trying to shout, his overused voice was emitting only a hoarse croak.

"Forget him," Packard said. "Let's get out of here."

"We can't leave him," Kinealy said.

"What?" Packard couldn't believe he'd heard right.

"He thinks we're grave-robbers. If we leave him, he'll tell that liveryman what he saw, and the law will be on our trail as soon as those men from the cemetery, whoever they are, get back to town."

Before Packard could answer, he heard a *thunk* on the far side of the wagon like someone thumping a ripe watermelon. McGuinn came around the tailgate, rubbing his big knuckles. "I took care of him, boss."

"You didn't kill him, did you?"

"Naw. He'll just be in the land o' nod for a spell."

"Good. Throw him in the wagon." Kinealy leaped up onto the driver's seat with a nimbleness that belied his size. Packard scrambled up after him, while the others were lifting the limp form of Corbett into the back.

"Hyah!" Kinealy popped the reins over the backs of the team, and the wagon started with a jerk.

"Hold up. Wait for me!" Mullins yelled, running and grabbing for the back of the wagon. McGuinn put out a meaty hand and yanked him with a quick heave over the tailboard and headfirst into the hay.

Kinealy seemed to know the terrain well. Apparently he had scouted the route thoroughly in advance because he shortly turned off onto a side road through a thick stand of timber and whipped the team to a gallop. They thundered along for a time between two black walls of trees, the moonshine silvering the frosty road ahead of them. Packard had no idea what hour it was, but it felt late — like a long time since darkness had closed down about five-thirty. When Packard tried to calculate the time, he figured it was probably between nine and ten. This team of Morgans, as good as it was, couldn't run, flat out and pulling this load, for thirty miles. And that's how far Kinealy said they had to go to arrive at the water stop ahead of the midnight express.

Packard was suddenly aware of a scuffling in back and twisted around to see McGuinn kneeling astride a struggling Corbett. As he looked on, McGuinn shrugged out of his coat, yanked off his galluses, and proceeded to lash the lunatic's arms to his sides while Corbett yelled and called down heavenly thunderbolts on their heads. But there was no one else to hear, and shortly even this ceased as McGuinn gagged him with a bandanna.

The patch of trees thinned out, and they came into rolling pasture land. The single-track road curved to the right, and suddenly they were back on the main road again, headed toward Springfield.

"Where you going?" Packard yelled over at Kinealy.

"Back to my saloon to get the crate."

"What?"

"The crate to hide the coffin in when we put it on the train."

In all the confusion, Packard had completely forgotten about the shipping crate. His heart began to beat faster. Town meant lots of people, and maybe a chance for him to slip away. But he determined to try the straightforward approach first.

"Good!" Packard yelled back at him. "My part of this job is done. Just drop me at the edge of town, and I'll disappear. When you get my share of the ransom, you know how to contact me at my post office box in Chicago."

Kinealy whipped the reins over the team to keep them running, and then looked across at Packard for several seconds before replying. His expression wasn't readable because of the deep shadow of his hat brim.

"Your job ain't over yet. Not till we get this body hidden on the other end at Saint Joe. So don't go getting any ideas about taking off early." He turned his attention back to driving.

So much for the up-front approach.

They drove right through town, past swarms of people on the streets. All the stores and saloons seemed to be open, and everyone was in a festive mood while they awaited the first election returns from the East to come in over the telegraph. Packard's heart was in his mouth most of the time, knowing what a cargo they were carrying under that pile of hay. But, by the time Kinealy turned the team into the alley behind his saloon, he had a grip on his nerves once more.

Kinealy jumped down, unlocked the back door, and went inside. In a few seconds, a match flared, and he reappeared at the door, lighted lamp in hand.

"OK, let's get this thing unloaded. We'll transfer it inside."

Mullins took the lamp and held it high, throwing light over the steaming backs of the black horses and the pile of tawny hay in the wagon. Corbett still lay, kicking and grunting, in the wagon bed. But with arms bound to his sides and a gag in his mouth, his struggles had subsided considerably.

"Mullins, I didn't mean for you to light up the world!" Kinealy gritted through his teeth. "Set that lamp down inside and keep an eye on both ends of the alley. We've got enough moonlight to see by."

The three of them slid the casket out the open tailgate and struggled to fit the heavy load through the narrow door. Packard could have sworn he felt something shift inside as they tilted the coffin. Maybe the lead liner didn't fit snugly, or it was the body itself sliding around. He tried not to think of it.

They finally thumped the coffin onto the floor inside the storeroom. Kinealy dragged a stout wooden packing case from a dim corner. Small slats were nailed to the corners for handles.

McGuinn looked at the coffin, and then at the crate. "Boss, this thing'll be so heavy once we get it into that crate, it may be too much for all of us to lift."

He and Kinealy were the stoutest of the quartet. If they thought it would be too heavy, Packard wasn't about to disagree.

"All we have to do is lift it into the wagon bed out in the alley and then slide it off at the freight dépôt," Kinealy replied. "Then it's up to the railroad people."

"Until we get to Saint Joe," McGuinn said. "How about we just dump this here cedar coffin as long as we got the packing box? Lighten it up some for the horses, too. They have a long ways to run with this load."

Kinealy considered for a few moments, rubbing a hand over his mouth and jaw under his thick mustache. "Maybe you're right. What about it, Packard? Think it'll work better that way? You're the expert."

Packard nodded sagely. "Probably so, although it's the lead that causes it to be so heavy."

He tried to sound as if he hadn't just stated the obvious.

"Let's do it, then," Big Jim decided. He grabbed the lamp and held it close to the polished cedar lid. "We need a screwdriver." He handed Packard the lamp and rummaged around in a drawer until he came up with a big screwdriver.

In a matter of minutes, he had the screws out and the lid off. A lead coffin in the approximate outline of a body rested inside. In a jiffy they lifted it out by four metal handles and placed it in the packing crate.

"Fits pretty good," Kinealy grunted. "Stuff some of that hay in around it for padding." He consulted his watch, holding it toward the light. "Hurry up. It's already a little after ten."

They all pitched in to help. Packard felt the same sense of urgency, even though he wasn't one of them. He was armed, but knew the time wasn't right to attempt an arrest by himself. A slip-up could well cost his life, although he knew coney men weren't usually killers. Even a successful arrest would ruin a well-planned undercover operation because the whole aim of the Secret Service was to get them for printing or passing bogus currency. On the other hand, if they couldn't nail Kinealy and his gang for counterfeiting, Packard's boss would settle for any conviction that might put them in prison for a few years. He would have to wait until the ransom demand was made to charge them with extortion. So, as long as the plan to stop the body-snatching had failed, Packard would go along with the gang for a time to see what developed. And, deep down, his decision was influenced by a desire to see Janice Kinealy again before the trap was sprung. He took a deep breath to calm himself. It looked as if he had a mountain lion by the tail and couldn't let go.

"What's wrong? You got a bellyache?" Kinealy's question was directed at McGuinn who was pressing his right hand to his stomach.

"Naw. Just holding up my pants. Popped a button off when I squatted to lift that coffin," the boxer replied.

"Mullins, make sure that lunatic is still in the wagon," Kinealy said, snatching up a hammer.

Mullins disappeared into the alley.

"McGuinn, forget about your pants for a minute and hold that lid on the crate while I nail it down," Kinealy ordered.

But, before he could swing the hammer, they were startled by — *Boom! Boom! Boom! Boom!* — from the front of the building. They all jumped at the noise and looked at each other with sudden alarm.

"The front door," Packard breathed, his heart beginning to race.

In spite of all their plans, maybe this operation was coming to an end, here and now.

Chapter Seven

"Open up, Kinealy!" came a deep voice from out front.

The door rattled under several sets of fists.

"Yeah. Let's have a drink!"

"I can see your light. I know you're in there. Why the hell are you closed on election day?"

The pounding became insistent. "Open the damn' door!"

"You've got a lot of thirsty customers out here. You got something against making money?"

Kinealy's eyes went wide, and his face ghastly pale in the lamplight. For the first time since this caper began, Packard saw the master of the coney men lose his composure. He opened his mouth a time or two, as if he couldn't catch his breath, but then managed to whisper: "Just a bunch o' drunks looking for a good time. Stay quiet. They'll give up and go away in a few minutes."

But the men outside weren't so easily discouraged. After some more banging and yelling, their voices subsided, and Packard could hear them talking and arguing among themselves. Then there was a terrific crash of splintering wood, and the voices were suddenly louder, closer.

"Why the hell'd you shove me for, Bill?" a voice complained. "Now look what you've gone and done. His door's busted."

"Well, as long as we're in, hunt up Kinealy and let's get those beer taps working."

"Beer, hell! Where's the champagne?" another man yelled.

"Big Jim! Show yourself, man! You've got some customers."

"Does he sleep upstairs?"

The door to the main saloon was standing ajar. Kinealy finally seemed to gather himself to face the situation. "Can't let anyone come back here. I have to go in there and stall them." He turned to Packard and McGuinn and said in a low voice: "Get this crate outside into the wagon. I'll join you as quick as I can."

"How long should we wait, boss?" McGuinn asked.

"Until I get there!" Kinealy snapped. "This shouldn't take long."

As they talked, they heard voices and glasses clinking as the customers helped themselves. Light flooded through the open door a few feet away, when somebody lighted the coal-oil chandelier in the main saloon.

Kinealy took off his hat and coat, squared his shoulders, and went through the door, pulling it shut behind him. They could hear his hearty voice greeting and chiding the revelers, then a general laugh.

"Let's get this lid nailed down!" McGuinn

said, taking off his bowler and wiping a sleeve across his sweaty forehead.

"No. We can't be banging around in here," Packard replied. "Let's just get it into the wagon."

Mullins had come back inside and nodded his agreement.

But they hadn't figured on the size of the crate. It was a good eight or nine inches too wide for the door. Packard had forgotten they'd had to tilt even the smaller coffin to get it in.

"Shit!" McGuinn spat.

"What now?" Mullins wondered.

They looked at each other.

"How'd he get this thing in here?" Packard asked.

"Through the front," McGuinn said.

"We can't go back out that way," Mullins muttered, looking worried.

"We'll either have to tear the crate apart or widen this doorway," McGuinn said. "We've still got that axe we busted the tomb with."

"It'll make too much noise. If those men in the next room catch us at this, it's all over," Packard said.

"I'll take the door off its hinges," McGuinn offered.

"That won't do it."

"Then we'll use a crowbar and axe to pry the door frame off," he said.

"That may give us enough room," Packard said. "If we can do it quietly enough."

"Why don't we just take the lead coffin out and wrap it in that canvas?" Mullins asked.

"How the hell we gonna get it on a train if it ain't disguised?" McGuinn retorted.

"Hell, I can't work one-handed," McGuinn said, distractedly glancing around the room. "Since I used my suspenders to tie up that nut in the wagon and then busted this button, I gotta get a piece o' rope or something to keep my britches up."

As McGuinn swung his coat open and hitched up his pants, Packard noticed he'd apparently added a few inches to his girth since his prize ring days. The pants were sliding down the rounded slope of his underbelly.

It was like wading through hip-deep molasses, Packard thought, as one problem after another delayed them. He was acutely conscious of the minutes ticking inexorably away. And trains, like time and tide, waited for no man. The only ones benefiting were the horses, which were getting a little more rest.

At that moment, the door to the saloon opened, admitting a few seconds of loud talk and cussing from the saloon. Then it was cut off abruptly as Kinealy came in and slammed the door.

"Quick! Into the wagon! They're drinking, and I got 'em into a big political argument."

"We can't get the crate through the door," McGuinn told him.

"What?" This news seemed to stagger him. He

leaned his back against the closed door. The argument was getting louder in the next room.

"We've got to get that thing out of here," he breathed. "Take the lead coffin out of the crate."

They obeyed.

"Put the cedar casket in the crate and put the lid on the crate." His face showed his mind was working furiously.

They complied.

"Shove the crate over into the corner," he ordered.

The crate grated across the rough-board floor. Hay was strewn everywhere. They looked expectantly at Kinealy.

Suddenly there was a wild yell in the saloon, and another man shouted: "Then, by God, we'll get Kinealy to settle this!"

"I still say Tilden wasn't the. . . ."

The door burst open, knocking Kinealy aside, and three men tumbled into the room.

"Oh, there you are, Jim. We want to . . . to. . . ." The drunk stopped, swaying slightly in the lamplight and focused on the four men and the lead coffin at their feet. His eyes went wide, and he pointed as he opened his mouth to speak.

But Kinealy's fist got there first, knocking the words back into his throat as the man stumbled into the two behind him.

The four pounced on the lead coffin and almost tore down the door frame getting into the alley all at once with the body.

The untethered horses shied sideways as

they came bursting out.

McGuinn's neglected pants immediately obeyed the law of gravity, dropped to his knees, and tripped the big man. He pitched hard against a rear wagon wheel, his crushed bowler rolling away on the cobblestones. When he fell, the other three nearly dropped the lead box, but barely managed to get one end of it onto the tail-gate. Corbett had gotten to his feet, his arms still bound to his sides. But they slammed the coffin up into the wagon box, cutting his legs from under him. He fell, face first, onto the coffin.

Heedless of the shouting as two men appeared at the alley door, Kinealy sprang to the driver's seat and grabbed a handful of reins.

"Hyah!"

The horses jumped when the lines popped across their backs, and it was all Packard could do to keep one knee and one hand on the tailgate as the wagon lurched forward. Mullins and McGuinn had to run, and finally caught up when Kinealy slowed to make the turn out of the alley some fifty yards away.

"Wait a damn' minute!" a hatless McGuinn panted, grabbing for the wagon with one hand while holding his pants with the other.

As they turned the corner, Packard caught a last glimpse of the revelers in the alley behind, one of them holding a lighted lamp.

Packard thought they were all in a state of shock because nobody even questioned why Kinealy was driving in the wrong direction —

north — out of town. The iron shoes of the horses rang on the cobblestones as they fled. Several blocks away they hit a dirt street, and Kinealy finally turned the team west, and shortly the last few darkened houses of Springfield were left behind. He urged the team to a brisk trot, and nobody spoke for a good thirty minutes.

McGuinn unbound Corbett's arms and helped him stand up so he could urinate over the side of the moving wagon. After the preacher restored circulation to his limbs, McGuinn tied the captive's arms behind him, this time using Corbett's belt and retrieving his suspenders. He even removed the gag until Corbett became abusive again, and then replaced it to give their ears a rest.

"Boss, I think we better be lookin' for a good place to dump this guy," McGuinn said, jerking a thumb at Corbett. "Otherwise, we can add kidnapping to our problems."

"In for a penny, in for a buck," Kinealy replied, a fit of shivering shaking his hunched frame.

Packard looked over at him. He had removed his hat and coat in the storeroom and was driving through the cold night in his shirt sleeves.

"Packard t-take the lines," he finally stammered, drawing the team to a walk. "I've got to climb in back and warm up."

"What time is it?" Packard asked, sliding over and accepting the reins.

"Don't know," Kinealy said as he crawled

over the seat and huddled down in what remained of the hay. "Just keep 'em pointed west down this road. We should be there in time."

Packard whipped the Morgans to a gallop for a brief run, then settled them back to a trot. They saw no other travelers on the road, for which Packard was grateful. He wondered what Kinealy planned to do about getting the lead coffin aboard the train since they had no container to disguise it. And a blind man couldn't fail to recognize the shape as a coffin.

But he didn't wonder for long. That wasn't his problem. Maybe the happenstance of the uninvited saloon visitors would yet prove the undoing of this plot. He shook his head in amazement. This gang had operated more like a bunch of bumbling fools than a group of professional criminals. But in spite of that, everything so far had somehow fallen into place. It was almost as if some higher power was looking after them.

The road was relatively level, and the team had settled into a ground-eating pace. As the moon was declining, Packard spotted a row of trees that signaled a meandering stream. Guiding the horses carefully off the road and down through the black shadows, he found a low bank with firm footing so the team could drink.

They all got down to stretch. Their breath was steam in the flare of a match as Kinealy checked his watch.

"Eleven twenty-five," he announced. "We're

making good time. We should be there with time to spare."

McGuinn got Corbett out of the wagon and loosened his bonds so he could flex his stiff arms.

"If you keep your mouth shut, I'll take that gag out," McGuinn said.

Corbett nodded, so the boxer removed the soggy bandanna. The unbalanced preacher seemed to have lost his zest for berating them, or else he just didn't want to be gagged or punched by McGuinn again. Crazy he might be, but stupid he wasn't. Corbett leaned his forearms against the side of the wagon and wearily rested his forehead on them. The rest of the men walked a few steps away, so they could talk sotto voce among themselves.

"Reckon this would be a good place to leave him?" McGuinn asked. "We're far enough from town so he can't do us any harm."

After taking a drink from the stream, Kinealy was pacing up and down, slapping his arms to restore some circulation.

"No. There are a few farm houses in this area. If he walks to one of them, someone could drive him to town and give the alarm."

"Hell, those guys at the tomb have probably already sounded the alarm," McGuinn grunted. "What difference does it make?"

"The difference," Kinealy replied slowly, as if his jaw was frozen, "is that no one, so far, knows what direction we went. Even those men at the saloon saw me turn north toward Chicago. We have to keep them off our track for as long as possible if we hope to make Saint Joe."

They fell silent for a few seconds with their own thoughts. It was true they had seen no one after they had turned west.

"Wonder how those men at the tomb knew we would be there?" Kinealy said thoughtfully as he turned to look in Mullins's direction.

"Hell, it wasn't me, boss!" Mullins objected loudly. "I didn't say a damn' word to anybody!"

"Well, it's mighty funny they were there waiting for us," Big Jim continued.

"Well, I didn't leak nothing about it," Mullins said in an injured tone. "I learned my lesson last time."

Kinealy let it drop. In the uneasy silence that followed, Packard hoped the big boss wasn't beginning to suspect him, as the most recent addition to this gang.

Finally Kinealy said: "Let's move out. The team has rested and watered enough."

Another fifteen uneventful miles brought them to the deserted freight dépôt. It was nearly one o'clock in the morning. The wind had ceased some time earlier, and a hard frost was forming and seeping into Packard's bones. But he forced himself to ignore the weather as Kinealy drew them all out of earshot of Corbett who still sat, bound and again gagged, in the wagon.

"OK, here's the new plan," Kinealy said, snapping a lucifer to the bull's-eye lantern, and then setting it on the wooden platform. He was once more the confident commander of the operation. "That train should pull in here to water and pick up freight within fifteen minutes. We'll wrap that coffin as tightly as we can with that canvas and tie it up good. From now on, I will be Doctor Lyle Desmond, Professor of Antiquities, Harvard University. I am transporting this rare and valuable Egyptian mummy to an exhibition in San Francisco. We missed our train in Chicago, and, in order to keep to our schedule, we hired a hack to bring us here. Hmm . . . no, that won't work. Here it is . . . we've heard rumors of thieves plotting to steal this valuable relic. So, in order to throw them off, we left the train in Chicago and hired a series of hacks to bring us to Springfield and to this out-of-the-way freight dépôt. You men are my hired guards and escorts."

He reeled off this new scenario as if he were a director, revising the scene of a play.

"That should work," Packard said, feeling a bit easier about what was coming. "What are you going to use for identification and documentation?"

"The conductor and express messenger won't need that as long as we're traveling with the box. I'll pay for everything in cash. You've got to go along with me. Remember, my name is Doctor Desmond. Just take my cue and let me do most of the talking. Act confident enough, you can bluff your way through anything."

If Big Jim Kinealy had ever uttered a truth, this was it. Any ordinary man would have been quaking like an aspen leaf at the prospect of what he was about to face. That's probably what had made Kinealy a successful counterfeiter — intelligence, careful planning, and, above all, audacity. He was a living example of an old Roman proverb Packard suddenly recalled from his schoolteaching days — *Fortuna audaces iuvat* — Fortune favors the bold.

"Sounds good, boss," McGuinn said. "But how do we explain him?" He nodded at Corbett.

"We won't have to. This is where we part company with the fire and brimstone man. Mullins, you're now in charge of the wagon and team and our prisoner. Drive him as far as you can before daylight. Then turn him loose somewhere out in the country. Make sure he's not close to any farm houses or towns. I'd suggest you head southwest from here. Got that?"

"Yes. Then what?"

"Go a few more miles and sell the team and wagon wherever you can. Maybe Saint Louis, if you can make it that far before the horses give out. Then disappear. I'll contact you in the usual way as soon as this is over, and we have the ransom."

"Got it," Mullins nodded, his chest expanding, obviously pleased to be entrusted with so important a mission. Packard thought Mullins was also relieved that he wouldn't have the perilous task of riding the train with Lincoln's body.

"Here's a hundred dollars for expenses. And that doesn't mean you buy any liquor with it. Now, get going before the train gets here. That lunatic might later guess which way we went, but. . . ."

"Hell, boss, he explodes in more directions than a mortar shell. Nobody's going to listen to any babbling about us stealing a body or kidnapping him," Mullins said effusively, glancing back at the darkened wagon where Corbett was sitting up, his back braced against the coffin. "They'll think he's just reliving the war, or holding a revival meeting."

"Let's hope so," Kinealy said.

"He's a wanderer, probably without any family," Packard added. "There shouldn't be anyone to report him missing."

"OK, let's do it," Kinealy said, rubbing his cold hands together. "Lend me your coat, McGuinn. I've got to look a little more like a real professor." Then he dug out a pocket comb and ran it through his wavy, graying hair, relining the middle part.

As they lashed the tan canvas tightly around the lead coffin, and lifted it down to the freight platform by the light of the bull's-eye lantern, Packard was struck by how much the shape of the bundle actually did resemble a mummy case.

Mullins then climbed to the wagon seat and, with a few parting warnings from Kinealy, rumbled away into the darkness, carrying the bound and gagged Corbett.

They'd been gone less than five minutes when the mournful wail of a steam whistle sounded in the distance — the midnight express, blowing for a crossing about a mile away. Shortly, the weak beam of a big oil headlamp came swinging through the trees as the locomotive rounded a curve, and the train began to slow for the water tank.

Kinealy shrugged his shoulders, then buttoned McGuinn's tweed jacket. "OK, boys, get ready." He smoothed his mustache with one hand. "The curtain is about to go up on the Professor Lyle Desmond show."

Chapter Eight

The big drive wheels of the American locomotive ground slowly to a halt within a few yards of them, a cloud of steam hissing from the escape valves. By the light of their lantern, Packard read **Toledo, Wabash & Western** in gold letters on the side of the tender.

Two brakemen clambered atop the train to pull down the counterbalanced spout from the water tank as the locomotive lay quietly panting like some great, thirsty, black beast. The train was composed of an engine, tender, Wells Fargo freight and mail car, two passenger coaches, and a caboose. At this time of night, the lamps in the day coaches had been turned down so they were barely illuminating the square windows.

Hardly had the train stopped rolling than a black-coated conductor was on the ground, lantern in hand and thumping a fist on the door of the mail car. As they watched from the platform, the big door was slid open from the inside, and the messenger jumped down. There was a mumbled exchange, then the two came forward.

"What have we got here?" the conductor asked as the messenger went on past and jangled a ring of keys by the door of the unattended freight shed.

"Professor Lyle Desmond," Kinealy said, drawing himself up to his full height. "These are my two associates. I would like to put this box aboard your train and accompany it as far as you go. I believe your line runs to Hannibal, Missouri?"

"That's right," the conductor said, eyeing them rather warily. "What's in the box?"

Kinealy picked up their bull's eye lantern and flashed it quickly over the canvas-wrapped coffin.

"Oh, a dead body?"

"Not just a dead body, sir . . . a rare and valuable archaeological treasure . . . an ancient Egyptian case containing the mummified remains of one of the greatest of the Pharaohs . . . Rameses the Second."

"OK, OK." The conductor thrust out his hand. "Lemme see the papers on it."

"Papers?

"Bill of lading. Some kind of receipt."

"Well, I'm afraid we have a problem there."

Kinealy backed water with such convincing hesitation that Packard was almost tempted to believe what he said next. He plunged into the story he had just concocted about a gang of thieves trying to steal this prize to sell it to the highest bidder. He lamented that they had been forced to abandon the train along with their luggage containing all their documents in Chicago to throw the robbers off their trail. The newly created Dr. Desmond confided that they were on a tight schedule to get to the exhibition in San Francisco. It was an acting job worthy of Edwin Booth.

The conductor, a fleshy, middle-aged man with bushy side-whiskers that protruded from under the sides of his pillbox cap, looked very dubious. Three strangers showing up in the middle of the night at a remote water tank and freight dépôt with such a story and such a cargo. Evidently, except for the non-existing papers he demanded, he could detect no cracks in the story. But still he stuck to railroad procedure.

"I'm sorry, but I can't let you load that thing up until you can show the freight has been paid on it."

"Our lost bill of lading was for another rail line," Kinealy shrugged, "so it would not help now. But this is an emergency. I realize how irregular this is, but if we can't get to the West Coast by Friday, we will miss the opening of the exhibition. It was I who persuaded the board of directors at Harvard to allow this mummy out of the university's hands in Boston for this exhibition. I personally guaranteed its safe delivery. If I can't keep my word, or if these underworld body-snatchers catch up with us here in the middle of the night, it will undoubtedly cost me my job." His anguish certainly sounded convincing to Packard — until he realized that *they* were the body-snatchers. "If anything happens to this box, it won't be just my career." Kinealy almost sniffled. "The Egyptian government will lodge a protest with Washington and. . . ."

"OK, I haven't got time to listen to all that," the conductor interrupted, glancing around to see if the crewmen were almost finished watering up. The messenger was throwing two small boxes up into the open door of the baggage car. "Maybe I could take the payment for the rest of the run, and you can straighten it out with the freight agent at the Hannibal dépôt."

"That would solve everything! What is your name, sir?" Professor Lyle Desmond gushed gratitude.

"Perkins," said the conductor. "Of course, I couldn't do this if you weren't accompanying the body. And I'll have to have the fare for the three of you as well. It's another sixty-six miles to Hannibal at five cents per mile for each of you. Let's see . . . that's. . . ."

"Nine dollars and ninety cents," Kinealy prompted, when he saw the conductor was having trouble calculating this in his head. "Absolutely. That's no problem." Kinealy dug into his pants pocket for his billfold and began leafing through a thick wad of bills. "There you are Mister Perkins," he said, counting out three tens into the conductor's hand. "I believe that will more than cover the freight bill and the fare for the three of us. And here's a little something extra for your kindness." A double sawbuck went on top of the small stack.

"Well, I don't know. I'm not supposed to . . . I mean, I don't want this to seem like a bribe. I'm just trying to do what's right."

"If porters can take tips for good service rendered, then why can't conductors?" Kinealy concluded briskly, reaching out and closing the man's hand over the greenbacks. Packard fervently hoped those crisp bills had not been printed from some of Ben Boyd's plates, but he felt confident that, when Kinealy was playing for high stakes, he wouldn't do it with bogus money. That was the main reason Kinealy had not been arrested and brought to trial — he was careful never to let any of the fake money pass directly through his hands.

"Roscoe," the conductor addressed the baggage car messenger who had come up just then, "help these men load that box. There's no address label on it, but they're riding with it to the end of the run at Hannibal. I've taken care of the freight. We'll talk later."

"If you like, I could ride in the baggage car with it," Kinealy offered, all helpful smiles. "I'd actually feel safer about it, if it were in my sight all the way."

"I'm sorry but that's against Wells Fargo regulations," Roscoe said.

Enough, you big ham, Packard thought. Don't overdo it!

The three of them and the messenger grasped the tan canvas bundle by the tight rope lashings and lugged it to the train.

"*Ugh!* Those old dead guys are heavy," Roscoe grunted as they lifted the load into the open side door.

"It's the coffin," Kinealy said lightly. "Plus the gold masks and breastplates they're buried with."

Packard shot a hard look in his direction, wondering what had prompted him to make such an idiotic statement.

"Really?" The messenger's interest was immediately piqued.

"That's the main reason a gang of thieves is out to steal it," Kinealy continued, warming to his story. It sounded as if he were actually beginning to believe his own lies. The tale was expanding with the telling.

A sudden blast on the steam whistle cut off any further conversation. Roscoe looked as if he wanted to question Kinealy some more about the contents of the coffin, but he reluctantly jumped into the car and shoved the coffin to one side. As he slid the door shut, he called: "I'll take good care of this for you."

"Just give it the same protection as you would that safe in there," Kinealy replied with the tone of a worried parent as the three of them hastened toward the first passenger coach.

The conductor swung his lantern from the caboose, and they clattered up the iron steps of the car just as the train jerked into motion. At first, Packard thought of chiding Kinealy about calling undue attention to the coffin by his ridiculous story of it containing gold, but then he decided to let it go. Maybe Kinealy would just talk himself into getting caught, and Packard wouldn't have to do anything.

These thoughts were driven out of his head quickly by the welcome warmth of the coach. He took a deep breath and relaxed as they made their way down the aisle. By the subdued lighting of the three overhead oil lamps, he scanned the seats on both sides for some sign of Janice Kinealy and Rip Hughes. The car was three-quarters full of men and women and several children, most of them slouched in positions of strained repose, hats over eyes, shawls and overcoats thrown around the shoulders, feet up on carpetbags or the opposite seats.

Packard glanced over his shoulder at Kinealy and shook his head, then proceeded out the end door onto the swaying platform where the sharp wind took his breath. They stepped across the metal platform to the next car, the wheels and couplings grinding and clanking just below them.

The second coach was also stuffy-warm from the stove just inside the door. This car was less than half full, and most of these passengers were also dozing. Two men, who might have been drummers, were playing cards in the dim light as they faced each other across the flat side of an upturned leather case. All this registered automatically while Packard's eyes swept along both rows of seats, seeking their contacts. And, suddenly, there was Janice Kinealy, sitting near the back of the car next to Hughes. It was quiet in the coach, but Packard imagined her presence flashing across at him like heat lightning. He grabbed the seatbacks on either side of the aisle and took a deep breath to calm his heart rate. This was ridiculous — a man nearing forty reacting like a schoolboy at the sight of his first love. And her a married woman at that!

She and Hughes were very much awake, but they didn't acknowledge the barely perceptible nod Kinealy gave them. Kinealy and McGuinn slid onto the plush maroon cushions several rows ahead of them, while Packard flipped the seatback forward so as to sit opposite, facing the rear. If he was going to exorcise the devil of this woman from his emotions, he had to keep her in his sight and ignore the cynical laughter of his conscience.

After settling into his seat, he noticed Janice was dressed in a white shirtwaist and a short, gray jacket with a full matching skirt. She was hatless, and her brown wavy hair was swept back from her face, falling to her collar. Hughes was wearing a black suit, a white shirt with paper collar and string tie, his dark hair perfectly parted and pomaded. A typical, nondescript couple who would draw no attention from other travelers, as long as they stayed to themselves and kept quiet. Since the original plan had been just to leave the crate for pickup by the Wells Fargo messenger, Janice and Hughes were probably wondering why the others had boarded the train. She caught Packard's eye over her husband's shoulder. It was a curious but happy-to-see-you look. At least that was the way he interpreted it. He gave her a reassuring smile to let her know nothing was amiss. He would get an explanation to her soon enough.

The Toledo, Wabash & Western may not have been a long haul line like the Union Pacific, but it did make some pretensions of elegance. None of the newer Pullman sleepers were in evidence, nor did they haul a dining car, but the day coaches were well-appointed with plush seats and burnished woods, a closeted commode and washbasin at one end of each car, along with the standard potbellied stove. The conductor even kept a pot of coffee steaming on each stove for those who wanted it, along with a rack of porcelain cups and a jar of sugar.

By local railroad time, Packard guessed it to be about one thirty in the morning. He discovered the basic physical need for sleep took precedence over everything else shortly after he squirmed into a comfortable position on the double seat and the warmth began seeping into his bones. Abrupt relief from many hours of tension and physical strain and fear and frigid air was draining the strength from his limbs and the starch from his eyelids. He fell into an exhausted sleep.

Sometime later he was awakened by his head bumping against the glass of the window beside him when the train hit an especially uneven stretch of track. He sat up and stretched his aching muscles, twisting slowly against the pain of a neck stiffened from sleeping with his head cocked to one side. McGuinn was snoring, his head braced on one arm, while Kinealy slept with his mouth open, head thrown back against the seat.

He quietly eased into the aisle to stand up for a minute to get some circulation back into his left foot that was asleep. Nothing but blackness lay beyond the windows as the train lurched through the night. He braced himself against the swaying motion, half listening to the rhythmic clicking of the wheels rolling over the rail joints.

In this pre-dawn hour it appeared everyone in the car had succumbed to sleep. There was nothing he wouldn't have given at this moment for a nice feather bed and the leisure to stretch out on it. Why was it that problems always seemed worse and troubles insurmountable in the late hours of a sleepless night? Probably because that was the time when humans were at their weakest and most vulnerable, both physically and mentally. No wonder so many sick people finally let go and died early in the morning.

His mouth tasted like the floor of a chicken coop. He had gotten just enough sleep to make him feel worse than before, so he tried not to think about this bizarre mission, realizing that nothing but depressing thoughts of trouble would loom up in his fatigued imagination. His reverie was broken by a movement in the rear of the car. Janice Kinealy sat up and saw him, then silently gathered herself and stepped across her sleeping companion. She put a finger to her lips and pointed toward the far end of the car. He preceded her down the aisle to the stove where she signed that she wanted a cup of coffee. He retrieved two cups and poured each of them one, sweetening the bitter brew with several spoonsful of sugar. She looked her thanks at him over the lip of the cup as she sipped. Her eyes were slightly bloodshot, and her hair was crushed down on one side where she had been resting on it. But when she gave him a tired smile, he felt a surge of adrenaline that banished any thoughts of further sleep.

After a minute, she set her cup down and stepped to a mirror affixed to the wooden bulkhead just beyond the stove at the end of the car. By the dim light of the overhead lamp, she ran her slim fingers through her hair, then looked at him in the mirror with a smile and a hopeless shake of the head. She looked back at herself, and, for the first time, he noticed that the few threads of silver that had been scattered through her dark brown hair the last time he'd seen her were now gone. Apparently she had dyed her hair. It was his first indication that she had any vanity about her at all. As minor a thing as this was, he felt slightly let down by the discovery. He couldn't say why exactly, except that he'd idolized her from afar, bestowing perfection on a woman who was only human, after all. Who wouldn't want to stave off the signs of advancing age?

While this was running through his mind, she silently took his hand and led him toward the door. He turned the brass handle and thrust it open against the swirling air that smelled of woodsmoke. It was still November outside. They stood on the platform in the dark under the overshot roof of the car, letting the cold wind clear their heads. He braced his feet and leaned back against the wall by the iron railing.

It seemed like the most natural thing in the world to slip his arms around her, pulling her close, crushing her breasts against him. She was only an inch or two shorter than he, and she wrapped her arms around his neck as her warm cheek pressed against his cold, unshaven face. He was sure she could feel his heart pounding. But strength and reassurance seemed to flow from her, almost as it had that day years ago in the Georgia woods. And since they'd met again recently, he'd received subtle signals that she found him attractive. He couldn't imagine why, even though he'd been considered handsome in his youth. He was still lean and athletic, but the wear of the years was beginning to show in the bags under his eyes and some small creases in his face. Maybe all this was only in his imagination. Maybe she was simply giving him an affectionate hug that one good friend gives another. He didn't care — he would just enjoy the moment. Too much analysis would be like looking for pits in a free cherry pie.

After several long seconds, she drew back and regarded him. He was still smiling at the analogy.

"What are you grinning about?" she asked, holding his hands and giving him a mischievous look.

"Oh, nothing. Something I just thought of." He could barely see her face by the dim light filtering through the small glass in the door beside them. And when she spoke in a normal tone, her voice barely carried above the rattling and clanking of the running wheels beneath them. The train was probably traveling thirty miles an hour.

"I'm really glad to see you," she said. "But tell me what you're doing here."

"It's a strange story," he said, and then went on to relate briefly the tale of their adventures from the previous day. As he talked, she gazed at him intently, her attention never wavering.

"So the whole plan had to be constantly changed as you went along," she marveled. "It's amazing that you're even here at all."

"I'll have to give your husband credit," he said. "If it hadn't been for Big Jim's quick thinking, we probably would not have made it."

"Well, it's not over yet," she said after a few seconds of silence.

"Even if we get to Saint Joe safely, it won't be over," he said.

She didn't reply immediately. He got the feeling that she was not the same self-assured woman who had been involved in the planning meetings a couple of weeks before. He decided to probe a little to see if perhaps she was having second thoughts about this operation. Maybe he could win her over as an ally. He told her about Kinealy's mentioning that the "mummy" was buried with body ornaments of gold plate.

"That was stupid," she said. "Why would he say something like that?"

"I don't know," he shrugged. "I guess he just got carried away with his own story, trying to make it sound more authentic. Then, again, he had to come up on the spur of the moment with a explanation for the coffin being so heavy after the Wells Fargo man noticed it."

"I just hope nothing comes of it," she added. "We'll have to change trains in Hannibal, so there'll be somebody different in the next baggage car." She seemed to droop as she leaned against the railing next to him. "I wish this were all over, and we were back to dealing in bogus money. I'm afraid we've let the lions out of their cages with this. But Jim said he had to do something drastic to get Boyd out of prison."

"Do you know where he plans to hide the body once we get to Saint Joe?" he asked.

She shook her head and looked away. "No."

Was she telling the truth and embarrassed that Kinealy hadn't confided in her, or was she lying to keep his secret? Packard had no way of knowing. "Then I guess we'll all find out when we get there."

"I wish we were there already. I have a bad feeling about the rest of this trip."

"Well, we've been lucky so far," he said, trying to sound cheerful. "Maybe we're past the worst of it, and all the unexpected things have already happened. What else could go wrong?"

He was immediately sorry he'd said that, when she gave him a wondering look. "I can think of all kinds of pitfalls," she said, as if he had no imagination at all.

"The trick is," he hastened to add, "when you're in mortal danger, just concentrate on one thing at a time and ignore all the bad possibilities."

"I guess you're right," she conceded. "There's nothing else we can do now."

"If something should go wrong, all you have to do is pay no attention to it, as if you were just another passenger. As far as anybody else knows, you and Hughes have no connection to this operation."

"I couldn't leave Jim, and just walk away," she said simply.

"He'd want you to. That was the plan."

"Let's hope we don't have to worry about that," she answered, but her voice sounded forlorn. Here he was, trying to cheer her up, when a few minutes earlier he'd been drawing strength from her.

"What made you get into grave-robbing?" she

asked, suddenly changing the subject. "You just don't seem the type for that."

He shrugged. "It's a living. Times were tough, especially since the panic three years ago."

"Is that all you've done since the war?"

"Not really. I've tried various jobs but never really found what I'd like to do. Just drifted into this." He hated lying to her but had to maintain his cover. He consoled himself by vowing that he would tell her the truth someday, after all this was over. He tried not to think that someday might be when he had her and Big Jim in shackles.

"I guess the penalty for counterfeiting is worse than for grave-robbing," she observed somewhat wistfully, as if she were comparing the wages of sin.

He detected a note of regret in her voice, and pressed ahead. "Actually, it is. Bogus money hurts the country . . . cheats people who innocently accept it. A grave-robber steals the remains of somebody's loved one. It may seem like it's against common decency, but the bodies provide medical schools information that will help mankind."

"I always thought grave-robbers just stole jewels and valuables buried with the bodies."

"Sometimes a client hires me for that reason," he nodded. "Usually it's a relative who knows about a bracelet, a gold ring, or something like that. Then the coffin is re-interred."

She shook her head incredulously. "That's

such a macabre occupation. It just doesn't sound like you. Maybe I don't know the real Sterling Packard. If anything, I would have pictured you in some dangerous occupation."

"Well, very often the family puts an armed guard on the grave for the first few weeks," he said, repeating what he'd read in an old copy of *Leslie's Illustrated Magazine.* "So it can be very dangerous as well as illegal."

"But not as illegal or dangerous as counterfeiting," she mused.

"You're right," he said, seeing an opening. "I guess your husband has a central location in Chicago where all the bogus bills are printed and distributed from?"

"No. He doesn't tell me much, but I know he doesn't stay in one place long. I'm so tired of being in hiding and moving from place to place to avoid detection, and not being able to meet other people except a few shifty characters in the same line of work. He spends all of his time with his business associates, meeting with men from Saint Louis or New Orleans or some place. I never know where he is or when he'll be home. At first it was a lark. The danger and the secrecy of it was exciting. It was almost like a game of hide and seek when I was younger."

"Is that why you left me in that cabin in Georgia after you'd saved my life?" he asked, in spite of himself. "You thought I'd turn you in, if I found out what you were doing there?"

Her face took on a pained expression in the

dim light. "No. That wasn't it at all . . . at least, not on my part. It was Jim's decision to pack up and leave. I wanted to stay and nurse you."

It took the rest of his eroded will power to keep from reaching for her again. He swallowed hard, and, before he could speak, she said: "There was another man there, too, who was working with us, and he was in a panic to get out before the troops came and found us. That man left us shortly after. He's dead now. He went to robbing stores and got shot before the war was over."

"It's funny how a person's life just progresses from step to step until one day we look around and wonder . . . how did I get here?"

She nodded solemnly, looking off into the windy darkness. "I know. Sometimes I wish I had it all to do over again."

"What would you change?"

"I wouldn't get married until I found a man who worshipped the ground I walked on. And then I would want to have children."

Her incisive, straightforward answer jarred him for a moment. She'd said nothing about finding a man with a legitimate occupation. He knew counterfeiting had allowed her and Kinealy to live very well, so maybe money was not even a consideration in her plan for happiness. She'd mentioned the two things she would have changed in her life, and one of them gave him a hint that she was disappointed in her marriage. While he was thinking of an answer, the door beside him burst open, and Kinealy shouldered his way out.

"Oh, there you are."

Packard didn't know which one of them he was talking to.

"Packard, get back inside." Kinealy glanced quickly around, but the three of them were alone on the platform. "We're not supposed to know each other, remember?" he said in a deep voice, glowering at the two of them. "Let's keep it that way."

Packard nodded and, with one last look at Janice, stepped around Kinealy and opened the coach door. What would Janice tell him of their conversation? He was confident of her discretion as he noticed the coming dawn paling the sky behind them. What would the new day bring? They were less than an hour from Hannibal.

Chapter Nine

Janice returned to the car a few minutes later, her face flushed, mouth set in a grim line. Her eyes were downcast as she resumed her seat.

Big Jim came in shortly thereafter and flopped down across from Packard, his face like a thundercloud. Packard figured he might have been part of whatever transpired between them but just ignored the sinking feeling and tried to act nonchalant. He was even able to relax enough to doze off again for a short time.

The cars jolting together awakened him as the train slowed for the Mississippi River bridge. The coach creaked and swayed as the train crawled carefully onto the narrow structure. He rubbed his gritty eyes and looked out the window at the iron girders sliding past in the morning mist. Not far below, the mighty, slate-gray river swirled and eddied, sliding the ponderous weight of its mile-wide channel down the middle of the country.

Glancing around, he saw that nearly everyone in the car was now awake, shuffling dunnage under their feet, rubbing their eyes, standing up in the aisle to stretch, preparing to get off in Hannibal. Janice and Rip Hughes were sitting quietly alert. McGuinn and Kinealy were also awake, but looking like they'd slept on their faces. Packard felt pretty rusty himself but was determined to keep a low profile and not give Kinealy reason to see anything askance. His cover was still intact, but he had to proceed with great caution from this point on and play his rôle as the professor's assistant. The lump of the holstered Colt under his jacket gave him a reassuring feeling.

A few minutes later they were stepping down onto the dépôt platform, their breath steaming in an icy morning fog. He'd noticed from the train window that the Missouri shore just south of here was mostly high bluffs, but the town of Hannibal was built on an irregular shelf of land that gradually sloped down to a riverboat landing. Even at this hour, the dépôt was a busy place with porters pushing luggage carts and freight along, debarking passengers being met and hugged by relatives. As the door to the dépôt opened and closed, Packard could hear the faint rattling of a telegraph key from somewhere inside. The sound made his stomach tense up as he realized the news of the great Lincoln tomb robbery could be coming in over the wire at that very moment.

Kinealy shrugged his shoulders in McGuinn's wool jacket, raked his fingers through his thick hair, and said: "Gentlemen, we have a mummy case to transfer, and we'd best get to it."

Packard followed him forward along the bustling platform to the baggage car where the messenger, Roscoe, had the side door open and was handing down several boxes to a waiting porter to be stacked onto a push cart with large iron wheels. They waited a couple of minutes until he finished and the porter had moved away.

"Here we are, gents, safe and sound as promised," he said cheerily. "Ancient Egyptians travel safe with their gold by Wells Fargo."

McGuinn jumped up and helped him slide the canvas-wrapped box to the open doorway while Kinealy hailed a porter with a baggage cart. While they were sliding the load down, Packard glanced up and saw Janice and Hughes walking away from them across the street toward a building that had a sign over the door: Hot Meals. Only then did he realize how hungry he was. He hadn't eaten since noon yesterday, and even then a nervous stomach had allowed him only to nibble a few bites. But food would have to wait until they got this cargo aboard the baggage and freight car of the Hannibal & St. Joseph train.

Kinealy tipped the porter to trundle the cart with the coffin to the far end of the platform and park it next to the brick dépôt wall for the moment.

"The train to Saint Joe is making up in the yard and won't be ready to go for more'n two hours," the porter answered in response to Kinealy's question. "You got plenty of time to get you some breakfast at that eatin' house over yonder." He pointed at the building that Janice and Hughes had entered.

"Thanks," Kinealy said. "We can handle it from here." When the porter had moved away, Kinealy said: "Packard, stay here on guard while I go in and get our tickets to Saint Joe and pay the freight on this."

Packard nodded as Kinealy and McGuinn walked away. So far, so good. He took a deep breath and leaned against the wall, resting and watching all the activity swirling around the dépôt. But he didn't have long to relax. Less than five minutes later a newsboy came around the corner of the dépôt from the street, hawking papers. "Extra! Extra! Body of Abraham Lincoln stolen from tomb!"

The adolescent voice was like an alarm bell in the night that set Packard's heart to racing.

"Grave-robbers grab Lincoln's body!" the boy yelled.

Several people stopped the boy and thrust coins into his hand, and he was handing out copies of the thin tabloid as fast as he could jerk them out of a canvas sack slung across his chest. Packard was right there with them, getting one of the last copies before he sold out.

He moved back to the wall and glanced around. No one was taking any notice of him. Nevertheless, he had to dig out a bandanna and wipe his clammy forehead. His hands were shaking so he had to spread the newspaper out on the edge of the push cart to read it.

LINCOLN'S BODY STOLEN the banner

headline screamed. And in slightly smaller type beneath it: **Grave-robbers Snatch Martyred President's Body From Springfield Tomb.** Then, in descending size of type, **Ghouls Elude Police Trap** and **Bold Robbery Pulled Off During Presidential Election.**

Packard's mouth was so dry, he had trouble swallowing as his eyes scanned down the column, reading the hastily composed article that contained several typographical errors. The news had leapt across the wires ahead of their speeding express train. They'd gotten far enough away from Springfield so that maybe trains in Missouri wouldn't be searched, unless the law knew where to search. And that brought to mind Mullins and Boston Corbett. Even though Packard was on the side of the law, he found himself fervently hoping that Mullins had stranded Corbett far enough away from civilization so that he had not been able to spread his story. Or, if he had been able to get his tale of kidnapping and body-snatching to somebody's ears, no connection would be made between that and this caper. It seemed a forlorn hope. Even though Corbett was crazy, most policemen would have enough sense to make the connection. And that meant a telegraph message to sheriffs and constables ahead of them to stop and search the train. Even if Corbett's story didn't get out, Packard had no faith in Mullins. He was probably drunk right now and bragging to somebody how he had been one of the major players in the great tomb robbery that was making headlines across the country. Packard took a deep breath of cold morning air. Maybe they would have time to get across the state to St. Joe before any of that happened.

He looked back at the article, trying to pick up more details of what was known by law officers, but details were sketchy. Journalism hadn't changed; getting a story out rapidly still took precedence over detailed accuracy. The same thing was just repeated in different words, along with editorial lamentations about the audacity and gruesomeness of the business and speculation about whether the robbers would demand ransom. The report stated that the inept lawmen had sprung their trap on an empty tomb and wound up shooting at each other and wounding one Pinkerton man. There was no indication that the authorities knew where the robbers had gone, or possibly the police and Secret Service had not divulged the full story to reporters.

Then another thought stopped Packard. What about those drunks at Kinealy's saloon? They had seen the lead coffin. Kinealy had slugged one of them before running off with the box. Even as drunk as they were, they must have put two and two together after the story broke and told the police what they saw. So the law probably knew it was Kinealy's gang. The only hope was they didn't know what direction the robbers had gone. They had seen the body-snatchers drive north in the wagon, and that was it. As nearly as Packard could recall, he had seen no one else before they got out of town. And, with any luck, no one had seen them.

His fear of being caught was almost equal to his fear of not being caught. He didn't know how much longer he could stand up under the pressure of this ruse. He almost wished some lawman would come up and arrest them right now. It would be a great relief. On the other hand, he wanted to stick it out and see Kinealy and his men put away for a crime greater than destruction of property, or petty theft. He wanted to see them get the body concealed somewhere at the end of their flight and nail Kinealy for extortion when the ransom demand was made. Yet he could almost see the hurt look in the dark eyes of Janice Kinealy when his real identity was finally revealed. Lying to criminals was one thing, but to a beautiful woman he was smitten with . . . well, that was another matter entirely. He couldn't silence a voice in the back of his head that kept reminding him Janice was a counterfeiter as well. If not actively engaged in the business herself, she had condoned the work of her husband all these years and had lived on the illegal profits. *She's a thief,* the voice whispered to him. *She's no better than any of the others — just better-looking and more desirable.*

"Damn!" he said aloud in frustration.

"What's the matter?" Kinealy's voice asked.

He jumped and turned around. "Oh, you startled me."

"Something wrong?"

He handed over the paper without answering. Kinealy took it and scanned the page, his face a map of weathered seams. For the first time, Packard noticed the puffiness around his eyes in the harsh light of early morning. It was as if the vivifying force that normally effused his whole being had suddenly drained out, leaving Packard staring at the husk of a tired, middle-aged man.

"About what I expected," he said, handing back the paper. "I just didn't think it would be this quick." He smiled, and the corners of his eyes crinkled. "But what is this to us? Professor Desmond must get the mummy of Rameses to San Francisco for the exhibit. And, to that end, I have our tickets to Saint Joseph right here." The mask had slipped for only a few seconds, but long enough for Packard to catch a glimpse of the vulnerable man beneath. "Let's get this loaded, and then we'll get some breakfast," he said, glancing around for a porter. "There's the train, backing in, three tracks over."

A quarter of an hour later Kinealy, Packard, and McGuinn were seated in the eatery across the street from the station. Hughes and Janice were just finishing up their meal two tables away. They didn't look up, and Packard tried not to be obvious when he rested his tired eyes on her alluring face and form. They placed their orders with a mustachioed waiter who looked as if he hadn't been long out of bed. But the cooks must have been ready for rail passengers because the food — steak and eggs and fried potatoes — was prepared and served quickly. The desultory conversation ceased while they consumed their meal. After he'd washed it down with three cups of hot coffee with cream, Packard could feel his strength coming back. Confidence rose with his energy, and all morbid worries that had plagued his mind an hour before evaporated like mist in the rays of the rising sun.

Janice and Hughes paid their bill and left while the other three were eating. Janice raked Packard with a sloe-eyed look as she passed his table. This kind of flirting was as exciting as if he had been a young man, but it made him very uncomfortable, too. Her husband was sitting right there, and, even if he hadn't been, Packard wanted to maintain the appearance of a professional relationship while they were on the run.

The news of the tomb robbery had a few of the waiting passengers talking when the three returned to the dépôt, but the ticket agents, trainmen, and porters were still going about their jobs as if nothing had happened. They could no more take time off to hash over this news than they could any other sensational happening the newspapers trumpeted on a daily basis. Seeing these men work at their routine chores calmed Packard's nerves. It was good to realize the world wasn't going to stop just because of what had been done last night. It was all a matter of perspective.

Even so, the hands of the dépôt clock hardly seemed to move at all during the next hour. Packard killed some of the time by going across the street to a barber shop for a shave. Tilted back in the barber chair, his face wrapped in the comfort of steamy towels, he nearly went to sleep. Thirty minutes later he came out, feeling clean and smelling of bay rum. He was in the act of purchasing a handful of slim cigars from a street vendor when he looked up to see Rip Hughes, eyeing him from the dépôt platform. He felt himself tense. Was he watching to make sure Packard didn't run off? They weren't supposed to know each other. It wasn't likely Kinealy, who was the boss, had told Hughes to keep an eye on him. Something had aroused Hughes's suspicions, he thought, as he purposely walked out of sight behind the corner of a building and waited a few seconds. When he stepped out again, Hughes was walking swiftly toward him across the street, looking anxiously left and right.

"Lose something?" Packard asked.

"Uh . . . no," he said, pulling up short, and trying to act casual. "Actually, I saw you over here, and it gave me the idea of buying a few cigars before we get on the train."

"Help yourself," Packard said, gesturing toward the street vendor.

Two short blasts of the steam whistle announced the Hannibal & St. Joseph was ready for boarding, and Packard walked quickly away.

Hughes was humorless and didn't talk much. But Packard felt something he'd said or done had triggered Hughes's curiosity. It was just another reason to be on his mettle.

Chapter Ten

The squat mogul locomotive of the Hannibal & St. Joseph lay panting quietly, its black bulk beaded with the sweat of condensation, brass trim reflecting the sun that was burning off the cold morning mist. Packard had read that the locomotive's six drive wheels, the last two beneath the cab, made it a better machine for pulling loads over hills than the American-type locomotive with its four large drivers. And, as he followed McGuinn's broad back up the steps into the coach, he thought they would probably need that stronger engine to traverse the long grades and rocky hills of north central Missouri, a rugged change from the undulating farmland of Illinois. Every turn of those powerful drive wheels would take them and their morbid cargo farther from the scene of the crime. Strangely enough, he had reached the point where he was constantly thinking like a member of the gang.

He had no reason to feel any safer from pursuit, but he heaved a long sigh and relaxed as they left Hannibal behind. Maybe a man can stand only so much unrelieved tension before his mind and body relax automatically. He had apparently reached that point.

All of them sat in the same coach, but this time he positioned himself by a window, facing forward, so he had to look over his shoulder to see Janice and Rip Hughes who were across the aisle and slightly behind them. Hughes's stares were beginning to unnerve him. Maybe he had noted the way Packard was behaving toward Janice. At least, he hoped it was nothing more than that. He would have to be more circumspect. Without being obvious, Kinealy had made sure his wife and Hughes saw the newspaper headlines before they left the dépôt.

They made a brief stop in Palmyra, about twelve miles to the northwest, dropped a passenger, and picked up two. Then the train pulled out, heading west by south, and Packard stared out at the bare trees and hills that slid past his window. His thoughts drifted to the Wells Fargo messenger who had accepted custody of the canvas-covered lead coffin in Hannibal. His name was Louis Griffin, a grim-faced man in his thirties — the apparent opposite of the affable young Roscoe, the previous messenger.

"Why didn't you state on here that this mummy case contains gold?" Griffin had demanded, looking at the waybill when they slid the coffin into the open side door of the express car.

Kinealy had looked surprised, but still kept up his academic guise. "How did you know about that?"

"Roscoe told me," he had said curtly. "I like to

know what I'm responsible for."

"Actually, Mister Griffin, I didn't think it necessary to mention it," Kinealy had replied rather stiffly. "The mummy itself, as an archaeological treasure, is worth much more than any gold ornamentation surrounding it."

"Maybe to you," Griffin had grunted, pushing the coffin to one side. "But not to a lot of other folks. And I don't like surprises."

Maybe it was Griffin's surly manner or because Kinealy was tired and out of sorts, but, instead of currying favor with a tip and maybe a joke, Kinealy had just snapped: "It doesn't matter what's in that box. I paid the freight on it. Just do your job and guard it like you would anything else in this car."

Even though Packard was in a hurry to get to breakfast at the time, Kinealy's sharp reaction struck him as a mistake. If there was anything they didn't need, it was to draw attention to themselves by getting into some senseless argument with a Wells Fargo guard. He just hoped the blunt words were forgotten, and they'd have an uneventful trip to St. Joe. The sooner they could get this body hidden somewhere, the sooner he could formulate his own plan of action.

By his rough calculations, it was more or less a straight shot of just over two hundred miles across the state to St. Joe on the Missouri River. Depending on the number of stops, he figured they'd be there sometime the next morning. He popped open his silver pocket watch. It told him the time was ten thirty-five, but he could have guessed the time closer by observing the position of the sun, since every town and every railroad had its own version of the hour of the day. There was no uniformity.

"We're scheduled to arrive in Saint Joseph at seven fifteen A.M.," the conductor replied to Packard's question. As he handed back the punched ticket and reached for McGuinn's, his eye fell on the folded newspaper in Packard's lap. "That was a terrible thing that happened over in Springfield," he said.

"What's that?" Packard asked, feigning ignorance.

"That bunch that stole Abe Lincoln's body, of course," he said, jabbing his punch toward the paper.

"Oh, yeah, it sure was."

"Things have changed since the war." He shook his head sadly. "Attitudes are different. Nothing is sacred any more. Outlaws have more brass than ever. I hope they hang 'em up by their earlobes when they catch 'em."

"What makes you think they'll be caught?" Packard asked before he thought.

"Oh, it's just a matter of time," the lean conductor replied in a confident tone. "If the body's hid close by, the police will find it. It's not like you could slip something that big into your coat pocket, so they couldn't move it very far."

When he paused, Packard said: "It sounds like

you've given this some thought."

"Well, the stoker and I have a bet going. He says it'll be found within ten miles of Springfield. I say it only stands to reason that. . . ."

"When do we stop for lunch?" Kinealy interrupted, throwing Packard a warning glance.

"Well . . . uh . . . we don't make a regular lunch stop," the conductor replied, his train of thought derailed. "Just have to grab what you can during the few minutes while we're picking up passengers and mail. Supper stop will be at Chillicothe." He moved away down the aisle.

"Keep your mouth shut, Packard," Kinealy muttered between his teeth. "Professor Desmond will do any talking that needs to be done."

"Best way to throw off suspicion is to act normal and discuss the news," Packard replied under his breath.

"That's my decision. Shut up!" His face was suffusing red, and Packard knew better than to antagonize him further. He thought about saying something flippant to lighten up the big man's mood, but Kinealy was as serious as a new chairman of the board. So Packard just mumbled — "Sorry, boss." — trying to sound as abject as possible.

McGuinn had moved to the back of the car to warm himself at the potbellied stove. The stained bowler was still perched at a jaunty angle on his head, but he was in shirt sleeves, since Kinealy was still wearing his coat.

Packard could have used a cup of Arbuckle's about now, but this rail line didn't provide coffee of any brand, free or otherwise. So he just settled back and resumed looking out the window. It was a deceptively bright, sunny day. But he could see the bare tree branches and the few pines and cedars waving in the wind, even as the cold air was seeping in around the closed window.

"Gimme one of those cigars," Kinealy said a few minutes later. Packard pulled one from his shirt pocket and handed it over. Kinealy heaved his big frame from the seat and swayed down the aisle and out the end door to smoke on the platform. Packard slumped down on the padded, green velvet seat and let the rocking motion of the car lull him into a doze.

About mid-afternoon, somewhere east of Chillicothe, Missouri, Packard was nearly thrown from his seat as the train slammed to a sudden stop, the coach's couplings banging together. There was a thumping of bags falling from overhead racks and startled yells.

"Damn! What'd we hit?" McGuinn yelled, lurching over the arm of the seat.

"Must've derailed," Kinealy said, struggling to untangle his legs from McGuinn's as he staggered to his feet. But he fumbled under his coat for his holstered revolver.

Just as he cleared leather, the forward door banged open and two masked gunmen burst in.

"Drop that shooter on the floor, easy-like," a muffled voice ordered, as the man gestured with the long barrel of an Army Colt.

Kinealy let go of his pistol like the metal was hot.

A woman behind Packard screamed, and he looked back quickly to see Janice Kinealy helping to ease a fainting woman to the floor.

"You folks just sit still, and nobody will get hurt."

Both men were of medium height but looked taller because of the long linen dusters they wore. The outlaw who had spoken took off his hat and moved down the aisle like a man taking up a collection in church. His companion, who remained silent, stayed at the end of the car, gun drawn and eyes alert above the blue bandanna tied across his face.

Packard's heart was hammering, but he knew better than to make a move.

"I'll take that brooch, ma'am," the robber said brightly, slipping the pin from the high neck of her starched shirtwaist with his thumb and forefinger.

"Oh, please, no!" the woman pleaded, anguish in her eyes. "It belonged to my grandmother. It's a cameo. Not worth much."

"Huh! You're right. I don't need to be fooling with anything that hasn't got hardly any gold in it." He handed it back. "But those earrings are a different story, yes indeed!"

The young matron unfastened them with a

pained look and dropped them into his hat without comment.

"We're doing you a favor by relieving you of these trinkets of vanity," the bandit chuckled beneath the red bandanna as he moved on to the next passenger. "That watch and chain look a mite too heavy for you, sir." He turned his head to take in the rest of them. "You others, get your cash and gold ready!" he barked. "We haven't got all day. And I'm sure this train has a schedule to keep." He gave a snort of laughter.

A little farther along the robber set his hatful of loot on a seat, then jerked a well-dressed man to his feet and patted down his pockets. "That all you got? Gettin' a little chubby around the middle there, aren't you?" He yanked up the man's vest to reveal a leather money belt. With a sudden movement, the outlaw backhanded the man across the face with his gun barrel, knocking him back into the seat. A trickle of blood oozed from one nostril. With one hand the bandit unhooked the belt and pulled it off. "Now, anybody else want to try holding out?" He glared around, his eyes cold and hard above the mask.

He finished moving along the aisle, taking Hughes's billfold and a small wad of bills from Janice's handbag. Packard thought she was smart enough to secret some of the money before the robber reached them. The man behind him was dressed in worn corduroys and a coarse wool coat. He handed over a few bills and some silver dollars.

"Lemme see your hands!" the bandit demanded.

The man held them out, palms up.

The robber touched them. "Calluses. You a working man?"

"I have a small farm."

"Here. I don't steal from honest working men." The gunman shoved the money back into the man's side pocket and moved on. He took the fifty-six dollars and change Packard had, along with his silver watch, then relieved McGuinn and Kinealy of their cash and watches.

Cleaning out the few remaining passengers took only another minute. Then the two men backed out the door they had entered, slamming it behind them.

"Hell, we've just been robbed by Jesse James!" the man with the money belt yelled, holding a handkerchief to his nose.

"How do you know that?" Packard asked. "Just because we're in his home state?"

Kinealy was looking for his gun where it had been kicked under a seat.

"Didn't you notice how that man was limping?" the injured one whined. "Jesse was shot in the thigh in that bank raid in Northfield, Minnesota only two months ago. He hasn't been heard from since. Besides, robbing trains is his specialty."

"Why didn't you sing out, then?"

"What good would that have done? Maybe get my head blown off, if he knew I recognized him." He dabbed at his bleeding nose.

"Hell, Frank and Jesse aren't killers."

"Not unless they take a notion," the farmer said dryly. "I live around here. Just because they don't steal from working men don't mean they're like Robin Hood."

"I don't care who the hell he is," a third added. "I don't take kindly to anybody sticking a gun in my wife's face and scaring her half to death." The middle-aged woman stretched out across the seats was beginning to come around.

"What are we going to do about it?" the first man asked.

"Probably nothing. I reckon they're mounted up and gone."

"Naw. The train ain't moved yet. The big prize is likely up forward in the express car," the farmer said. "I'd say they're cleaning it out right about now."

Kinealy and Packard looked at each other.

"You reckon they'll bother the mummy?" Packard asked quietly, drawing his gun from his holster, while the other men in the car were still jawing back and forth, trying to convince each other they weren't scared. "Let's find out." Packard flipped open the loading gate of his Colt, turned the cylinder, and loaded the sixth chamber from his cartridge belt.

The men in the coach still talked and argued. It was apparent they were not going to challenge the James gang for the sake of some cash and a few personal possessions, no matter how dearly held. Rip Hughes stood as if carved in stone, staring in their direction. He carried no holstered weapon, but Packard felt sure he was probably armed with a small pocket pistol, or had a gun stashed in his bag. His blank expression gave no clue to his thoughts. Was he debating whether to come along, or possibly to warn them off? At the time, it never occurred to Packard that he might be paralyzed by fear.

Janice sat, worried eyes darting from Packard to her husband as the pair prepared to go out the forward end of the car. As McGuinn quickly drew his gun also, it suddenly dawned on Packard that the three of them were going up against an unknown number of armed train robbers, led by two of the country's most notorious outlaws. The realization made his knees as limber as rope.

Chapter Eleven

Kinealy led the way, shouldering aside the excited men and women in the aisle. He carefully opened the door at the end of the coach, but the platform was empty. In two jumps they were across to the adjoining car. While Kinealy looked through the window, Packard carefully peered around the end of the coach. Off to the left side of the train and about thirty yards forward one mounted man held four other saddled horses. So it was three against five. The other four robbers were apparently in the express car, just ahead of the coach they were entering. As Packard looked, the horse-holder's mount tossed its head and danced away from the acrid smoke that swirled down from the halted locomotive.

"All clear. Let's go," Kinealy said, opening the door.

The dozen or so passengers were talking in low voices, and several were at the windows. They turned to eye the trio as they passed through.

"Where are you men going?" The lean conductor blocked the way, looking at their drawn guns.

"Out of the way!" Kinealy said.

"You're not going up there. They've got the

rest of the crew at gunpoint. If you start anything, somebody will get killed."

"We must protect our cargo!" Kinealy said.

"What cargo is worth your life?" the conductor demanded.

"There is a very valuable Egyptian mummy in that express car," Kinealy said in his professorial voice. "I'm responsible for. . . ."

"To hell with your responsibility!" the conductor snapped. "The safety of passengers is my responsibility. You're not going up there. Besides," he added after a second, "those robbers aren't after any old mummy. They want something they can spend."

"They've got the brakeman as well as the express car messenger and the engine crew up there?" Kinealy asked.

"Right. So just stay put until they get what they want and leave. There's nothing we can do. Wells Fargo will make good any losses."

"What about the money and watch they took from me?" McGuinn growled. "And the stuff they snagged from the rest of the passengers?"

"I. . . ."

Kinealy shoved him roughly out of the way, and the three of them lunged past to the door.

Packard's heart was pounding and his mouth dry. This was carrying things too far, but, for some reason he couldn't explain to himself, he couldn't stand by and let the other two do this alone. The conductor was right. Jesse James would have no use for an ancient mummy, encased in a box too heavy and bulky to carry away without a wagon.

"Hold it!" Kinealy said, raising his hand as they crossed the platform and stopped by the windowless door at the end of the express car. He pressed an ear to the door, then shook his head. He placed a hand on the handle and carefully started to twist. It was locked.

"Maybe we better let it go," Packard suggested in a whisper. "The box should be OK." He hoped the nervous fear wasn't revealed by his voice.

"Not if that damned messenger tells them there's gold in it."

It was a possibility Packard hadn't thought of. "Surely he won't volunteer any information."

"I can hear voices inside. Apparently, they didn't have to blast the side door open," Kinealy said with some sarcasm. "The messenger doesn't seem to be putting up any heroic resistance."

Packard could think of other ways the robbers might have gotten inside without violence — but he held his tongue.

There was silence for a second, but he could tell Kinealy was itching to push ahead and confront Jesse and his boys. There was no way he could stall him any longer, so Packard volunteered. "Tell you what . . . let me slip around to the back side of this car and see if I can create some sort of diversion. Maybe I can pick off the man holding their horses. Or maybe I can slide the side door shut and hold them in there a bit until you and some of the passengers can be ready to pick them off when they come out."

He was only blowing hot air since he had no intention of doing anything except getting out of their sight and out of the way until these bandits were gone, but he had to put up a good front. He didn't know what had gotten into Kinealy. All of a sudden the man was going off half-cocked, as if he wanted to take on the whole gang of gunmen. Even if they were somehow successful in foiling this robbery, was Kinealy thinking of the glare of fame that would shine on him as a hero who had stopped the James gang — sudden fame that would be his undoing? Possibly it had something to do with acting the part of the heroic leader in front of his wife.

The conductor was of no help. Apparently, he felt he had done all he could to dissuade Kinealy and had not followed.

"Better yet," Packard continued, "let me see if I can get a look inside that car without being seen. If nobody's bothering the coffin, I'll just lay low until they leave."

Kinealy paused, as if having second thoughts about rushing headlong into this nest of coiled rattlesnakes. "Good idea, Packard," he finally answered. "Sing out if the coffin's in danger."

"Will do." Packard had hardly gotten the words out before he was down the off-side steps of the platform, feeling relieved for the first time since they'd been stopped some minutes before.

He was safe. He'd try to get a squint inside, but, if anybody was molesting that coffin, he'd eat his boots, heels and all.

As Packard crept along the tracks, crouching close to the express car, he realized for the first time that the outlaws had chosen a perfect place to hit them. They were near the top of a long, gradual grade and had probably slowed to no more than a dozen miles an hour by the time they had slammed to a halt. There was an identical sliding door on this side of the car as well, but it was closed and locked. From beneath the coach, he could see the legs of the horses on the other side. He stood up and examined the door to see how well it fit. The old car's blue-gray paint was peeling from the dried wood. The vertical planks in the door were not tongue-in-groove and had shrunk just enough to produce a crack perhaps a half inch wide. He pressed his face to the crack, and a limited portion of the interior came into view. The two men who had robbed their coach held pistols on Griffin, the express messenger. Packard moved his head back and forth, but couldn't see anyone else. The other two robbers were either out of his range of vision or maybe were in the cab of the engine, holding the train crew. The low rumble of voices was indistinguishable until he turned and pressed his ear to the crack. A voice he recognized as Jesse's came through. But now he had dropped all pretense of civility or courtesy.

"We've wasted enough time with you. Open

that safe before I count ten or tomorrow's papers will be praising you as a dead hero."

"OK, if you say so, but it's a waste of time, I tell you," came another voice Packard identified as Griffin's, but this time much less sure of himself. "There's no cash or bearer bonds or gold or stock certificates. You hit the wrong train." As he talked, his voice became muffled as if he had moved away. "I'll open it," he continued, his voice growing fainter. Packard could picture him, crouching by the big iron safe and working its combination. "If there was anything valuable in here, do you think I'd have opened the door so quick?"

"If you hadn't, we'd have blasted it off," came the reply. "You didn't have no damned choice." This came from a third voice Packard didn't know.

There followed several seconds of silence, then he heard a faint scuffling of someone moving around.

"See? I told you we weren't carrying anything much this trip," Griffin said.

"Damn you!"

There came a couple of thumps, and someone grunted. Packard applied his eye to the crack again, and Griffin was sitting on the floor, his back to him. He listened again.

"You think we went to all this trouble just so's we can go back with a few watches and a couple hundred in cash?" Jesse snarled.

"I can't help it that nothing valuable got

shipped on this run," Griffin whined.

"Hell, I got a good mind to tie you to that safe and blow this whole damned car to splinters," came the third voice.

"Leave him be, Frank. It's our own fault for believing our source about what this train was carryin'."

"Well, it'd give me a lot of satisfaction to take it out of this arrogant little bastard's hide," Frank grated in a deadly tone. There was another thump and a cry of pain.

"Wait! Don't hit me again. I'm just the messenger," came Griffin's suddenly high-pitched voice.

"What other freight you got in this car?" Frank snarled.

"Nothing much. A few cases of dishes, some boots, couple barrels of pickles. . . ."

"Pickles!" Frank was flying into a frustrated rage.

"Please, don't!" Griffin begged. "I've got a wife and child at home."

Packard expected to hear a gunshot at any moment as Frank snarled: "I reckon your wife and child'd be well rid of a snivelin' coward like you."

"There's something here you might want," Griffin's terrified voice continued. "It's an Egyptian mummy case."

"What?"

"I hear tell the body's encased in solid gold."

Packard reeled away from the door as if

McGuinn had punched him in the ear. He would have bet Kinealy would have gone straight, and Janice would suddenly have turned into a toothless, hooked-nosed witch before the James gang even glanced at the canvas-wrapped lead coffin. But now the unthinkable had happened! The messenger had given them away to save his hide. His heart pounded and his mouth was dry as he took another look. But all three men had moved out of his limited vision. Desperately, he pressed his ear to the crack again but could hear only muted voices for a few seconds. Then Jesse's voice said: "Hell, this thing's sealed in lead. We gotta find something to bust into it."

They'd gotten the canvas off! He had to do something quick. He could yell for Kinealy and McGuinn, but a shoot-out could end in several men being wounded or killed, and possibly the contents of the coffin being revealed. The trainmen weren't shootists, and it appeared none of the male passengers was eager to stand up to the robbers, so no help could be expected from that quarter. This flashed through his mind in a second or two as he considered, and rejected, a half dozen plans. It was apparent he had to create some sort of diversion to take their minds off the coffin.

An idea suddenly hit him, and he scrambled toward the front of the express car where the tender, stacked with cordwood, shielded him from view of anyone in the locomotive cab. He was sure the brakeman hadn't had time or opportunity to set the brakes on the individual cars. If he could uncouple the express car and send it rolling back downhill, that would surely distract the gang's attention quicker than anything he knew to do, short of violence. The cars were connected with a simple link and pin coupling. Simple, but stout, he quickly discovered when he tried to pull the iron pin. The locomotive's brakes were holding the whole train on this slope and were putting a strain on the coupling that would probably take three mules and a circus strongman to disengage.

He looked around frantically for some kind of tool. Nothing suggested itself at first until he noticed some detritus along the roadbed. It was that or nothing, he thought, as he selected a rock slightly larger than his head and mostly flat on two sides. It was heavy enough to be an effective hammer, but not so heavy that he couldn't swing it with some force. Bracing his knees wide, he knelt beside the coupling, grasped the rock on the edges with both hands, and swung upward with all his strength. Limestone chips stung his face, but the pin didn't move. He swung again, and yet again, grunting with the effort of the blows. Swinging upward, trying to punch the pin out was awkward, and he couldn't get enough force behind the blows. On the fourth hit, the rock split in two and fell out of his hands. He scrambled to find a thicker stone, conscious of another banging noise that was probably the outlaws, pounding on the lead coffin inside the car.

He started again, and sparks flew as his rock hit the iron pin a glancing blow. Cold wind chilled the sweat beginning to trickle down his face and neck. His breath was coming in gasps before the pin began to inch up from its link. Encouraged, he hammered like a madman. With one last mighty effort, the iron pin popped out far enough to let the heavy link slide free.

"Hey, you!"

Apparently alerted by the noise, the horse-holder was looking at him from about twenty yards away. The mounted outlaw dropped the reins of his own horse and jerked his pistol with his free hand.

Packard fell back out of the way as the man fired. The slug whanged off the iron rail hardly a foot away. Packard yanked his own Colt and threw himself flat on the far side of the slight embankment beside the tracks. He snapped off a shot and then saw that his cover was disappearing as the train separated from the locomotive and tender. The express car, two passenger coaches, and caboose very slowly began to roll backward. It was as if a snake's body had been chopped from its head. The gap widened to several feet and then to several yards as gravity began to pull the heavy coaches back down the long slope.

The horse-holder fired again, but his startled animals were jerking, and the bullet kicked up dirt several feet away. Packard heard shouting from the direction of the express car and knew he had succeeded in diverting the attention of the robbers who were trying to force open the coffin. He suddenly remembered the brakeman was being held captive in the locomotive. There was no one to stop the runaway portion of the train he had just unleashed. As the severed portion of the train began to pick up momentum, Kinealy's head poked out from the platform at the far end of the express car. He shouted something, but his words were whisked away by wind and increasing distance.

Packard's throat constricted as he watched. The train wouldn't merely roll to a stop after a mile or two. At the bottom of the grade was a long curve. With the speed this train would be traveling by the time it reached that point, there was no way it could stay on the tracks. And it wasn't just the two outlaws and the body of Abraham Lincoln he was sending careening down that hill. He could almost see the terrified face of Janice Kinealy when she realized that she and all the other passengers were hurtling toward destruction.

Chapter Twelve

Packard's inertia lasted only a matter of seconds. Then he bounded away after the retreating train with the speed of a sprinter. Fear shot so much adrenaline through his system that a mad grizzly couldn't have caught him. His boot soles barely touched the rough ballast and cross-ties as he flew toward the end of the express car.

The gap closed quickly at first — until a rock turned under his right foot. He felt his ankle going, and instantly tucked his shoulder and rolled into a fall. Momentum brought him back up onto his feet immediately. His ankle hurt, but he'd taken the pressure off it so quickly that he knew it was all right. The train had gained several yards on him. He redoubled his efforts, running just outside the tracks with one eye on the uneven ground ahead of him. It was an unequal contest; he had the advantage of desperation, while the train was only obeying the laws of physics.

He finally edged close enough to make a lunge for the iron railing. One hand snagged it, and then the other. But his feet failed to keep up, and for several seconds he was stretched out nearly horizontal, boots plowing a furrow through the dirt and stones. Pulling with both arms, he got his legs windmilling under him and, with a mighty bound, landed on the bottom of the metal steps.

His breath came in ragged, painful gasps, but he had no time to recover. The ties were flashing past just beneath, faster and faster until they looked like one continuous blur. He dragged himself to his feet and swayed up the two more steps to the platform. The door into the end of the express car was locked, for which he breathed a prayer of thanks. Even armed with his Colt, he had no wish to face Jesse and Frank James. His hand went automatically to the holster beneath his wool jacket as he tried the door. The gun was gone! It had apparently been flung out when he took that tumble. It couldn't be helped now. He had to stop this train.

As he stood there panting, he made a quick assessment of the situation. The two outlaws and the express messenger were inside this car. One side door was open, but both end doors were locked. He assumed Griffin, the messenger, had a key and would probably use it to unlock one of these doors once he realized their peril. But, by then, they would be going too fast to jump. Kinealy and McGuinn were still on the platform at the other end of this car, if they hadn't retreated into one of the coaches. He would have to climb over the roof to reach them.

His main concern, however, was to stop the train. Every car had a brake wheel at each end to apply a brake manually to the four-wheel truck just beneath. He grabbed the small iron wheel that stuck up about a foot from the hand railing and began to turn as fast as possible. He spun it until it would turn no more. If the brakes were being applied, there was no resistance through the wheel itself and no squalling of brake shoes against metal — nothing but the rumble of the heavy car and the screech of wheel flanges against rails as they picked up more and more speed.

He cursed himself roundly and loudly for doing such a stupid thing as uncoupling these cars. But cussing himself produced about the same effect as spitting into the wind. His next move had to be a lot more productive. To that end, he climbed quickly, but carefully, up onto the hand railing and grasped the rungs of the iron ladder that led to the overhanging roof. When he pulled himself over the top and looked down the length of that train, his nerve nearly failed him. Wind was whipping into his face at forty to fifty miles an hour, and each of the four cars was swaying dangerously. He hoped that Kinealy, McGuinn, and Hughes and maybe some of the other passengers were already trying to set the brakes on the cars. It was their only chance.

He'd never had an ambition to be a circus high-wire walker, but the next minute or so gave him plenty of training for it. With the car dancing a jig beneath him, he had to negotiate a three-foot-wide ridge that ran a full sixty feet. On either side of this raised ridge were small windows to admit light and air when the car was sealed. Also on either side of this ridge the roof sloped off to nothingness. Not even a seam or rain gutter to grab onto if he slipped.

He dropped to all fours and scuttled forward, trying to keep his weight low and centered as the coach whipped from side to side like an angry bull. The cold wind tried to rip him off backward. Half the distance was covered when the car suddenly lurched, and he was flung sideways, both hands sliding on the smooth roof. The toes of his boots snagged the ridge just before his upper body went over the edge. Holding his breath and straining to keep his toes hooked, he carefully placed his palms on the roof and pushed backward until his body was lying athwart the center ridge of the car. He lay there, heart pounding, and turned his head away from the wind to breathe easier. It was then he realized his face was close to one of the narrow, dirt-streaked skylights. Moving gingerly to keep his balance, he rubbed a spot clean and looked down into the express car. Griffin lay on his back on the floor, and the outlaws were gone! He raised his head and looked back up the hill. The locomotive and its tender were growing smaller in the distance, but the outlaw with the horses was nowhere to be seen, and he saw no one along the right of way. Somehow the robbers had gotten away into the woods, while he was plunging toward his death!

Crawling and gripping with fingernails, knees, and feet, he scrambled to the end. The whole trip couldn't have taken more than ninety seconds, but it seemed an eternity. He fully expected the train to be near the bottom of the grade, but a quick look showed the curve still at least a mile away as he climbed down between cars. Kinealy and McGuinn were not where he had left them. He flung open the door to the first passenger coach.

"Runaway!" he shouted. "Help set the brakes!"

"Already got six men on it," a rough-looking man in miner's clothes replied.

"Then come on and help me out here!"

"We've done set those," the miner replied, indicating the two brake wheels on the adjoining platforms where Packard had just entered. "They don't work worth a damn."

Packard pushed through several terrified passengers and out the other end of the car. Kinealy and Hughes were twisting the iron wheel on the platform, and this brake was working. A high-pitched squeal of agonized metal nearly pierced his eardrums. Across the platform Janice Kinealy was helping turn one of the brake wheels until a brawny man with a full beard gently pushed her aside and lent his muscle to the effort.

Packard bounded across the platform, grabbed Janice by the shoulders, and pulled her inside the coach. Her brown eyes were wide with fear. "Are we going to crash?"

"I hope not," he replied, somehow seeing everything clearly and calmly. "Are there men on the caboose brakes?"

"Yes. The conductor and three or four others."

"I'll go help."

He dashed out the lower end of the car with Janice right behind him. But his help wasn't needed. In fact, there was no room for him to get close to the brake wheels; they were being fully manned by the male passengers. For the first time he felt they might have a chance. Their efforts to save themselves could make the difference. He and Janice stepped back into the coach and waited. He stuck his head out of a window and saw the curve coming up fast. The air was full of rumbling, grinding, and the smell of scorched metal. Their freewheeling speed was gradually being checked, but not nearly quickly enough.

A few seconds later the caboose careened into the curve, and all passengers in the following coach instinctively threw their weight to the inside as the car leaned outward, wheel flanges screeching against the rail. He grabbed Janice and pushed her into a seat against the window, wedging himself in against her. The men outside clung to the brake wheels and railings to keep from being flung off the platforms as centrifugal force pulled them toward the trees and rocks. He could have sworn he felt the inside wheels of the truck lift clear off the rail. Tortured steel screamed. The coach tilted at an impossible angle and hung there, suspended, for the space of several heartbeats. Packard held his breath and hugged Janice tightly, bracing for the crash.

Limestone ledges and tree trunks flashed past in a blur, and then the coach settled back onto its wheels as the curve flattened out. His breath escaped in a long sigh. Now that the weight of the train was on nearly level ground, the inefficient mechanical brakes took hold and pulled them to a stop within a quarter mile. The sudden silence was deafening.

For several long seconds, nobody moved, nobody spoke. Packard thought they were all amazed that they weren't mangled beneath a pile of jagged splinters and twisted metal.

"My God, Sterling, that was close!" Janice breathed. He was suddenly conscious of her rigid form clinging to him.

"About one mile an hour faster and we wouldn't have made it," he gasped, his voice a little shaky. He was in no condition to appreciate her nearness as they numbly disengaged themselves and stood up. The reaction was setting in, and his knees were so wobbly he had to hold onto the seat backs to stay erect.

Finally somebody muttered a joke and someone else laughed. The tension was broken, and everyone began stirring and talking at once, the relief obvious in their voices.

Kinealy, McGuinn, and Hughes came

through the milling passengers, many of whom were making for the doors to get outside.

"What the hell happened?" Kinealy demanded, looking at Packard. "Why did they uncouple these cars?"

With a start he realized that no one had seen him knock the coupling pin loose. Rather than try to justify his actions, he quickly decided to let the James boys take the blame.

"Damned if I know," he said, seemingly baffled, but actually stalling while he struggled to concoct some sort of plausible tale. He said in a low voice. "I heard that damned messenger tell them there was gold in the mummy case."

"I thought that might happen," Kinealy nodded.

Now that suspicion was deflected from him, Packard continued: "Before I could figure out how to stop them, or give you the high sign, the one holding their horses started shooting at me." He affected a disgusted look. "My gun's lying back there along the track somewhere."

"Let's step outside a minute," Kinealy said, taking his arm. McGuinn followed, while Janice and Rip Hughes stayed inside.

They stood away from some of the other passengers on the lee side of the train out of the cold wind. The pale afternoon sunshine felt good, and Packard began to relax.

"Did they get into the coffin?" Kinealy asked, striding along the left side of the train toward the open express car.

"Don't think so. I got a quick look inside from the skylight," Packard replied. "Griffin was on the floor, and the James boys were gone. But I didn't have time to look for the box." He had a sudden thought to elaborate on this lie. "Maybe they were rolling the train back down to a waiting wagon."

"They had no way of knowing there was any loot big enough to require a wagon," Kinealy said over his shoulder.

By then they were close enough to see the conductor and the farmer helping Griffin down out of the express car. Blood smeared the side of his face.

"I'm all right," Griffin said, waving them off as they came up. "Let me sit down here a minute." He accepted a bandanna the farmer was offering and dabbed gingerly at his bloody, matted hair.

"You shot?" Kinealy asked.

"No. They clubbed me before they jumped off," he replied, sitting down weakly on the bleached grass.

Kinealy, McGuinn, and Packard all scrambled up into the open side door. The ropes had been cut, and the canvas cover thrown aside. The coffin was in plain view and showed numerous hacks and dents from an axe, but the lead had not been breached.

Before they could cover it, the conductor hopped up nimbly beside them. "Is that your mummy case?"

"Yes."

"They didn't get it, then." He took a second look at the coffin. "I didn't know those things were encased in lead."

"The university had that done to protect the fragile wood," Kinealy lied quickly.

"Oh."

The success of their ruse continued to rely on the ignorance of most people as to what a real Egyptian mummy looked like. Actually, Packard's only contact with one was a detailed woodcut he had seen once in a *Harper's Weekly* article.

McGuinn grabbed up the discarded canvas cover, and the three of them began quickly to rewrap the heavy box.

As they worked, Packard reflected that Kinealy might do some more probing when things settled down. But his basic story, with a few elaborations, should stand up to any questioning. By the time they had found enough intact pieces of rope to retie the coffin securely, the sound of the chuffing locomotive was coming closer as it backed down toward them.

Just to keep Griffin on his heels, Packard caught him momentarily by himself, still sitting on the grassy bank.

"You're lucky those robbers jumped off," he said quietly to the messenger.

Griffin looked up.

"If they'd gotten away with that mummy, you'd have something worse than that bump on the head."

He colored slightly at the veiled threat.

"I heard you tell them there was gold in there," Packard continued.

Griffin looked surprised, but couldn't deny it.

"I won't say anything about it to your superiors at Wells Fargo. But if I hear that you've breathed a word about that mummy to anyone else, you'll answer to me and to him." Packard gestured at the burly McGuinn a few yards away. "We're Doctor Desmond's escort and guards for that case. You understand?"

"Yes," he mumbled.

Packard moved away, satisfied he'd given Griffin something to think about that would head off any suspicions the messenger might develop about their cargo. He was also learning a thing or two about tactics from Kinealy.

"Everybody back aboard!" the conductor yelled, waving the excited passengers toward the coaches.

The miner and the farmer helped Griffin to his feet and into the express car.

"I'll stay with him until we get to Saint Joe," Kinealy said, soaking a bandanna with a canteen of water he had scoured up somewhere. "Just to make sure," he added as Griffin started to object. "You could have a concussion."

"I'm all right," Griffin said slowly and without much conviction.

"Well, I'm staying with you," Kinealy concluded, climbing into the car. "Besides, it was my cargo they almost got, thanks to you."

Griffin turned a mournful face in his direction.

"You need any help, Doctor Desmond?"

McGuinn asked.

"No. We'll be fine," Big Jim replied.

Packard was relieved to be away from Kinealy for the rest of the trip; he didn't want to be pressed for any answers until he'd had time to yank all the kinks out of his story.

With hand signals from the brakeman guiding him, the engineer eased the locomotive into position to recouple the train. While the brakeman was reconnecting the tender to the express car, and then going from coach to coach releasing all the hand brakes, Packard walked over to the cab of the locomotive and yelled up at the engineer: "I lost my gun on the track just this side of where you were stopped."

"We'll get it," he replied.

"Anybody hurt?" Packard asked as an afterthought.

"Naw. Just scared the hell out of us. They made for their horses as soon as they saw the rest of the train take off."

The stoker was behind him, throwing short chunks of wood into the firebox.

"Did the two in the express car jump?" Packard asked.

"Yeah," the engineer replied. "Before you got going too fast. You didn't see 'em?"

Packard shook his head.

"Pure dumb luck they didn't break their necks," he snorted. "Reckon 'cause they rolled down the embankment in the grass." He pulled off his gauntlets and leaned both elbows on the padded armrest in the open window. "They was on their feet in a jiffy and running for their horses like the devil was after 'em. Too bad nobody boosted 'em on their way with some hot lead. But I reckon you all had other things on your minds right about then."

"You bet. We were mighty lucky that runaway didn't fly right off into the woods."

"Who in the hell uncoupled us, anyway?" the engineer wanted to know, pushing up his cap.

Packard shrugged.

"I reckon it kept them from cleaning out the express car, though."

"Griffin said there wasn't much worth stealing this trip," he replied, walking off. "Don't forget about my gun."

Packard was the last passenger to climb aboard, just ahead of the conductor. With two short blasts of the steam whistle, the locomotive jerked them into motion. Caught off balance, Packard staggered in the aisle and nearly fell into Janice Kinealy's lap.

"Sorry, ma'am," he nodded, catching himself and smiling at her as if she were merely an attractive stranger.

"Quite all right," she replied, squeezing his hand surreptitiously.

Hughes glared, but Packard only smiled to himself as he moved away. He was feeling invincible after that harrowing brush with death and considered Hughes no more than a pesky mosquito.

Chapter Thirteen

They reached Chillicothe some time after dark with no further problems, other than Packard's personal problem of a growling stomach and a billfold that was flatter than a mallard's instep.

"Hope they sprained their ankles when they jumped," he grumbled, feeling for his absent watch. At least, he had retrieved his gun from alongside the track.

They all filed off the train for the supper break. Packard paused on the platform, thinking to stretch his legs and get a drink of water in the hope that hunger wouldn't keep him awake through the night. He knew neither McGuinn nor Kinealy had any hide-out money left. He wondered idly, if hunger might induce him to pass some of Kinealy's counterfeit money, had some of the bogus bills been in his pocket at the moment. Luckily, he wasn't faced with that temptation.

As this hypothetical situation was passing through his mind, somebody bumped him in the crowd, and he whirled, ready to defend himself from a pickpocket.

"Shhh!"

He could barely see Janice in the lamplight

from the dépôt. Hughes wasn't glued to her side as usual. She slipped a coin into his hand. From the size and weight he recognized a five-dollar gold piece.

"Share it," she whispered. Then she was gone into the crowd.

Packard caught up with McGuinn who had found Kinealy. They went into the dining room adjacent to the dépôt, but there were few diners since most of the passengers were in the same financial condition. They bought three sandwiches, and Kinealy kept the change. He took part of this to pay for a telegram. Packard overheard him give a Chicago address to the Western Union telegrapher who was on duty behind a wire cage in the dépôt.

"Isn't that dangerous . . . sending a telegram like that?" Packard asked a few minutes later, when they were warming ourselves by the dépôt stove and eating their sandwiches.

"Can't be helped. We've got to have money," Kinealy replied. "I encoded the message just as I always do. How do you think I've stayed in business all these years?" he asked with a hint of pride. "We'll have some money waiting for us in Saint Joe."

"Who was it to?" Packard inquired innocently, munching his food.

"Nobody you know," he replied shortly.

"We won't have to worry about being broke for long," McGuinn grinned around a mouthful of food. "We'll be rolling in gold and greenbacks when we sell that damned box back to them."

"Keep shut about that!" Kinealy grated, glancing furtively around. "You never know who might be listening."

Packard looked up and caught a glimpse of Janice and Rip Hughes entering the dining room. Apparently Janice had been able to hide more than just the five she'd slipped to him. Of all of them, she alone had had the presence of mind and opportunity to hide some money from the robbers, and, being a woman, she was also less likely to be searched than the men. In spite of his reputation, Jesse James didn't impress Packard as the type to abuse a woman in the course of a hold-up.

An hour later they were back aboard the train and chugging away into the Missouri darkness. By this time, Packard was very fatigued. About a dozen passengers had detrained, freeing up extra seats. Packard took advantage of the space to stretch out on a double seat and sleep for four solid hours, waking only for an hour or so around midnight, then dozing off and on until daylight.

A few of the people in the coach were stirring when he got up and stretched. Janice was asleep in her seat, leaning her head against the window. Hughes was just returning from the commode at the end of the car, and avoided his eyes as Packard strode out the opposite end of the coach to get some fresh air on the platform. The sun was just tipping the horizon behind them, its rays glittering off the frost-covered trees and grass. The biting air cleared his head quickly, and he shivered in the wind that was whirling around the moving car. The pleasant smell of wood smoke drifted back from the locomotive. As the train rounded a slight curve, Packard leaned out and squinted into the cold wind. Through watering eyes, he was surprised to see a scattering of houses atop a slight rise about a half mile ahead. He could only guess at the local time, but the position of the rising sun indicated the engineer had made up the lost time. St. Joe was coming up on schedule.

Their only luggage was the wrapped coffin, so he and McGuinn were at the side door of the express car less than a minute after the train finally ground to a halt at the St. Joseph dépôt. Griffin unlocked the door and slid it open. From the looks of him, Kinealy had apparently spent a sleepless night on the hard floor, and Packard doubted anyone could have been happier that their trip was over. The original plan had been for Janice and Hughes to rent a wagon and take delivery of the crate that would be labeled harrows. The three men were not supposed even to be aboard. But circumstances had altered the scheme, and now Professor Lyle Desmond and his two guards were responsible for the Egyptian mummy. Janice and Rip Hughes would go about their business and disappear. At least, that's what Packard assumed.

The three of them and Griffin off-loaded the

coffin onto the platform and waited while McGuinn hurried off to hire a wagon and team, without any money, as it turned out. Kinealy and Packard waited by the coffin, standing back out of the way of the milling passengers and porters who crowded the dépôt platform at this busy terminal. Packard saw no sign of Janice and Rip Hughes, but assumed they'd show up later. He still had no idea where Kinealy planned to hide their gruesome cargo, but just held his peace as they waited. He nervously lit a cigar, hoping it would take his mind off breakfast.

They needed to be gone from here before the train crew reported the robbery and the law showed up, asking questions. Kinealy was unusually silent, and from the look on his face Packard didn't think it wise to generate any small talk, and there were too many people nearby to discuss their real business. Finally, when he had about decided McGuinn wasn't coming back, he saw him edging a span of mules and a wagon through the jam of buggies and drays that crowded the far end of the loading platform beyond the dépôt. McGuinn waved, and Kinealy and Packard quickly got a porter to help them lift the coffin onto an iron-wheeled luggage cart so they could trundle it to the wagon. Kinealy tipped the porter what Packard figured was their last dollar, and they got the heavy burden aboard the wagon.

"That way," Kinealy said, pointing. "Down toward the river."

McGuinn's big hands had a delicate touch on the reins, and he seemed to have a natural way with the team as he backed them gently, clucking to the strange mules. They started off along the dirt streets, Kinealy sitting on the driver's seat with McGuinn while Packard rested on the floor of the wagon bed with the coffin. He was finally going to find out where Kinealy planned to hide the body while he contacted the governor with his ransom demands.

"Had to leave my gun for security at the livery since I was fresh outta money," McGuinn said.

Packard was surprised the stable operator would accept a twenty-dollar gun for a wagon and team, until he remembered that McGuinn's pistol was a nickel-plated, engraved Colt with ivory grips — a true work of art worth at least a hundred dollars. He had displayed it once when the two were discussing firearms. The fancy scrollwork had been done by Ben Boyd, the engraver of counterfeit plates whose release from prison Kinealy was planning to negotiate.

"Are Janice and Hughes going back to Springfield?" Packard asked as the wagon clattered over the cobblestone streets near the waterfront.

"No. They'll be putting up at the Patee House."

"They've got the cash for that?" Packard wondered aloud, turning to look at the big, six-story brick hotel that dominated the town from a hillside several blocks above them.

"They won't have to pay until they check out.

And we'll all be solvent again as soon as the bank opens and I get the money I wired for," Kinealy replied.

"And I need to get me a coat, boss, if you're going to keep mine," McGuinn said. He was still in his striped shirt and derby hat.

Kinealy stripped off the wool jacket and handed it over. "Here. I'm done with it. I'll get one later."

"Thanks."

"Turn right at the next corner."

Packard saw the tall stacks of several steamboats, lying at the long, sloping landing about two blocks to the west. They were in an area of brick warehouses, saloons, and boarding houses. The buildings alternated with a few muddy fields. Scattered among the patches of dead grass in the vacant lots were bottles, rusty cans, and broken wagon wheels. Since the big rush to the gold fields a quarter century ago, St. Joe had taken on the aspect of a well-settled, permanent — even a run-down — river town. The trio drew no more than casual notice from the pedestrians and drivers of other buggies and wagons and men on horseback who were passing up and down the streets of the busy port.

"Stop here," Kinealy ordered.

"Whoa, mules, whoa!"

Kinealy hopped down. "I'll be right back."

He strode away down the street and rapped on the front door of a saloon that appeared to be still closed this early in the day. He had to knock again before the door was opened, and he disappeared inside.

Packard and McGuinn sat for what seemed a long time but, in reality, was probably only a few minutes.

"What's he doing?" McGuinn finally asked.

"You got me," Packard said, looking over the twitching ears of the mules at the closed door. "He never mentioned the rest of his plan beyond just getting here to Saint Joe." He felt very exposed, waiting in an open wagon with the President's body while people were passing up and down the street.

Finally the door opened, and Kinealy reappeared, followed by a bald man in shirt sleeves and vest. They walked around to the side of the building and motioned the wagon forward.

McGuinn popped the reins over the backs of the team, drove about fifty yards, and swung into a vacant lot next to the saloon, pulling the wagon up near a side door.

"This here is Andy Riley, an old friend of mine," Kinealy said. "Jack McGuinn and Sterling Packard," he said, pointing at the two. They nodded at each other without shaking hands.

Riley was nearly as stout as McGuinn, except it appeared that most of the black hair had slipped off his head and come to rest on his chin. His upper lip was shaved, giving him the stern appearance of a Mormon elder or a Nantucket whaling captain.

Following the quick introductions, they slid

the coffin out of the wagon and squeezed through the door with it, two of them at each end. Packard had probably toted Abraham Lincoln in and out of more places than his original pallbearers, he thought grimly, as they struggled down some steep, narrow wooden stairs into a basement. A lantern hanging from the seven-foot ceiling cast a dim light through the interior of the dank, chilled room. The walls were mortared rock, but the floor was packed earth. In the center of the small room was a grave about three feet deep, with the freshly turned earth piled to one side.

"Right down in there, boys," Kinealy grunted.

They lowered the coffin by its tie ropes. The bottom of the damp hole was thickly padded with newspapers. For some reason Packard was glad to see this, even though the sealed coffin would keep the corpse from any kind of dirt or outside contamination.

Riley then took a scarred wooden door that was leaning against a wall and laid it over the grave. "Now we'll just throw a little loose dirt over this so it won't be obvious." He picked up a shovel.

If anyone saw this floor, the disturbed earth would certainly be obvious, Packard thought, but he said nothing.

"You the only one who has a key to the door that leads down here?" Kinealy asked, as if confirming something he already knew and wanted repeated in their presence.

"That's right," the bearded saloonman nodded, scooping dirt over the wooden cover. "Just like you asked. There's a trap door behind the bar that opens into this ceiling, but I never use it. It had a ladder that reached down here, but I took it out when I heard you were coming with this . . . this . . . box. That door we came in is the only way down here."

"OK, good. Let's go upstairs and have a drink to celebrate," Kinealy said, rubbing his hands together. His confident good humor had returned, and he seemed well-pleased with himself as he led the way back up the stairs and outside into the pale sunshine. Riley was last out with the lantern and locked the door, making an obvious motion of slipping the padlock key into his vest pocket.

They all went through the saloon's front door, and Riley locked it after them.

"What's your pleasure, gents?" the saloonman asked in a deep voice, going behind the bar. "It's on the house."

"It better be, considering what I'm paying you," Kinealy responded good-naturedly. "Besides, we're all broke. You won't believe what happened to us on the way."

Riley brought a bottle of Kentucky bourbon and one of brandy from the back bar and set them on the table with four shot glasses.

"A little early in the day for me," Packard said. "Just draw me a beer."

Riley complied as Kinealy began the tale of the

robbery and their wild train ride. To Packard's great relief, he gave one of the bandits credit for uncoupling the train.

They sat there around a table in the closed saloon for nearly an hour, while McGuinn and Kinealy unwound with several shots each. The setting took Packard back to the blustery night in October when they had met in Kinealy's saloon in Springfield, finalizing the plans for this caper.

"By God, Andy, the last two or three days have been the greatest adventure of my life!" Kinealy declared. "And that's saying something, 'cause I've had a few adventures in my time." His tongue seemed to be getting a little thick as he refilled his glass and held it up. "Here's to the success of our enterprise."

Packard raised his mug. "And may Honest Abe be resting in Springfield shortly after a bundle of cash is resting in your pocket!" he added to the toast as they all touched glasses and drank.

"Well the hardest part is over," McGuinn said, leaning back and crossing his legs. "Smooth sailing from here on."

"Don't be relaxing too soon. Negotiating with the Illinois governor won't be any picnic," Kinealy replied. "He's gonna be mad as hell." Then he smiled. "But I'll have him over a barrel . . . or, rather, over an empty tomb." They all laughed, except Riley.

"The police and the Secret Service won't think it's too damned funny," he commented, sipping at his brandy. Packard noticed he was drinking much less than the other two — a good trait for a saloon owner.

After the second beer, Packard got up. "Where's the outhouse?"

"Straight through that back door," Riley said, pointing.

Packard thought this might be his best opportunity to get away as he made his way through the tables, out the unlocked door, and across the broad alley to a rickety outhouse.

His heart was beginning to beat fast with excitement as he hurriedly relieved himself, trying to decide which way to run and where might be a good place to hide.

But as soon as he opened the door, there was McGuinn. "I had to go, too," he said, showing a crooked grin. He went in and left the door open, talking to Packard over his shoulder as he took care of business. It was the second time he had conveniently thwarted Packard's plans to blow the whistle on this gang. And Packard was beginning to think it wasn't just by chance. As they went back inside, he consoled himself with the thought that he would soon have other opportunities.

When they finally got up to leave, he noticed that Kinealy was slightly unsteady and seemed more talkative than normal. It was the most hard liquor Packard had ever seen him consume at one sitting, and on an empty stomach at that. But, had he been in his shoes, Packard probably would have been in a mood for celebration. It seemed incredible that, under Kinealy's direction, they had traveled, undetected, with the body of the late President more than two hundred miles by wagon and train while the country and the authorities were in an uproar and looking for them.

Big Jim had best enjoy it while he could, because as soon as he made his ransom demands, it would be all over. Yet, somehow, Packard instinctively felt it probably wouldn't be that simple. Nothing ever was.

Chapter Fourteen

It might have been the result of three beers for breakfast, but Packard was awash in a sea of well-being as they left the saloon and Kinealy drove the wagon toward the bank. The day was brisk, but sunny. Lincoln's body was safely hidden, at least for the time being.

When Kinealy came out of the bank and climbed back onto the wagon seat, he was obviously still feeling the effects of the whiskey.

"No problem, boys," he grinned, patting his hip pocket. "It's good to have a smooth-running organization . . . and men you can trust."

Packard winced slightly at this last statement, feeling like the Judas he was about to be. Even though entrapment was the whole purpose of his being here, he still had contradictory twinges of conscience, and they weren't just because of Janice. Kinealy had been good to him, and all of them had gone through considerable turmoil together. Working with these men had created a human kinship. In fact, Packard had to keep reminding himself that it was his job to stop these counterfeiters from undermining the economic health of the country. But staying focused on the job at hand was more readily resolved than done.

He was caught up in the camaraderie of the adventure.

Kinealy pulled out his billfold and counted out a hundred dollars to each of them. "That should hold you for now."

He shoved the leather billfold back into his pocket and took up the reins, clucking to the mules.

The next stop was the livery barn where they turned in the rig, paid the rent, and redeemed McGuinn's gun. Then they walked the four short blocks, mostly uphill, to the imposing Patee House Hotel. Now that they were away from the train, Kinealy apparently didn't care who saw them with Rip Hughes and Janice, who were waiting in the lobby of the hotel. Packard realized Janice had probably shared the last of her money so they could all buy something to eat the night before.

Kinealy and Janice registered as John and Lisa McCarty from St. Louis. Packard expected Hughes quietly to disappear at this point, but he promptly rented a room by himself under his own name. Before Packard could do the same, McGuinn leaned over to the clerk. "My friend and I will take a double room." He snatched up the pen from its inkstand and signed the registration book with their real names.

"Yes, sir," the clerk replied, reaching into one of the cubbyholes behind him for the keys.

Packard was hoping to get some measure of freedom by having a room to himself, but it was not to be, and he became more convinced than ever that Kinealy had set McGuinn over him like a guard dog. But he flattered himself that he could give the ex-boxer the slip long enough to send a telegram to his Chicago headquarters. For now, he had to act as if these rooming arrangements were immaterial.

After agreeing to reassemble in the lobby at four that afternoon for supper, they all retired to their rooms to rest. Complete exhaustion was the only condition that ever allowed Packard to sleep during the day, so his nap consisted of lying on the big bed, hands behind his head, letting his mind wander. McGuinn paced restlessly about the room, staring out the window, cleaning his fingernails with a pocketknife, and examining the lithographs on the walls.

Except for registering under an assumed name, which was probably second nature to him, Kinealy was leaving a trail that anyone could follow, provided they knew where to look. And the law would immediately know where to start looking if he sent a ransom demand from St. Joe.

"Hell, let 'em sweat for a day or two," Kinealy replied when Packard inquired about his plans for the ransom demand. It was later that afternoon as they all sat in a mid-town restaurant. The place was nearly empty since they'd arrived a good hour before the normal supper crowd. "They'll be a little more desperate, then," he smiled smugly. "When they can't find the coffin anywhere around Springfield, they'll be ready to deal a lot quicker." The effects of the whiskey had apparently worn off, but he was still in an expansive mood.

Packard nodded at his answer, but cringed inwardly. It was very irritating to have to wait even longer for the extortion attempt before he could make a move. But he took a deep breath and sat back, pretending to examine the menu. After coming this far, it wouldn't do to set the hook too soon and risk losing the fish.

Putting the whole thing out of his mind as the waiter came over, he ordered a steak, baked potato, and a glass of burgundy. Their table was near the front window where they could look out on the late afternoon traffic of wagons and pedestrians. The sun was sliding down toward the solid line of bare trees that fringed the far shore of the Missouri River.

They chatted and joked in low voices, all feeling relieved to be off the train and checked into the best hotel in St. Joe.

"This chair feels like it's moving," Packard said to Janice who sat opposite him.

"I know," she smiled. "I don't like to be on a train that long. But I'm sure we'll get our land legs back by morning."

He stifled a yawn. "Hope so. I wasn't sleepy this afternoon. Now I could fall asleep on a bed of nails. My appetite is the only thing keeping me awake." He looked at the blue pinstripe dress she was wearing, and at her thick brown hair brushed and fastened with tortoise-shell combs. "How do you manage to stay so fresh and clean?"

"You forget that Rip and I were able to prepare for this trip. I've got a grip packed with clean clothes. I even had the maid bring the bathtub and some hot water up to our room a little while ago."

The mental image of her bathing sent a strange feeling through Packard's stomach. Kinealy was a lucky man. Although faint shadows under Janice's eyes indicated that she was still not well-rested, to Packard she was more alluring than ever. He must be careful not to focus all his attention on her, lest Kinealy or Hughes take notice.

The waiter brought their food. Conversation flagged as they ate, the silence broken only by the clink of silverware and favorable comments about the food. They finished a bottle of wine and ordered another. Before the meal was ended, Packard noted that Kinealy had drunk most of the wine.

Afterward, they strolled down the street in the chilled evening air toward their hotel. The streets were in shadow as the last rays of the setting sun were hitting the tops of the low buildings. Kinealy was still without a coat but didn't seem to notice. The good meal had raised all their spirits, and they acted like a group of good friends on vacation.

Kinealy hailed a newsboy who was hawking the *St. Joseph Daily Gazette* on a street corner. The paper bore no headlines, but one entire column on the front page of the four-page newspaper was devoted to detailing the Lincoln tomb robbery. Kinealy scanned down the page, mumbling to himself as they walked along. "Just rehashing the same old things," he said. "Let's see. . . ." He continued reading. "Ha! Just as I suspected," he finally chortled, folding the paper and handing it to Packard as he glanced around to make sure they were alone on the street. "They haven't got the slightest idea where we are."

"Says here," Packard quoted from the article, " 'police are co-operating with federal authorities in the investigation. Chief Wilkinson of the Springfield police force stated that his department is following up several leads, and he expects the perpetrators to be apprehended very shortly.' "

"Just a lot of bluster," Kinealy said. "Have you ever heard a copper admit that he was baffled?"

"Boss, I'll have to say that was a mighty slick job we pulled off," McGuinn said, contentedly working some steak out of his teeth with a wooden toothpick.

Packard wondered what might have been the cause of Chief Wilkinson's public optimism. His own Secret Service boss knew only that he had vanished with the robbers and might very well be dead.

Elmer Washburn walked back into his office and slammed the door with unnecessary force. "Close that transom!" he ordered James Brooks, his assistant chief who shared the office with him. "There've been enough damn' leaks. I don't want anybody else hearing what I have to say. Everybody, including the charwoman in this building, seems to have an opinion about this case."

He sat down heavily in the swivel chair behind his desk and pulled out a blue and white polka dotted handkerchief to mop his red face, while Brooks obediently climbed up on a chair and pushed the glass transom closed over the door.

Washburn stared at the wall, deep in thought for a few minutes. "Where the hell is Packard?" he finally asked aloud, without directing his question at Brooks. His assistant, a younger man of forty, got down and dusted off the chair. Unlike Washburn, who sported a huge, gray, walrus mustache, Brooks was clean-shaven and neat to a fault, the creases of his pants sharp, shoes shined, and not a speck of lint on the charcoal gray suit. His thinning hair was neatly trimmed and parted just low enough to keep the creeping baldness from being obvious.

"Chief, just tell me what you want to say, and I'll deal with the reporters next time."

"It won't matter. They'll print whatever they want, regardless." He sighed heavily, his florid face beginning to subside to its normal color.

"We had 'em dead to rights," he continued, as if speaking to himself. "Like shooting fish in a barrel. And they got away!" His tone was incredulous.

"Packard never gave the signal," Brooks said simply.

Washburn nodded. "Yeah. But he's not here to take the blame. Even if he were, I'm the boss in charge of this operation, so the responsibility falls on me." He exhaled and seemed to wilt. "Well, that'll teach me to go out on these field operations. If I hadn't been there, I could've bluffed my way through this somehow. But I was there, in personal charge, and we wound up not only letting the grave-robbers get away with the body of the President, but wounding one of our own men in the process. I'm the laughingstock of the whole state . . . the whole country by now. Did you see that political cartoon in the morning paper?"

Although Washburn didn't say it, Springfield Police Chief Wilkinson was also making public statements to the effect that, if his department had not been left out of this secret ambush attempt, they would have captured the miscreants. In his twelve years as a public servant, Washburn had never experienced anything as embarrassing. One of his worst duties had been explaining to an unsmiling Robert Lincoln what had happened. The late President's son had not said much, but his silence had spoken volumes. He had simply gotten on the train and left for

Chicago, requesting that he be informed of any developments.

Washburn swiveled his chair and stared out the window at the low clouds scudding in over the city from Lake Michigan. His mood was as bleak as the gray November weather. He didn't need to look at it again — that blistering telegram from Washington that lay on his desk blotter. What would he do if he were fired? As one of the gospel parables put it: "To dig I am not able; to beg I am ashamed."

The men at Kinealy's saloon had reported what they had seen to Police Chief Wilkinson, who had brought them to Washburn's office this morning on the overnight train from Springfield. What day was this, anyway? He'd almost lost track. It was Thursday, November 9th, and the grave-robbers had been gone almost two full days. The men who were celebrating at Kinealy's saloon had reported seeing the reputed counterfeiter in his back room with four other men and a coffin. The witnesses at the saloon all agreed that Kinealy had slugged one of the revelers and then had fled with his four accomplices and the coffin, going north out of town in a wagon. There was another detail of their story which Washburn didn't understand at all: they swore there was another man in the wagon who was bound and gagged. Could it have been Packard?

Washburn mentally reviewed their statements, which a clerk had written down. Could it possibly be that Packard had betrayed his trust and gone over to the criminals? What other explanation could there be for his not having given the password so the law could spring the trap? The pay of a Secret Service agent was not great, while the dangers often were. Perhaps they had made him a much better offer.

"Brooks, get me Packard's personnel file out of that cabinet."

The assistant obediently delivered the folder to his chief and withdrew to his own desk in silence.

Washburn turned to the last two annual performance evaluations by Packard's previous supervisor and ran his finger down the pages, sifting the pertinent details.

athletic . . . fearless in dangerous situations . . . skilled with a hand gun . . . carries out assignments appropriately, but tends to question authority. Sometimes proceeds on his own and exceeds instructions. Well-liked by fellow agents, but can be insubordinate at times if he disagrees with a directive. . . .

Washburn's finger stopped on this last line. It was all he needed. He had found his scapegoat. He closed the folder and stood up, smiling faintly to himself. Perhaps something could be salvaged out of this fiasco. If not his reputation, then maybe his job.

Chapter Fifteen

That evening Packard lounged in the hotel lobby, smoking a cigar and scanning a recent issue of *Harper's Weekly* someone had left lying on one of the overstuffed chairs. By ten o'clock he was upstairs in bed, and he slept a solid nine hours.

He awoke, feeling almost human again, and a breakfast of ham and eggs in the hotel dining room finished bringing him back to his normal robust self. Except for the slight stitch in his left side from the old wound that he'd aggravated with the wild escapade on the runaway train, he felt fit enough to tackle anything. Like providential manna in the desert, food and rest seemed to be available just when they were most needed.

"What's the plan for today, boss?" McGuinn asked, leaning back in his chair with a second cup of coffee.

While appearing to be attentive to Kinealy's reply, Packard was really casting furtive glances at Janice who, to Packard's eager eyes, was as radiant as a spring morning in Tennessee.

"Well, first of all, you and I and Packard need to buy some clothes, get shaved, and cleaned up. Then I plan to send a wire, and begin to rattle some official cages."

"I thought you were going to let 'em sweat for a few days," McGuinn replied, obviously disappointed that he wouldn't have some time off to eat and drink and run through the money Kinealy had given him.

"I've reconsidered," Kinealy replied, all business. Apparently the celebrating and relaxing were over. He was once again the cool, calculating leader of the coney men. "I've got an encoded message ready to send to my contact in Chicago. Then he will relay my message by telegraph to the Illinois governor, demanding two hundred thousand dollars and the release of Ben Boyd. The message will be signed . . . The Coney Men." This last was said with a hint of pride.

"So the governor will think you are in Chicago," Packard said. "Clever. But where and how will he send the money? And how will your contact correspond by telegraph with him without getting caught?"

"The governor will be told to respond publicly by having his reply printed in the Chicago *Times*. His answer will be relayed to me by encoded telegraph messages. Anyone with the price of a daily newspaper will be able to follow these negotiations. There will be no secret deals or subterfuge. This will be a very public affair."

They all digested this information in silence for several seconds.

Kinealy chuckled. "As to the money, you leave that to me. I've got a plan that will keep us safe beyond the reach of the law. If they don't have anyone smarter than that bunch who tried to grab us at the tomb, we haven't got a worry."

"I wouldn't underestimate the enemy, if I were you," Packard cautioned. "Not all of them will be shooting at each other."

Kinealy fixed him with a hard stare that he found uncomfortable. "You don't think I've gotten by all these years without ever seeing the inside of a jail by being stupid and careless, do you?" he snarled with the arrogance of a treed cougar.

Packard didn't reply and resolved again to keep his opinions to himself. Let Kinealy bet all he had on this pot, Packard still held the winning hand. "How will your contact keep from being identified by the Western Union operator, if he sends your decoded demand to the governor?" Packard finally asked, trying to think of weak links in the chain of events.

"How the hell should I know?" Kinealy waved his hand impatiently. "There are a dozen ways. Maybe he'll seal the message and the fee in an envelope and hire a street urchin to take it to Western Union. Maybe he'll go himself in disguise. He's smart, and I trust him to cover his tracks."

Not having lived a life of crime, Packard apparently didn't think as deviously as Kinealy. It was immaterial to him how it was accomplished, anyway, as long as it was done.

"Let's get to it," Kinealy said, rising from the table.

They followed. Janice retired to her room to wait. Hughes opted to lounge in the hotel lobby while McGuinn, Kinealy, and Packard walked down the hill a few blocks to a general merchandise emporium and outfitted themselves with new clothes from the skin out. Then they visited a Chinese bathhouse and, while they scrubbed and soaked, left their old clothes next door to be laundered.

"Wait for me at Riley's saloon," Kinealy instructed McGuinn and Packard as they exited the steamy washhouse. "I'm going to Western Union." He spoke casually, as if he were going to lunch. "I'll join you in less than an hour."

"Right, boss," McGuinn said as they parted company.

It was still mid-morning, and only two early customers were in Riley's place. They were dressed like riverboat deckhands. Packard and McGuinn stood at the opposite end of the bar and ordered beer. Riley waited on them, a sour look on his face. "What're you doing here?" he muttered as he worked the beer taps.

"The boss is meeting us here," McGuinn said.

"Damned bad idea," the barkeep replied, sliding the foamy glasses across the polished wood. "Stay out of here unless you got business with me."

"Friendly sort," Packard remarked, as Riley walked off without even taking their money.

"Nervous as a mouse in a cage of rattlesnakes," McGuinn muttered under his breath.

Riley studiously avoided them as he washed glasses and mugs in a tub of water behind the bar. The saloon-keeper kept glancing out the front window, worry lines creasing his high forehead as if he half expected blue-uniformed police to come bursting through the door at any moment.

"Barkeep!"

Riley nearly jumped out of his white apron. One of the rivermen was holding up an empty glass.

"Kinealy could've picked somebody a little steadier," Packard remarked, sipping his beer.

"Yeah. Don't know why he's so on edge," McGuinn replied under his breath. "All he has to do is keep his mouth shut and collect his money."

"But after the ransom is paid and the law comes to claim the box, Riley will be implicated."

"He'll probably be long gone by then," McGuinn said. "Once the ransom's paid, Big Jim's going to move the box, anyway."

"He is?" Packard tried to keep the surprise out of his voice.

"Yeah," McGuinn nodded. "But I don't know where," he continued, heading off the obvious question. "And I don't ask too many questions. He keeps us in the dark until he's ready to make a move. It's kind of insulting, but that's the way he's been able to stay on top all these years . . . by not trusting anybody but himself."

"What about his wife?"
"What about her?"
"He doesn't trust her?"
"Hell, I don't know what he tells her in private. It ain't really my concern. But he don't seem to involve her in most of his business dealings."
Packard nodded. This squared with what Janice had told him on the train car platform that night.
"Fact is, she was more involved in this operation than she's ever been in anything I've been part of," McGuinn added.
Kinealy sauntered in some thirty minutes later and had a drink. By then fifteen or twenty customers were lining the bar and sitting at the tables. Another bartender had come on duty, relieving Riley who was nowhere to be seen.
"I got the ball rolling," Kinealy said, excitement lighting up his eyes. "Now all we have to do is wait."
"Yeah," McGuinn said. "We'll all wait together."
They headed back to the hotel, stopping to buy razors and toothbrushes, then taking time for a leisurely lunch in the hotel dining room.
While all this was going on, Packard's mind was working to form a plan to elude his muscular watchdog — at least long enough so he could get off a telegram of his own. It would probably have to be at night. He was fairly certain most Western Union offices kept a telegrapher on

duty twenty-four hours a day. But he would wait until the first reply was received from the Illinois officials. Then he would have to move fast, to prevent any ransom from being paid and to get word to his superiors before Kinealy moved the body again.

They had less than a day to wait. Before noon the next day, Kinealy picked up a telegraph message from Western Union.

"Here it is!" he said gleefully, holding up the telegram. The boyish excitement and anticipation was unlike him. Packard sometimes wondered if Kinealy lived more for the thrill of danger than for the profits of his counterfeiting business.

They gathered in Kinealy's room at the Patee House while he sat down to decode it. He worked with pencil and paper at a table near the light of a window.

Packard caught Janice's eye as she stood by her husband's shoulder. She gave a warm, reassuring smile, as if she already knew the answer from the Illinois governor.

Packard's heart was pounding; he wasn't so sure. The outcome of this whole venture could very well depend on what Kinealy was translating. He swallowed hard and tried to return Janice's smile.

It was a long message, and Kinealy was about three minutes decoding it.

"I'll be damned!" he finally muttered, his face clouding.

"What's he say?" Hughes demanded.

Janice was reading over Kinealy's shoulder, a frown on her face.

"Governor Beveridge says he's not paying a cent to recover the body."

"What?" McGuinn exclaimed.

"He can't do that!" Hughes put in.

They were all taken aback. It was the one answer none of them had expected.

Kinealy held up his hand until they fell silent. "The governor refuses to pay or release Ben Boyd from prison because Lincoln's body is not in that coffin."

Chapter Sixteen

Packard felt foolish — like he'd thrown a haymaker at Kinealy's big jaw, missed, and fallen flat on his face. How many thousands of people were reading this in the Chicago paper and howling with laughter at the gang that snatched an empty coffin? There was stunned silence in the room for a few seconds. He dared not look at Janice, and turned away to take a deep, calming breath. His insides felt as empty as a Guinness keg after an Irish wake.

"Just another stalling tactic," Kinealy said, his voice sounding a little forced, as if he were trying to convince himself.

"How do you know that?" Hughes asked.

"Just put yourself in the governor's place," Kinealy said with more assurance. "He wants to give the law time to work on this. He has to have time to decide what to do."

"What if he's right and there's no body?" Janice asked, voicing all of their worst fears.

"After all, there was someone waiting to ambush us," McGuinn added. "And when they failed, they never bothered to chase us 'cause we didn't have nothing but an empty box."

"I've heard rumors off and on for years that his

body wasn't really in that big new mausoleum they built," Hughes remarked. "But you know how rumors like that get started."

"Well, there's only one way to be sure," Packard said.

"All we need is a small hole by the face," Kinealy said thoughtfully. "Riley has some experience as a plumber. He should be able to cut that soft lead so it can be replaced without any damage to what's inside."

"If there is anything inside," Packard said.

"If there's nothing left but dust and bones, how we gonna know it's him?" McGuinn asked.

"The governor says the coffin's empty," Kinealy said. "If there's anybody's remains in there, they've got to be Lincoln's. I'm betting there's enough left to identify him." Kinealy got up and stuffed the decoded message into a pocket. "Janice, stay here."

"Jim, I've been part of this from the start, and I'm not going to miss seeing what we've really got," she told him firmly.

A half hour later they were all in Riley's saloon. The Irishman saw them coming and was sliding toward the rear door when Kinealy caught up with him. They watched as the two talked. Riley was shaking his head and gesturing at the customers in the room. Kinealy clearly intimidated the smaller man. Then the two came back toward the front, and Kinealy motioned them all outside. They moved off down the sidewalk a half block and paused by a vacant lot. In spite of the fact that Riley was dressed in shirt sleeves and vest in the cold air, he pulled a bandanna from a hip pocket and began mopping perspiration from his face and bald head. His eyes had the mournful air of a Basset hound as he faced Kinealy and the rest of them.

"Jim, I can't go messing around down in the basement with a houseful of customers. It's just too dangerous." His thick beard bobbed up and down as he talked, putting Packard in mind of what an Irish gremlin might look like.

"I told you why we gotta know," Kinealy said. "And right quick."

"I know. I know." The little man bobbed his head. "Tell you what . . . wait until the crowd thins out in a couple hours. Then I'll close early this afternoon, and we'll open 'er up and take a look." He tucked the bandanna away. "I got some tools that'll do the trick. But. . . ."

"But what?" Kinealy was pressing.

"It ain't just lookin' at the body . . . it's . . . well, there's something else almighty funny going on with that coffin."

"Like what?"

"I live in the back room of my place, and I heard and saw some things in the night that you just wouldn't believe. Strange, eerie things." He looked at their solemn, expectant faces, then slowly shook his head. "Never mind. Come back about half past three, and rap on the side door. We'll get the job done then."

"OK," Kinealy said, and led them away.

When they were out of earshot, he muttered: "I believe the old boy has been sampling too much of his own stuff. I just hope he holds together long enough for us to collect the ransom."

"Provided we've got a body," Hughes said.

Kinealy nodded, not appearing as sure of himself as he had earlier.

They returned to the hotel, bathed, shaved, and were back at the saloon at the agreed time. The place appeared deserted as Kinealy knocked on the side door. It was opened, and he signaled the rest to come ahead from where they'd been lounging separately down the street.

The basement was as dark and dank as Packard remembered it. But this time the acrid smell of burning charcoal assaulted his nose. There was a slightly smoking brazier setting on the floor off to one side. The one, tiny window open near the ceiling did little to dispel the noxious fumes. Riley and McGuinn scraped most of the dirt from the old wooden door and lifted it off the hole. They pulled the canvas cover off the upper half of the coffin, and Packard held the lantern as Riley took a hammer and sharp chisel and began tapping carefully at a spot near where the head would be. Cutting at an oblique angle, he gradually carved a hole big enough to insert one blade of an oversize pair of metal shears. Then it was just a matter of working the shears around in an oval, cutting the half-inch thick lead. As he struggled with the long handles of the big shears, beads of perspiration glistened on top of his bald dome in the lantern light. His harsh breathing and the slight scuffing as he shifted his position every few seconds were the only sounds in the room.

Finally, when he had only about two inches left to complete the cut, he inserted the chisel and wedged up one edge about an inch. "Get your fingers under there and bend the flap back," he said, looking up at Kinealy. Riley's big, dark eyes told Packard he was fearful of inserting his own hands even that far inside the death box.

Kinealy wiggled the fingers of both hands under the lip of the oval cut and bent the soft lead back like the lid of a tin can.

All of them but Riley crowded in to see.

"Hold that light down closer!" Kinealy snapped when Packard got jostled out of the way.

"Ah, just as I thought . . . the governor was bluffing and stalling," Big Jim said while they all stared down at what remained of the late President. Packard held his breath against the strong odor of mildew and chemicals that wafted out of the coffin as curiosity got the better of revulsion. Lincoln was in a remarkable state of preservation for having been dead eleven and a half years. The craggy features were darker than in life — almost a mahogany hue. The great head lay on a silk pillow, eyes closed as if he had just laid down to take a nap. The coarse black hair and beard, slightly tinged with gray, appeared to be exactly as he had seen them in Matthew Brady's famous photographs. Even the mole on his cheek was intact.

"Damn! That's spooky," McGuinn breathed. "He looks like he could sit up and talk."

"Henry Cattell of Brown and Alexander, Surgeons and Embalmers, did one helluva job on him," Hughes said, showing off his superior knowledge of these useless facts. He leaned down closer to the opening and sniffed. "Since they hauled the body around the country on display for almost three weeks before they buried it, Cattell probably had to pump him full of arsenic, bichloride of mercury, and zinc. The skin appears desiccated. I'm sure the drying process turned the skin darker and helped to. . . ."

"Enough!" Kinealy snapped, holding up his hand. "We don't need a lesson in embalming."

The dank cellar couldn't account for a chill that passed over Packard as he suddenly visualized his own body in that coffin. Reportedly, Lincoln had experienced a recurrent dream of seeing his assassinated remains lying in state in the White House. A premonition? Mental strain from the war? Who could say?

They all stared silently for several more seconds. Then Kinealy said: "OK, everybody had a good look?" It seemed to break the trance, and they muttered their satisfaction.

Even though Packard personally had had no doubt that it was the body of Lincoln they had been hauling, it still felt strange actually to behold the dead face with his own eyes. He had never seen the man alive, but it was like looking at a legendary figure such as George Washington, or Alexander the Great. This much-loved and much-hated giant of a man who was stretched out at his feet had been at the center of a great storm — a storm that had blown away most of an American generation in the space of four years.

Packard looked across at Janice. She had not spoken since they had entered the cellar. As she returned his glance, her lips were compressed in a thin line and her face appeared pale in the lamplight.

"Close it back up, Riley," Kinealy said, standing up with a grunt and stepping back out of the way. "Sorry to put you to this trouble, but I had to be sure."

Riley came forward from the shadows and quickly bent the lead flap back down to cover the face. Then he pulled what appeared to be a running iron or a short poker from the iron brazier and examined the tip of it. Apparently not satisfied, he thrust it back into the red-hot charcoal and took up a set of small, hand-operated bellows, pumping them several times with a *whooshing* noise. Fine, white ash went everywhere, and angry red eyes of fire glowed even fiercer. It was several minutes before the end of the rod was glowing, and he started the painstaking job of sealing the flap back into place, melting the edges of the soft lead together. He could do only a couple of inches at a time before reheating the rod, and the sealing process took the better part of a half hour. They waited and watched patiently and silently. Once the Illinois authorities had the body back, they would probably go through this same procedure to ensure they had recovered the actual corpse of Lincoln. It was most unlikely they would take Packard's word alone for something this important without other witnesses.

While Riley was at work, Kinealy was wasting no time. He squatted in the lamplight, encoding his next message to the governor, writing laboriously on a small pad of paper on his knee. By the time the saloon-keeper had finished his job, and McGuinn had slid the old door over the hole, Kinealy was done, and the pad was tucked away in his pocket.

They all trooped back up the stairs and outside. It was like coming back into a world of commonplace realities to see the daylight and the buildings and people passing along the street. The late afternoon sun had been snuffed out by a gray overcast, and a cold November wind was blowing up from the direction of the river.

Kinealy walked directly to the Western Union office and sent his coded message to Chicago while the others returned to the hotel. When he joined them later in the Patee House dining room, his face betrayed no sign of his feelings. He seemed quietly confident as if his plan was on track.

Janice had apparently shaken off the somber mood of the burial cellar and was talkative at the table, laughing at some remark McGuinn made about the food. Packard wondered if she missed female companionship. But she seemed totally at ease with just the four men. He watched her over the lip of his coffee cup, thinking perhaps her unsettled life had rendered her completely comfortable in just about any surroundings and any company.

The gang now had the upper hand. The governor's bluff had been called, and he had to show his hand. What would his answer be? It wasn't exactly like a kidnapping case where someone's life was at stake. Yet Governor Beveridge couldn't very well ignore the demands. Now that he had publicly responded, everyone knew a ransom demand had been made. The governor's claim that the coffin was empty wouldn't fool the public for long. And that same public would demand he do something to obtain the return of their late President's remains. Not only would the public demand it, but the state and federal politicians would also put pressure on him.

Packard held the key to this stalemate. It was time for him to make his move. Considerable thought had led him to the conclusion that he had to stay with the gang until they were arrested. At first, it had seemed a simple matter to make his escape and keep going, sending a telegram to the Secret Service while *en route* home. But then it dawned on him that this would not do. When Kinealy realized he was gone, he would immediately know he'd been betrayed and either move the body, or make his own getaway, or both, before anyone could arrive to arrest him. Maybe Packard could alert the local police in St. Joe to detain them before Kinealy could make a move. But he didn't know if the local constabulary could be relied on to hold them. Kinealy and Hughes were smarter than the average bandits. Besides that, he would be calling down the political wrath of his own superiors if he allowed anyone but the Secret Service to capture this gang. So it was up to him to get loose somehow, send his message, and get back without any of this group being the wiser. Tonight seemed a good time to make the attempt. Attempt was not the right word. He *would* do it. There was no room for doubt. A man who walks the high wire dares not look down or think of anything but reaching the other side.

Packard scraped up the last morsel of apple pie and popped it into his mouth. "Ahh . . . that was delicious." He set his fork down on the plate. "The perfect ending to a perfect meal."

The legs of his wooden chair scuffed on the floor as he pushed back from the table and looked across at Janice who was sipping a cup of coffee. "Would you care to join me in a little stroll outside?" he asked. "I need to work off some of this food and get a breath of fresh air."

She nodded, but slid her eyes toward McGuinn and Hughes who had walked to the colonnaded archway leading to the lobby. Both were lighting cigars and having an animated discussion.

"Don't worry about them," he said in a low voice. "Where's your husband?"

Kinealy had finished before the rest of them, excused himself, and left the table.

"Gone to our room, I expect."

"He didn't bother waiting for you," Packard observed.

He saw the hurt in her eyes before she could glance away. "He doesn't care," she murmured, standing up and flashing him a rather forced smile. "Shall we walk?"

"Where you two going?" McGuinn demanded as they passed, headed toward the front door.

"Out for some air," Packard answered, not looking back.

"The boss wants all of us to stay in the hotel," Hughes said.

"He won't care," Janice said lightly. "We won't be long."

Packard heard their boots thudding on the carpeted floor as the pair followed.

"Big Jim's ordered everyone to stay inside after dark," McGuinn insisted.

Janice paused and fixed him with a hard stare. "I think I know Big Jim a little better than you do. Even if he told you that, he doesn't order me."

McGuinn looked uncertainly at Hughes. "Then we'll walk with you," McGuinn stated, moving to grab the door handle.

"No, thanks," Janice said, slipping outside as he opened the door. Packard maneuvered himself quickly to face the two of them, his back to the open door. "I think she made it clear she doesn't want your company." His voice had an edge to it. This was not the time or place for a confrontation, but he was at least glad he was armed if it came to that. With just the right touch, he could make it appear that he was simply protecting a lady's wish for privacy — nothing more.

McGuinn hesitated as if unsure what to do next. "Go tell Big Jim about this," he said to Hughes.

"Tell him yourself," Hughes retorted. "I'm not your errand boy!"

The tension was broken, and Packard had them at each other. He stepped aside, allowing a well-dressed older couple to enter the hotel, and took advantage of the interruption to slip outside, closing the big door behind him.

He vaulted off the porch and joined Janice who was waiting for him.

"Let's go."

They quickly disappeared into the night. It had been dark less than an hour, but what warmth the weak November sun had provided was now gone, and she shivered as he helped her wrap the hooded cape around her shoulders.

"I missed being able to talk to you alone," he said.

"Me, too. Jim's so caught up in this business that I don't think he even knows I'm in the same room with him."

She slipped her cold fingers into his hand as he guided their steps down the hill in the general direction of the Western Union office. Gas lamps lighted the cobblestone streets for several blocks in the downtown area. A few carriages and men on horseback were still in evidence, but most of the pedestrians had disappeared. The business of the town was winding down for the night.

He was trying to devise some innocent excuse to get away from her for a few minutes — long enough to send a telegram — when she interrupted his thoughts with a sudden question. "What do you plan to do once this is all over?"

"I really haven't given it much thought," he said truthfully.

"There doesn't seem to be much future in grave-robbing." The distaste in her voice was obvious. "Why don't you join us?"

"I don't think your husband trusts me," he said before he thought.

"Why?"

He regretted having brought up the subject, but answered, "Oh, maybe it's just a feeling."

"You must have some reason for thinking that," she persisted.

The gears were whirring and meshing in his head. "I believe he knows there's something between us besides just friendship." He couldn't let on that Kinealy or Hughes suspected him of treachery. "Did you notice how eager McGuinn and Hughes were to keep us in sight just now?"

"Yes. And I think I know why. Rip Hughes is after me."

"What?" It was his turn to be surprised.

"He was constantly making advances to me, especially before the three of you got on the train. I used to think he was harmless, but I've seen the other side of him on this trip. I'm glad I've got a Derringer in my handbag." She smiled slightly. "Actually, I had an easier way of dealing with him. He always managed to find a whiskey when the train stopped for meals or passengers. Twice I was able to slip a few drops of laudanum into his drink, and he slept for several hours after that."

"You carry laudanum with you?" Packard frowned. He wondered what else he didn't know about her.

"Oh, I'm not sick or anything. It's just that I sometimes have trouble sleeping. It helps me relax." She gave his hand a squeeze. "Anyway, what I was getting around to saying is that Hughes is jealous of you."

Packard was flattered, but covered his embarrassment by saying: "I've had the feeling since the first night that Big Jim has had McGuinn keeping an eye on me. He never lets me out of his sight. I'm sure that's why we're in the same room. And when I went to get a shave in Hannibal, Hughes came looking for me."

"Maybe that's just your imagination," she said slowly.

"No. When I offered to drop out of sight in Springfield after we had escaped from the cemetery, your husband practically ordered me to stick close until it was all over. I was hired on just to help rob the grave. That's all."

She was quiet for a moment and then said softly: "You didn't want to stay around a little longer to see me?"

His heart melted at this. He stopped walking, and they turned toward each other. Her face was framed by the big hood that partially hid her dark hair. His heart pounding, he slid his arms around her and kissed her gently on the mouth, then more passionately as she melted into his embrace.

Finally, she backed away, somewhat breathless. "I guess that answers that question."

"What question?" He'd already forgotten.

She threw back her hood and gave him a smile that penetrated to the depths of his soul. Her expression held the unspoken question: *Where do we go from here?* The last, slight barriers between them had been broken, along with any shreds of his remaining resistance. Had the time and the place been appropriate, he thought they probably would have fallen into bed together. Again he mentally scourged himself for succumbing to the spell of this attractive woman. What was it about her that was so irresistible? Certainly there were other unattached women his age and younger who were just as beautiful and charming and interesting. Maybe it was gratitude to her for having saved his life more than a dozen years before. After all, wounded men tend to fall in love with their nurses. Surely she was a strong part of his past; without her he would have no present. But, deep down, he knew the real answer. It was plain, old, perverse human nature that made him want what he couldn't have. The lure of forbidden fruit had been the bane of the race since Adam and Eve.

Just then, he saw a movement out of the corner of his eye. Looking over her shoulder, he saw something that turned the fire in his veins to ice. No more than thirty yards away, three men emerged from the railroad dépôt. One of them wore a blue police uniform. The second was a tall man in a gray overcoat and hat. The third man was shorter and talking excitedly. The longish hair, the way he moved, the sound of his voice — all rang a faint alarm bell in the recesses of Packard's mind. Then the man turned, and the light from the gas street lamp fell fully on his face. It was Boston Corbett!

Chapter Seventeen

"Oh, no!"

"What?" She turned to follow his gaze.

"Boston Corbett," he breathed. "I hoped I'd never set eyes on him again."

"The crazy preacher you told me about?"

"The same." He pulled her into the shadows of the brick warehouse a few feet away.

His heart was hammering again, but this time not from passion. A dozen thoughts flashed through his mind in the next several seconds. Corbett had obviously gone straight to the law with his story of being abducted. Mad or not, he had convinced someone in authority to listen to him. They had put two and two together, connecting his tale with the theft of the body. And, thanks to him, the law had picked up the trail. Packard knew his boss, Elmer Washburn, would be desperate to follow up any leads, however remote.

Now was his chance to blow the whistle on this whole operation. All he had to do was draw his gun and turn Janice over to these men. He had no identification on his person, and Corbett knew him only as one of his abductors, but that could be cleared up very shortly with a telegram to the Secret Service. He would direct the police to Riley's saloon and to the Patee House to grab the rest of the gang. Newspaper headlines around the country would again proclaim the mad hatter as a national hero — this time for leading the law to the recovery of the body and the capture of the extortionists. But that couldn't be helped.

His right hand went halfway to the gun under his coat before it faltered. His left arm was around Janice's waist as they stood close to the wall. He could feel her hip pressing against him. Even if he'd had no feelings for her, could he really hand her over, just like that? *Where are your thirty pieces of silver?* a mocking voice asked from somewhere.

"There you are!"

He nearly jumped out of his coat at the sound of McGuinn's voice only a few feet away.

"Big Jim wants to see both of you back at the hotel."

The ex-pugilist and Rip Hughes moved out of the shadows and stood on each side of them. It was an obvious maneuver to make sure he was trapped. Packard ground his teeth, looking from the square jaw and bent nose of McGuinn to the shaved, suave, sneering face of Hughes. Of the two, he preferred the bulldog to the serpent. Hughes wore a smug smile. His right hand rested on the pistol at his hip.

Packard's chance was lost. A quick glance showed Corbett and the two lawmen walking away from them into the darkness beyond the dépôt. He could still faintly hear the preacher's voice yammering away.

Janice also looked toward the departing Corbett, so he quickly took her arm and started for the hotel. When they got a few steps ahead of Hughes and McGuinn, he leaned over and whispered: "Don't say anything about the preacher."

She looked her curiosity at him, but nodded silently.

Just to irritate the jealous Hughes, he held her hand all the way back to the hotel. A stupid, juvenile thing to do. But his mind was occupied more at the moment with what he had just seen than with Janice. By the time they reached the hotel, he had decided to tell Kinealy about Corbett. This would do two things — solidify his own shaky position in the gang and, secondly, allow him to choose his own place and time for springing the trap on them. But what about the woman who held his affections? Would she also have his loyalty? Not if he did his job properly. Once again he just put off the decision by thrusting this problem to the jumbled storeroom in the back of his mind.

McGuinn and Hughes escorted them to the Kinealys' room as if they were two miscreant schoolchildren being taken to the principal's office. Hughes rapped on the door.

"Come in."

Hughes opened the door for them, then departed with McGuinn.

Kinealy sat at a small table by the window, writing something by the light of a coal-oil lamp. He immediately put his pen down and got up, his face clouded like an approaching storm. But Packard had been with this man long enough to know that the best defense was always a good offense.

"Jim, it's a damn' good thing I went out for a little constitutional. I just saw Boston Corbett."

Kinealy stopped short, his mouth half open and eyes wide, like a man who'd caught a punch in the solar plexus.

"He and a cop and some other man were coming out of the train dépôt about fifteen minutes ago," Packard continued before Kinealy could recover his breath. "I didn't say anything to Hughes and McGuinn. Thought you ought to know about it first."

He glanced over at Janice as if for confirmation of his statement. She nodded, but her eyes held a questioning look.

Kinealy rubbed one big hand over his mouth and jaw, staring at nothing. Finally he said: "Did he see you?"

"No. I was probably thirty yards away, and he was standing under a street light, gabbing with these two men."

"You say one of them was a policeman?"

"Yeah."

"Damn!" he exploded. He dragged up the wooden chair he'd been using and sat down heavily.

Janice walked over and seated herself on the bed while Packard continued standing by the door.

There followed a long minute or so of silence.

"No telling what that crazy bastard is telling the law," Kinealy muttered then, as if thinking out loud. "If they're questioning the train crew and the station agent and the porters, they'll be able to track us easily enough. Their next stop will be the livery stables and hotels, starting with the largest . . . this one." He lapsed into silence once more.

Janice and Packard looked at each other. He'd apparently forgotten their presence entirely.

She undid the clasp at her throat and threw off the cape, laying it across the bed.

"OK, we'll fall back on the alternate plan," Kinealy said, looking at them. "We have to move fast. Tonight." He got to his feet, once more clearly in command. "Janice, go tell McGuinn and Hughes to get their stuff together. We're checking out right now."

"Where are we going?" she asked, standing up.

"We're taking that body out of Riley's basement. Then I'll show you."

"I thought we were done moving that thing," Packard muttered quietly to Janice after they stepped out into the hallway and Kinealy closed the door behind them.

"So did I. Are you sure that was the same crazy preacher you got tangled up with the night you boarded the train? It couldn't have been somebody who just resembled him, could it?"

He shook his head. "Once you've seen and heard this man, there's no mistaking him."

To keep her from being alone with Hughes, he paused by the door while she rapped. He opened it and gave Packard a cold look.

"Boston Corbett's in town and has the law looking for us."

"Who?"

"The crazy man who shot Wilkes Booth," Janice said. "You remember, I told you that Jim had to kidnap him because he was going to give the whole show away."

"Oh, yeah. How'd he find out we're in Saint Joe?"

"I don't know, but Jim says to get packed. We're leaving here tonight."

Janice went with Packard to his room to tell McGuinn. At first he was incredulous, then said: "Why didn't you tell me this when we were out on the street just now? Hell, we could have grabbed him again and kept him quiet."

"Grab him away from two cops? Not likely. And the way he was running his mouth, they already had the full story, anyway. Somebody probably escorted him out here on the train."

"I hate the idea of running from that runty, little loud mouth," McGuinn grumped as Janice nodded to Packard and ducked out of the room. "We should've done for him when we had the chance."

"You mean killed him?"

He balled a knotty fist under Packard's nose. "I could have punched him a lot harder than I did."

"And swung for murder if you were caught. Right now, all you've got against you is body-snatching and property damage, which are only misdemeanors."

"Missed . . . what?"

"Small offenses in the sight of the law. Why do you think I've never done anything worse than robbing graves? That way, if I was caught, I wouldn't get the death penalty."

"Some things are worth the risk," he said, angry as he snatched up his spare shirt and rolled his razor and toothbrush into it.

Packard borrowed a towel from the washstand to hold his few items of spare clothing and the personal effects he'd bought.

Ten minutes later they were in the lobby, checking out. Janice and Rip Hughes were the only ones carrying small grips.

"I have to charge you for tonight," the desk clerk said primly, peering over his half glasses. "You might as well stay until morning."

"Urgent business," Kinealy grunted, shoving several bills at him.

As they trooped out the front door, Packard glanced back and saw the thin clerk look up at the big wall clock. It was only nine-twenty.

They were virtually silent as they walked the several short blocks to Riley's saloon. When they were several doors from the place, Kinealy turned to Hughes. "Stay here and keep an eye on Janice. I don't want anyone thinking she's alone in this part of town."

"I'll go with you," she said quickly, throwing a fearful glance at Hughes.

"No. The place looks pretty busy. You'd draw too much attention. I won't be long."

"I'll stay with her," Packard offered, trying to sound disinterested.

"Why is everyone starting to question my orders?" Kinealy exploded, turning to face them. "I said Hughes and Janice will stay here. You two come with me." He gestured at Packard and McGuinn.

The three of them went on ahead and entered the saloon. The frosted glass door let in a wave of cold air that stirred the hanging haze of tobacco smoke. Three or four men nearest the door looked up, but they occasioned no notice from the rest of the two dozen men in the place as they headed for the bar. Riley was helping his bartender. In the minute or two it took him to wait on them, Packard used the back-bar mirror to study the clientele in the room and was relieved there was no sign of Boston Corbett or anyone else who looked like he might be a law officer.

They ordered beer, and Kinealy gestured that he wanted to see Riley in private. Riley nodded toward the back room. The two of them slid away, leaving Packard and McGuinn.

Time dragged as they leaned on the polished

mahogany and sipped their tepid beer. The big, wall clock slowly cranked itself around to ten after ten. Packard was beginning to worry that something was amiss, but, just as he started to suggest they go find out what was taking so long, the door to the back room opened and the two of them emerged.

Riley went back behind the bar, and Kinealy slid up alongside McGuinn. "He's got a buckboard in a shed out back we can use. We can borrow his team to pull it . . . as soon as he gets rid of this crowd."

"Gentlemen!" Riley called, walking out from behind the bar and raising his hands. "Gentlemen! Let me have your attention!"

The hum of voices gradually died.

"Afraid I've got some bad news. I've just been told that my sainted mother has been struck down with apoplexy and is in a bad way. She lives some ways out of town, so I'll have to close early and go see about her."

There was a murmur of disappointment, and someone said: "Why can't your bartender run the place?"

This met with general agreement.

"Sorry, gents, but that's not the way I do business. But I'll be open at the regular time tomorrow. Just to show I appreciate your business, everyone have a drink on me for the road."

With a clatter of chairs and comments of approval, the men at the tables moved toward the bar.

For the next few minutes Riley and his young barkeep were kept busy pouring the free drinks. Then, one and two at a time, the men put on their hats and drifted out into the night.

As the last customer left, followed by the bartender, Riley closed and locked the door behind him. McGuinn, Kinealy, and Packard went out the back way, following Riley who carried a lantern. Across the alley and some way behind the privy was a small, wooden building that served as a wagon shed and stable. The place smelled musty and was festooned with cobwebs and layered with dust. But instead of the neglected, dried-out, old trap Packard half expected, the buckboard showed considerable care. The axles had been greased, the wood recently varnished. The harness, hanging on a peg, was also in excellent condition, the leather cleaned and oiled. One of the two duns they backed out of their stalls to harness up was apparently Riley's saddle horse, but the saloon-keeper seemed almost gleeful that they were taking his only means of transportation.

"We'll get this rig back to you as soon as we can," Kinealy was saying as McGuinn, Packard, and Riley set about hitching up.

"Don't worry about it," he chattered. "Just keep it as long as you want. In fact, you can have it. Yes, it's yours. You don't have to bring it back."

Kinealy looked at him curiously. "I'll pay you for it right now, then." He reached inside his coat and drew out a wad of bills. Apparently he had gotten more from his contact in Chicago than Packard realized.

"You'll get your regular fee later, after I get paid," Kinealy continued, handing over three or four one-hundred-dollar bills.

"I know. I know. No rush about that," Riley said, stuffing the bills into his pocket without even looking at them. He went to the stable door and peered through a crack into the dark alley. "Just take that coffin and go." He seemed both nervous and relieved, as he pulled out a bandanna and mopped his face and head.

After the team was harnessed, Riley extinguished the lantern, opened the door, and they walked the horses and buckboard around to the side door of the saloon. The sky was still overcast, and the only light showing came faintly from several other saloons up the street. Riley unlocked the door and held the duns while the three of them went down into the basement once more with the lantern. Kinealy struck a match to the wick and set the smoky light on the floor while they made short work of uncovering the lead coffin, wrapping and tying the canvas around it, and muscling it up the wooden steps to the wagon outside.

"Just keep your head down and your mouth shut," Kinealy said in a low voice as he mounted the seat and took the reins. "I'll be in touch in a few days."

"You can count on me," Riley answered, stepping back out of the way as Packard joined Kinealy on the wooden seat, and McGuinn climbed into the back.

Kinealy clucked up the team, and they again began the perilous task of moving the body through a town that was not deserted or asleep. They paused a block away to beckon Hughes and Janice out of the shadows of the building where they'd been left. They quickly clambered in over the tailgate and joined McGuinn in back.

People were still up and about even though it was around eleven o'clock. Kinealy took a circuitous route to avoid the well-lighted saloons near the waterfront. They passed the old, brick Pony Express stable, and within a few short blocks had left St. Joe behind. Kinealy whipped the team to a trot, and the buckboard made good time, running north along a deserted road that roughly paralleled the Missouri River.

Packard wondered if the others had any idea where they were going, but he had learned his lesson about asking Kinealy too many questions. Nobody spoke, and Packard hunched forward and sat on his hands to dull the bite of the wind.

They traveled about four miles as nearly as he could estimate before Kinealy pulled the team to a walk and guided them off the road and across a flat field, bumping in and out of shallow washes and holes. Then they were back on some sort of overgrown road, and, by the time they began winding up into some steep hills, the horses had their second wind and were pulling strongly.

They were apparently in a range of low hills, northeast of town, some distance back from the river.

Finally, after several twists and turns, Kinealy drew up in front of a large, white house Packard could dimly make out.

"Here we are," he said, setting the brake and stepping down.

"Where?" Packard asked. It appeared to be an abandoned two-story frame house.

"The old Hanrahan place."

This told him nothing, but Packard kept silent until he continued.

"Thomas Hanrahan made a fortune in textiles in New York. Retired here with his money and had it built around Eighteen Fifty-Two. Unfortunately, he got to meddling in politics, got crossways of some Southern border raiders who killed him and his wife just before the war. Tied up and stabbed in the cellar. I heard there was a big wrangle among his relatives about the estate." He paused as the four of them dragged the heavy coffin off the buckboard and started toward the house. "Anyway, nobody's lived here since the murders. Had an idea about stashing the body here to begin with, instead of fooling with Riley. Probably should have. Would've saved time and money." He grunted as they leaned into the slight incline with their burden. "We'll take it in the front door. Watch your step on this porch. The boards could be rotten. This place has been deserted for years."

"Just what I wanted to replace the Patee House," Janice muttered under her breath as she walked beside Packard.

"What's that?" Kinealy snapped, catching her words.

"Nothing," she replied wearily.

"If you don't like it, you can go back to Springfield, or any place else you want to go," Kinealy replied coldly. "It was your idea to be part of this operation, so quit complaining!"

"The least you could do is tell me in advance where we're going, so I can be prepared," she retorted. "But, no. You drag us up here to some ratty, old, haunted house. I thought you could find something better than this."

"Would it have made any difference if I'd told you?"

This exchange was going nowhere so she lapsed into a sullen silence. Packard was thankful for the darkness, because he didn't want to look at either one of them. Marital arguments made him very uncomfortable, and even more so since he was enamored of her.

They set the coffin down on the porch while Kinealy shoved the front door aside with a gloved hand. It squeaked open on rusty hinges and glass tinkled as the remaining shards of an oval window fell out.

"Fetch the lantern from the buckboard," Kinealy ordered his wife.

She obeyed without comment, and a couple of minutes later they had the canvas-wrapped coffin inside the front parlor with the door shut. "I hope this house sets far enough back in the hills that no light can be seen from the road," Kinealy said, striking a match to the lantern and sending warm, welcome light flooding the space around them. The house had been left furnished, and the dust of years lay over a horsehair sofa, wingback chairs, marble-top table, and Oriental carpet. "Even if somebody should see it," Kinealy continued, "we can count on them believing it's the spirits of the dead, so nobody will come to investigate. You can see how nobody has stolen or vandalized anything in here. Fear of murder victims is a powerful deterrent. The Hanrahan house has the reputation of being haunted, as Janice says." He added with a touch of sarcasm: "But, just in case, better make sure the shutters are closed."

"Hell, boss, about half these shutters have fallen off," McGuinn said, examining the front windows. The heavy, moth-eaten drapes looked as if they would drop into a dusty heap if anyone so much as touched them.

"No matter," Kinealy said. "Let's get this box down into the cellar, anyway."

"Damn it, boss, do we have to carry it down more stairs?" McGuinn groaned. "Let's just set it in one of these empty rooms. We'll be here the whole time, I reckon. Nobody's going to bother it."

"Well, maybe you're right. Janice, lead us into the back parlor with that light. We'll just set it across a couple of chairs."

This accomplished, they explored some of the other rooms, trying to find some reasonably comfortable place to bed down for the night. Candelabras were still intact on the big sideboard even containing a few candles that hadn't been chewed up by hungry mice. This gave them a little more independence, since they could each have a light of sorts.

"What a magnificent mansion this must have been before the war!" Janice marveled, as her initial disgust with the state of the place began to ebb. By the wavering light of her candle, she was examining the ornate furnishings and the darkened oil portraits that glared down from heavy frames.

"I imagine this house has a magnificent view of the river from this height," Hughes said, sliding into their conversation with an oily persistence. "You know, of course, that we are in the lower end of the Loess Hills."

"The what?" Janice asked.

"The Loess Hills," he said, then smiled. "An irregular string of hills that stretches from the Dakota Territory down into northern Missouri. Formed eons ago by wind-blown dust. There are no rocks in these hills." He was obviously trying to impress her with his knowledge.

"Oh, really?" Janice sounded less than enthusiastic with her geology lesson.

As she and Packard and Hughes stepped into one of the front bedrooms, she gasped and jumped back as something scuttled away from the light and disappeared under the bed.

"Wouldn't be surprised if there wasn't a nest of pack rats up inside that mattress somewhere," Hughes remarked.

"I think I'll sleep in the front parlor," Packard said with a laugh, but laying the groundwork for the escape he planned before daylight. "And, speaking of sleep, I guess we'd better see to the horses before we settle in." Packard had to know exactly where the horses were so he could lay hands on one of them in the dark.

He went back into the kitchen where he found Kinealy working the handle of an indoor water pump. In a minute or so water came gushing out into the deep sink. "Ah, good! It still works. Water, but no food. I'll pick up some food, when I go back in to the Western Union office tomorrow. If everything goes well, we can stash the body somewhere out of sight around here and then head on up the river to Nebraska City. Maybe get a steamboat from there to Omaha. Once the body's well hidden, we can move on and deal with the governor from anywhere."

This was more information than Kinealy had ever divulged at one time. Even though his plans sounded tentative, and he had shown he was capable of improvising on the spot, Packard filed away his remark in the back of his mind for later use in case Kinealy managed to get away from here before the Secret Service could nab him.

While the others were selecting places to bed

down, McGuinn and Packard went out and drove the buckboard behind the house. By the light of the lantern they unhitched the team and put them in a small barn. Rodents had chewed through the sacks of oats and corn. What hadn't been eaten or scattered was mingled with droppings, or had gotten damp and sprouted. They did manage to find a few scoops of dry corn that had been sealed tightly in a hogshead.

"Looks like everything was left just as it was when the Hanrahans died years ago," Packard observed, dumping the grain into the feed box.

"Yeah," McGuinn said, without offering any further comment. He seemed more tight-lipped than usual, as he shook the dirt out of two empty buckets and carried them through the back door into the kitchen to pump water for the animals. When he returned, Packard silently picked up the lantern and led the way back to the house. His cover as a gang member was wearing as thin as the leather soles of his old boots. The time had come for him to escape. It would have to be tonight.

When he reëntered the parlor, Janice was wiping off the slick surface of the black horsehair sofa with a damp towel from the kitchen and was preparing to lie down on it with her hooded cape for a cover. He was surprised she and Kinealy hadn't claimed one of the bedrooms. But then he remembered the pack rats in the front bedroom and assumed she had refused to move any deeper into the recesses of this old mansion.

He was on edge himself, but not because of sharing sleeping space with any vermin. Sagging with fatigue, he knew there was a good chance he wouldn't wake up before daylight. His only hope, if he couldn't discipline himself to stay awake, was to rely on the cold and the hard floor to wake him after an hour or two. Betting that Kinealy would not post a guard, he needed to make sure the others were comfortably asleep. To that end, he took up a lighted candle and went down the hall, looking for a linen closet that might have some blankets. Behind him, he heard McGuinn mention building a fire in one of the brick fireplaces.

"Sure. Build a fire. Be comfortable. We'll hold a public Lincoln exhibition up here as soon as everybody sees and smells the smoke," Kinealy snapped.

"We get the point. You don't have to be so sarcastic," Janice complained, slapping a cloud of dust out of a sofa pillow.

As Packard walked off, he heard a low-voiced exchange between Kinealy and his wife. He could distinguish only a few words, but what he could hear and her vehement tone indicated she was refusing to take a room with him.

Under the staircase he found a musty-smelling linen closet piled deep with quilts and towels and sheets and carried an armful back to the parlor. Just as he'd hoped, everyone helped themselves. To his relief, Kinealy and McGuinn opted to seek the bedrooms. Kinealy even climbed the creaking steps to the floor above, possibly to have a better lookout point from the upstairs windows, come daylight.

"I'll just curl up on the floor in the back parlor to keep an eye on the body," Packard said with a grin. Nobody answered, but Hughes carried his blanket only as far as the next room that had once been a library. Packard pulled the big sliding door out of its wall recess partially to shut off the view from the front parlor. The dry rollers squalled on their metal tracks. His last view, before he snuffed his candle and lay down on the quilt on the carpet, was of the wrapped coffin, setting across two chairs a few feet away. He purposely didn't wrap up in the quilt to keep from getting too comfortable.

But, in spite of his resolve, and the chill that pervaded the deserted mansion, he must have dozed off, because suddenly consciousness returned and he lay there with cold-stiffened muscles, wondering what had awakened him. It was either his mental alarm clock or something external. A shiver ran over him as he heard the wind moaning around the eaves. The old house creaked and groaned, like the timbers of a ship in a seaway. These noises were normal, as were the faint scratchings of what he assumed were mice or rats in the baseboards. No human sounds reached his ears except the slight snoring from McGuinn in the front bedroom.

He had not removed his boots, coat, or gun belt, so he was ready to go. Very carefully rolling over on his hands and knees, he bowed his back, stretching all the muscles he could before getting to his feet. Then he rose and felt his way around the open edge of the big sliding door. Proceeding by memory only, he placed one foot ahead of the other across the front parlor past the sofa where Janice lay. He paused two or three times, when she sighed or shifted her position on the couch. The sound of her regular breathing stopped, and he wondered if she had awakened. He took two more steps and cringed as the floorboards creaked loudly under his weight.

"Who's there?" she whispered in a tremulous voice.

He didn't move or breathe for the space of at least thirty seconds, hoping she'd think it was only the timbers of the old house working. He couldn't have been more than four feet from her and realized she probably felt his presence. It was almost as if he could hear her heart pounding with fear. Finally, he took one more step — and kicked over the lantern. It rolled on the floor with a metallic clatter that could have been heard in St. Joe.

Chapter Eighteen

"Oh, my God!" Janice screamed.

Packard made a dash for the front door, got the handle, and flung it open.

"Hold it right there!" Hughes yelled.

Darkness covered Packard as he leapt outside, but his first step was his last as his right boot crashed through a rotten spot on the porch floor. One leg went down at least two feet, throwing his upper body forward, and he did the splits. It was the only thing that saved him as a shot blasted, and the slug clipped a porch post.

Cursing, he yanked his own gun and twisted around to fire blindly into the darkness behind him. But, at the last instant, he thought of Janice and barely had time to tilt the barrel up before his hand reflexively squeezed off a shot that shattered glass in the big chandelier.

He put both hands on the floor, desperately trying to jerk his leg out of the hole. Rolling over, he finally pulled loose, raking skin off his leg with the jagged edges of the boards.

"There he goes. Get him!" Hughes cried.

Packard sprang to his feet and turned to flee. Someone slammed into him with a tackle that nearly crushed his ribs. The two of them went flying off the porch and landed hard in the yard, jarring the pistol out of his grasp. He lay stunned on his back, unable to breathe. He had never been hit so hard in his life and was hardly aware that his assailant had gotten up.

"Get the light! Quick!"

Packard's spinning head began to slow, and his eyes picked up the bobbing, weaving light of a lantern coming toward him.

"Damned if it ain't Packard!" McGuinn said. "You ain't hurt, are you?" he asked, reaching down with a big paw and yanking him to his feet before he was ready. Packard's head was still reeling, and he staggered and fell against McGuinn.

"Whoa, there. Take it easy."

"Where the hell you think you're going this time o' night?" came Hughes's suspicious voice.

Packard shook his head and only half pretended to be dazed as he sat down on the porch step.

Just then Kinealy appeared in the light, puffy-eyed and gun in hand. He was wearing only his long johns.

Before he could open his mouth, Packard spoke up. "Thought I heard something outside and was slipping out to take a look," he said, holding his ribs and moving gingerly to pick up the gun that had been knocked from his hand. "But the floor gave way, and then that son-of-a-bitch started shooting at me." He gestured at Hughes. "Lucky for me, his shooting is as rotten as this porch." He couldn't resist needling the man.

"I tackled him before I knew who it was," McGuinn added.

"If you can punch like you tackle, I'd hate to face you in the ring," Packard said, drawing a deep, painful breath. It never hurt to throw a compliment to keep your enemy off balance.

Kinealy lowered his gun and blew out a deep breath, rubbing his sleep-swollen eyes. "Well, thanks to you idiots, probably half the county heard those shots and knows somebody's up here."

Hughes was giving Packard a baleful stare, but said nothing.

"Aaww, boss," McGuinn groaned. "Don't tell me we're going to have to lug that body some place else."

"Not tonight. But, as long as you can't sleep for hearing things, Packard, you can stand guard for the rest of the night. Daylight couldn't be more'n three or four hours off."

It had been a desperate fabrication, but they seemed to buy his story. He looked at Janice who was standing with her cape around her shoulders and eyeing him with a very strange look. Intuition must have told her that his story was a sham, but she still wasn't sure what he was up to.

Their breaths were smoke in the frosty night air as Kinealy said: "Get that lantern out of the doorway. This house may be visible to anybody on the road down below."

It was unlikely any travelers were abroad on the river road at this hour. Nevertheless, they moved inside and shut the door. McGuinn turned the lantern low, but left it burning as he set it on the parlor floor.

Kinealy clumped back up the stairs, using the banister to steady his heavy tread.

"Helluva way to wake up from a sound sleep," McGuinn yawned, stretching and heading back into the front bedroom. He mumbled something unintelligible as he pushed the door partway closed.

Rip Hughes seemed reluctant to return to his interrupted sleep in the library and leave Packard awake with Janice in the front parlor, but, finally, he pointedly shoved his pistol back into the waistband of his pants. He had removed only his wool suitcoat, gun belt, and boots. With his shirt-tail out and his pomaded hair splayed comically erect on one side of his head where he had been lying on it, he gave the general appearance of an unmade bed — totally unlike his usual debonair self.

Baiting this man was something Packard's reason told him to avoid as long as he was trying to retain his cover as a member of the gang. But it was almost a reflex, or a compulsion — something he couldn't help doing at every opportunity. It wasn't as if he were trying to win Janice from him; she had already expressed her revulsion at his advances. There was just something about the man that irritated him, like fingernails raking a slate blackboard. He didn't know exactly what it was — maybe something as subtle as his facial expressions, or his demeaning attitude. At least with McGuinn he knew what to expect; he came at you like a battering ram. There was nothing devious about the ex-boxer.

Hughes reluctantly turned to leave, giving Janice a look that slithered over her like a lascivious tongue. She recoiled as from a physical touch, averting her eyes and wrapping her cape closely about her.

Packard moved to her side in a protective gesture as Hughes went back into the library. When he disappeared, Packard drew his gun and punched out the one empty shell, replacing it with a fresh cartridge. He also filled the sixth chamber which was normally kept empty for safety reasons.

"Don't worry about him," he said, his mouth close to her fragrant hair. "I'll be on watch the rest of the night."

"I know," she replied, moving away from him and sitting on the sofa. "Come here and let me look at your ribs."

She had apparently noticed him favoring his left side. He dutifully stood before her and pulled up his shirt and undershirt. "Turn toward the light." He turned. Her touch was light, but he still winced at the pressure on certain spots. "Left an imprint. Can you take a deep breath without pain?"

He tried it. "Yes."

"Don't think any ribs are cracked, but you've got a good bruise there."

"I guess I'll live."

Her fingers trailed down below his rib cage, and he looked to see her touching the livid scar where the Yankee ball had ripped into his side. The spot was still white, thirteen years after the wound had healed. He shivered, and it wasn't just from having his skin exposed to the chill in the room.

She looked up at him. "Remember this?"

"It aches in cold weather. But I don't mind, since it brings back pleasant memories. I'd be bones and dust now, if you hadn't found and taken pity on me."

"It wasn't all pity," she said softly, running her smooth hand over his belly. He began to grow warm.

"What about your leg?" she asked, suddenly the practical nurse again.

He glanced down at the few small spots of blood that had wet his right trouser leg. In all the excitement, he'd forgotten about the splintered boards raking his leg, just below the knee, and had not even felt it after the first sting.

She tried to push up his pants leg, but the torn material wouldn't slide up over his calf. "Let down your pants so I can see how bad those cuts are," she said matter-of-factly. "You might even have some splinters."

He hesitated.

"Go on. I'm not going to hurt you."

He unbuckled his trousers and slid them down, feeling very self-conscious.

"Just some scratches. Nothing deep. Probably need to wash it off with some clean water and alcohol first chance you get."

"You should have been a nurse," he said.

"Actually, that's what I always wanted to do," she said. "But sometimes life gets in the way of dreams. I'm sure you know how that is."

"Yes." He was distracted by the embarrassment of standing there in front of her in his white cotton drawers and his trousers around his boots. But she was using her own clean handkerchief to wipe off the half-dried blood.

"Sterling, what were you really doing a few minutes ago?" she asked as she continued wiping his leg.

"Like I said, going to check on a noise I heard."

She shook her head. "No, you weren't."

"What makes you say that?"

"When I asked who was there, you never answered." She looked up at him. "I was scared. You at least could've whispered to reassure me."

"I didn't want to scare off anyone who might have been outside," he said lamely.

"When Rip yelled for you to stop after you kicked over the lantern, why didn't you sing out? You were almost shot, running like that."

"I can't tell you everything now," he finally said, as gently as he could, stroking her hair as she sat in front of him, still cleaning his scratched leg.

"I don't understand."

"Trust me," he continued, hating himself for deceiving her. "You'll find out everything later," — *much to your regret,* he should have added, feeling like a heel. Even this cryptic remark put a dangerous crack in his façade. With any persuasion at all, she could get the whole story from him.

"I suspected there was more to you than just being a grave-robber," she whispered, not looking at him. "Tell me who you really are and what you're doing."

He hesitated, trying to think of how to answer.

That few seconds of silence was suddenly shattered by the sound of a pistol cocking behind him. Janice gave a slight gasp, and he slowly turned around.

"Figuring to make your guard duty a little more pleasurable, eh, Packard?" Hughes's face above the steady gun barrel was positively demonic. "After I put a bullet in you, I'll just tell Big Jim I caught you seducing his wife."

"It wouldn't have been a seduction," Janice said scornfully. "Put the gun away. Nothing is going on here."

"Big Jim will be glad to hear his wife is an adulteress."

"Huh! You just wanted me for yourself," she goaded him. "If Jim hears anything, it will be how you tried to take me every time we were alone."

"You think he's going to believe that when he

finds your dead lover by your couch with his pants down? Which reminds me . . . let's make this even better. Drop those drawers, too."

Anger was slowly building, driving out the initial fear. "If I'm going to die anyway, I'd just as soon not go out bare-assed and with genitals showing."

For some reason this struck Hughes as funny. Packard had never heard him laugh before, and then he knew why. Hughes burst out in a high-pitched giggle.

"What's so funny?" Packard asked loudly, hoping to wake McGuinn. The ex-boxer was no ally, but maybe he would create enough of a distraction to provide Packard with a few more minutes of life. At this moment, he would do just about anything to keep Hughes from pulling that trigger. Didn't the Bible say something about a live mouse being preferable to a dead lion? He thought desperately of diving for the lantern and trying to snuff the low flame. Once they were in blackness, it would be Packard's gun against his. But the lantern was on the floor about four feet away, on the other side of Janice. He was quick, but not that quick. Besides, there was a chance, instead of putting out the light, he'd spill the fuel and set the house afire. He thought of yelling for Kinealy, but knew he'd be dead before the shout was done.

"That's all right," Hughes continued, obviously enjoying the situation. "I can always yank down those drawers after you're dead and before Big Jim gets here."

"What's your real reason for wanting to shoot me?" Packard asked, louder than necessary. "It's not just because you were jilted by a married woman. Coney men aren't murderers."

"I've suspected you of being a traitor from the start," Hughes replied. "And so has the boss. My hunches aren't often wrong. You're slick, and I can't prove it just yet. But it won't matter now that I've caught you with her."

"Might as well hang for a hog as a ham," Packard muttered to Janice.

"What'd you say?" Hughes demanded, thrusting his weapon forward.

"I said . . . where the hell is McGuinn?" Packard bellowed. "Don't you want a witness to back up your story?"

"What's all the damned noise about this time?" McGuinn grumbled, appearing in the bedroom door and squinting in the dim light.

What happened next would remain a mystery to Packard, but he would always give credit to the Great Emancipator for freeing him. Just as their attention was diverted by McGuinn, he heard a moaning, groaning noise and looked toward the darkened hallway behind Hughes, expecting to see Kinealy coming down the stairway. The stairs were empty, but a wavering, luminous ball of mist was floating about six feet off the floor. It looked like a cloud of steam, venting from the escape valve of a locomotive. The steam — if that's what it was — did not evaporate, and there was no hissing noise. The only sound that came from that writhing vapor was something akin to the agonized groans of a man in great pain.

They all stared in silent apprehension at this phenomenon. What was it? Possibly some kind of escaping gas that needed only a spark to set it off? Or had Kinealy gone against his own orders and built a fire in an upstairs fireplace? There was no smell of smoke or gas, and the vapor cloud didn't grow any larger. But now it was drifting upward toward the ceiling in the dark hallway. The moaning had taken on a very human, very pitiable sound. A hard chill ran from Packard's heels to the top of his head even as logic kept telling him it was some kind of natural occurrence.

"Oh, God," Janice breathed behind him. "Spirits. The murdered Hanrahans. They want us out of their house."

But then a bright ball formed itself in the middle of the diaphanous cloud. As Packard gawked in disbelief, the bright spot evolved into a face — a face all of them knew, a face they had seen only yesterday — the long-dead features of Abraham Lincoln.

Chapter Nineteen

Packard's scalp prickled with fear. Was he having hallucinations? Sheer terror at his imminent death had surely unhinged his mind. But, no, Janice was seeing it, too.

"Aaahhh!" An agonized cry was wrenched from McGuinn. His knees buckled, and he crumpled to the floor as if in adoration of some vengeful god. "Please . . . please . . . don't hurt us," he croaked in a voice hardly recognized by Packard whose attention was yanked away from the vision for a few seconds to the strange sight of the muscular fighter reduced to a quivering mass. But he shouldn't have been surprised, since the presence of the dead in the Springfield mausoleum had even brought on a nervous sweat.

Hughes stood rigid and staring, his back to Packard, gun at his side.

A chilly breeze on Packard's legs through the broken window of the front door suddenly reminded him of his condition, and he reached down to pull up his pants and buckle his belt. In the few moments it took to do this, his eyes never left the moaning, disembodied head that was moving slowly toward them, eyes open in an accusatory stare. He couldn't tear his eyes from it, even though instinct was yelling at him to fight or run. His mind was simply not functioning. Everything was slowing down, as if he were wading through hip-deep molasses in a dream.

His hand moved to his gun, and, without thinking, he pulled his Colt and fired two shots at the oncoming head. The blasts crashed against his ears as the two flashes and the powder smoke obscured the vision for a few seconds.

Hughes jumped as the gunshots seemed to break the spell. He turned around, and Packard struck him across the head with the barrel of his pistol. Hughes dropped like a sack of wet sand.

A quick glance showed McGuinn still groveling on the floor. Packard grabbed Janice with his free arm. "Come with me!"

"Wha..a..t?"

"Now! Quick! Let's run!"

She turned stunned, uncomprehending brown eyes on him. She was in shock. He hesitated a few long seconds. The face of Lincoln was gone, and the vapor was blending into the drifting gunsmoke.

Footfalls thundered on the carpeted stairs as Kinealy came lumbering down, gun in hand. The paralysis was gone, and, without hesitation, Packard raised his Colt and fired. The bullet splintered the newel post. The big man reacted with a nimbleness that would have done a gymnast proud. He leapt over the banister and crashed onto the floor near the end of the hallway. A second later an answering shot flamed out of the darkness. The bullet tugged at Packard's coat sleeve, and he dropped to the floor atop the broken pieces of glass chandelier.

"No! No! Don't shoot!" Janice cried, coming to her senses and jumping between them.

They had no choice but to hold their fire. A movement caught Packard's eye, and he glanced over to see McGuinn getting to his feet and reaching for the gun stuck in his belt. Two guns against him and possibly three when the stunned Hughes rallied. It was time to move. He sprang up and darted out the front door, leaping over the hole in the porch.

Packard didn't think he'd ever moved so fast in his life. In a matter of seconds, he was into the blackness of the stable behind the house. Giving thanks that he'd helped with the horses, he quickly found one of them in a stall and got him out. There was no time to look for a saddle or bridle. He'd have to attempt an escape bareback on a strange animal. He jammed his gun into the holster to free up both hands as he led the skittish horse outside with one of his hands wrapped in the hair of his mane. Walking him carefully, he went around the opposite side of the house from where he'd come. Voices were near, and feet clumped on the porch. He stopped to determine which way they were going, and heard Kinealy order someone around the other way. Then his heavy panting was coming closer as he ran toward Packard's side of the house.

"Here goes!" he muttered to himself, lacing the fingers of his left hand into the mane of the dun. He vaulted up onto its back, kicking with his boot heels. The startled animal bolted, knocking Kinealy spinning. Packard was nearly unseated by the sudden lunge and just barely managed to hold on. The big dun went thundering downhill along the winding road in the dark, as if he knew exactly where he was going while Packard swayed around like a drunken man. He didn't know if faith could really move mountains, but he could testify that desperation could make a bareback rider. It was hands, elbows, knees, and thighs clutching to hold on as he was all over the horse's back. On a steep slope, he was pitched forward far enough over the withers to get both arms around the neck, but was quickly jarred loose from that position. Every minute he could stay aboard the hurricane deck of this plunging animal was another half mile between him and that house on the hill — and several more minutes added to his life span. Stinging tips of the mane lashed his face while his tailbone took a fearful pounding.

When the dun began to tire and slowed to a lope, Packard blinked away the wind-whipped tears and saw they were headed toward St. Joe — possibly due to the animal's instinct to return to his familiar stable behind Riley's saloon. Whatever the reason, it was fortunate for Packard, since he had no reins, bit, or hackamore to guide him. Being a rider of less than average skill, he had to let him go where he wished. The river road was the path of least resistance, and they headed straight for town.

Finally the big horse slowed to a walk, his coat lathered, and his sides heaving. Packard was able to sit upright on his back in a more or less natural position. They must have covered at least three miles. Bushes and trees along the road began to take on ghostly shapes as the eastern sky slowly lightened with the coming dawn. The heavy overcast remained, but at least the northwest wind had subsided. He wiped a sleeve across his sweating face, breathing as heavily as his mount. He looked again at the eastern sky, wondering what time it was.

While his attention was thus diverted, the horse apparently shied at something — a 'possum, a shadow, he never knew what — and jumped sideways. In the blink of an eye, Packard hit the ground hard. The horse skittered off a few steps, and then trotted on toward town while Packard sat up, holding his left arm and shoulder. By the time he got painfully to his feet, the horse was fifty yards off, and it was useless trying to catch him, even if he'd felt like running. There was nothing for him to do now but start walking, and get as far as possible before full daylight forced him to get out of sight down along the river. Once there, he could probably work his way toward town through the trees and undergrowth.

What kind of pursuit would be coming? He'd

never seen it done, but assumed it was somehow possible to hitch only one horse to a buckboard. Or maybe Kinealy would find a saddle in the barn and send Hughes or McGuinn after him on horseback. He had to assume his cover was shredded. Hughes would convince Kinealy that he had run because he was a traitor and had set up the ambush at the tomb, and not just because he'd been caught with his pants down. None of Janice's explanations would carry any weight, since she was hardly a disinterested party. Kinealy could not afford just to let him go. There was too much at stake. Even if he wasn't sure of Packard's rôle as an undercover Secret Service agent, it was vital that Kinealy catch and hold him *incommunicado* until the ransom was paid. He wondered if Kinealy would try to kill him; somehow the chief of the coney men didn't impress him as a murderer. Hughes was a different breed. He would shoot first and justify it to Kinealy later.

Packard trudged on another mile or so, turning over the thought of the strange apparition in his mind. Was it truly a supernatural vision? An actual ghost? All four of them had seen the same thing, so there was no doubt something was visible. Beyond that, who could say? The groaning head of Abraham Lincoln was adrift in a cloud of vapor while his body lay in the next room. Try explaining that to a hard-edged lawman in the cold light of dawn. He resolved to give it more thought later, but this "ghost" may have been the reason Riley had been so nervous and anxious to be rid of the body. Whatever it was, the specter had provided a chance to escape that den of thieves — a chance he wouldn't have had otherwise.

The sky lightened to a dull gray as the sun rose behind the overcast. Full daylight came, and he felt very exposed, glancing back over his shoulder every few steps. His ears were attuned to anything that sounded like hoofbeats or an approaching wagon.

It was then his body began complaining about the accumulated abuse he'd put it through — the bruised ribs, the cuts on his leg, the pummeled backside that ached with every step, the left shoulder he'd jammed falling off the horse. Every muscle and joint were strained. He felt like someone who'd been romped on by a playful grizzly. All this was in addition to the fact that he'd been sleepless for twenty-four hours and was dirty, unshaven, and wearing a cologne of horse sweat. To top it off, his stomach was growling and his throat dry.

But things began looking up. The gables and roof cornices of some buildings were just coming into view over the bare trees, possibly two miles ahead along the straight road. He lowered his eyes and trudged on, blotting out the discomfort by figuring his next move. Besides chasing him, Kinealy would have to get back to the Western Union office in St. Joe to pick up the reply from the Illinois governor. If Packard could reach the police or county sheriff and tell his story, maybe the law could be waiting for him. Or, better yet, he would try to get off a telegram to his superiors first. In spite of all the hitches, he began to feel that everything was going to work out at last. But he couldn't let down his guard now as he mentally examined this scenario for problems. He found only one — Janice. He consoled himself with the resolve to swear that she was an unwilling participant who was forced to go along by her husband. His conscience immediately excoriated him for such a weak excuse. Any decent prosecutor could show that she had been Kinealy's willing partner in crime for years. It was doubtful if any testimony of Packard's would get her off easier, especially if it leaked out that he was in love with her. And Hughes would gladly supply such testimony. But he had heard it was illegal for a wife to testify against her husband. Was the reverse also true? Even if Kinealy couldn't or wouldn't accuse her, there was always Hughes and McGuinn.

Yet he was getting far ahead of himself. The Kinealy gang had to be caught first, and to that end he quickened his painful strides toward St. Joe. A few minutes later the jangle of trace chains made him whirl around. A wagon was coming along the road toward town. The span of mules pulling it told him it wasn't Kinealy. But he didn't want to meet anyone just now, and looked around frantically for a place to hide. No bushes or trees large enough to conceal him on this open stretch of road. He reached under his coat, put a hand on the butt of his gun, and waited.

A lone man was on the driver's seat of the farm wagon and pulled the mules back from a trot to a walk.

"Want a lift to town?" he hailed as he got within earshot.

"Sure. Thanks." Anything to get him there a little quicker.

The driver drew the team to a halt, and Packard climbed aboard. As he settled himself on the wooden seat, his back and legs groaned with relief at finally being able to sit down and relax.

The driver was a man of medium size, wearing a slouch hat, gray canvas coat, and mud-spattered boots. What Packard could see of his face was weathered and creased. A two-day growth of gray stubble covered the lean jaws.

The man clucked the mules into motion again.

"Thanks for the ride. I was getting kind of tired of walking."

"Glad to help," the man replied slowly, eyeing Packard slantwise from under his hat brim. "You ain't from around these parts." It was not a question.

"No, I'm not."

"Come down from Ioway, did ya?" the man prompted when Packard didn't continue.

"Actually Nebraska City," Packard lied. "Got a ride a few miles, but had to wind up sleeping in a barn last night," he said to explain his scruffy appearance. "Yes, sir, these nights are gettin' mighty nippy, even if I did have a good pile of hay to burrow into."

"I've got a son-in-law and daughter in Nebraska City," the driver said. "Name of Wardlaw. You wouldn't know 'em by chance?"

"No. I was just passin' through on my way to Kansas City. Got a sister there. Got a job waiting."

Packard was afraid he'd hooked up with some lonely, nosey old farmer, who would want to pump him for any and all information he could get.

"Would've been a lot quicker if you'd got on a steamboat and gone straight down the river."

"You're right about that, friend. But even deck passage costs money. Besides, I warn't in that big a hurry. You see, my sister ain't exactly expectin' me, and I'm hoping to bunk in at her place a spell until I get my first paycheck."

"If you're hard up for money, you could probably sell that shootin' iron for enough to see you to Kansas City, and then some," he remarked, noting the holstered Colt as Packard leaned forward and his coat fell open.

"That may be, but a man might as well go nekkid as travel unarmed these days. You never know what kind of riff-raff you might meet on the road."

"That's a fact," the man replied, eyeing him again as he slapped the lines over the mules who had slowed down to a walk.

Apparently the driver concluded Packard was a lost cause as a source of news or conversation because he stopped talking for the last mile into town. Packard didn't dare look back for fear the driver would then assume he was on the run from somebody. So he just pretended to stretch and yawn and, in the process, managed to twist around far enough on the seat to get a quick look at the road behind them. It was still empty.

The trotting mules ate up the distance a lot faster than his shanks mare would have, but his nerves still counted it as a long time before they reached the edge of town.

"I'll just be getting off here," he said as they passed the first three widely spaced buildings.

"I can take you a few blocks farther."

"No need. Got some things to do. Sure appreciate the ride." He waved and jumped off the side while the iron-banded wheels were still turning. The farmer gave him a strange look as the heavy farm wagon rumbled on down the street.

Packard waited until it was a block away before making a dash for the Western Union telegraph office. It was several short blocks away, and he made it a point to detour away from Riley's saloon. Riley would probably be sleeping at this hour of the morning, but his dun horse might be wandering the streets somewhere near his place.

Packard's worn boots were never made for running, and his body hurt with every pounding step as his soles slapped the cobblestones and thundered across the occasional boardwalk. He was praying the Western Union office would be open and ready for business because he was like a racehorse in the home stretch. Once his message was on its way to the Secret Service in Chicago, his job was essentially over, and he could handle whatever came after. By the time he rounded the last corner and spotted the Western Union sign hanging over the sidewalk several doors down, his breath was coming in rasping gasps. He forced himself to slow down to a walk and enter the office under some control.

He opened the door and went inside, still breathing heavily and perspiring. Two men were just turning away from the counter, and he brushed past them toward the telegrapher.

"I need to send a telegram right away," he gasped.

"Certainly, sir." The beefy man in the green eyeshade, striped shirt, and galluses shoved a pad of paper and a pencil across the worn oak counter toward him. Packard's hand was shaking from exertion, and he had to take several deep breaths before he could begin to write.

He put pencil to pad, trying to concentrate on how to word a succinct, but complete, message to his chief in Chicago. They had never worked out a code for such situations, but that hardly mattered. He was the law, and there was no need for secrecy. He would stand here until the message was transmitted, and wait for an acknowledgment from the other end.

"That's the man. I'd know him anywhere!"

The voice grated into his concentration, and he glanced up. Boston Corbett stood about six feet away, pointing him out to a tall man in a gray overcoat beside him. Packard realized these were the two he'd rushed past as he came in.

"What?" He was momentarily taken aback and didn't know just how to react to this man.

"You're certain this is one of the men who kidnapped you?" the tall, graying man said, sliding back his overcoat to rest his hand on his gun.

"Who're you?" Packard stammered.

"Cyrus Morgan, Special Police Detective, City of Saint Joseph." His calm manner was much more reassuring than the wild demeanor of the mad preacher, in spite of the fact that the blue-gray eyes regarding him were as cold as the November dawn.

"My name . . . is Sterling Packard," he said, still panting. "I'm an undercover agent . . . for the United States Secret Service out of Chicago. I'll be glad to give you the whole story . . . and believe me . . . there's more than kidnapping involved. Just let me send a telegram to my chief, first."

He turned to take up the pencil again, when he felt the muzzle of Morgan's gun pressing into his back. He froze, then, very slowly, turned to face him.

"If you're an undercover agent, let me see some identification."

"I told you I'm working undercover. You don't think I'm carrying anything like that on me, do you?"

He eyed Packard's rough exterior. "If you're an undercover agent, I'm President Grant."

Packard held his hands out. "Look, I know this sounds ridiculous, but I haven't got time to explain right now. I've got to get a message off to my boss. There are three men after me. They're the ones who stole Abraham Lincoln's body and are holding it for ransom."

"You're one of them!" Corbett yelled, wild-eyed.

Morgan reached out, flipped open Packard's coat, lifted the Colt from its holster, and shoved it into the side pocket of his overcoat. "Let's go."

"Where?"

"To the jail. My chief will want to question you."

"Am I under arrest?"

"Not unless you resist."

"But I'm a lawman! I'm on your side. All you have to do to verify that I'm who I say I am is send a telegram to this name and address and wait for an answer."

"Even if a reply comes back that they have an agent named Sterling Packard, how do I know that's you?"

He could feel it all slipping away again. McGuinn or Hughes or Kinealy himself might be coming down the street right now, and here he was, arguing with these idiots and trying to defend himself. "This can't be happening," he muttered.

"That's it, Cy," Corbett said with gleeful familiarity. "Don't let him talk you out of it. I was there. They tied me up and beat me. Him and three other men. And they had that body right with them in that wagon."

"OK, OK, you've told me all that several times," Morgan interrupted with some irritation. "Come along, you. We'll get this all sorted out at the station. And don't try anything foolish, because I haven't lived to be this age by taking any chances with prisoners."

Packard sagged dejectedly as Morgan deftly ran one hand over him, feeling for hidden weapons. He determined to make one more try. "Just let me send this telegram before I go. What can it hurt?"

"No. If you really are an agent. . . ."

"He's no agent of the government," Corbett interrupted. "He's an agent of the devil. Don't listen to him, Cy. He'll have you all twisted in knots. That's the way Satan fooled Adam and Eve in the Garden of Eden."

"Will you shut up and let me handle this?" Morgan exploded. "Let's go Packard, or whatever your name is. The chief should just be getting to the office about now."

"I've got to get a telegram off to my boss or these extortionists will get away," Packard insisted, a note of desperation in his voice.

Morgan shook his head firmly.

Packard played his last card. "Do you want the newspapers all over the country spreading the word that Cyrus Morgan was responsible for this gang of grave-robbers escaping again, just when we almost had them?"

"If you're telling the truth, we have some good policemen right here in Saint Joe who can take care of arresting these men," he said unperturbed, then gestured with the gun. "Let's go down to the jail where we can talk in private." He threw a glance at the telegrapher who had taken off his eyeshade and stood, looking from one to the other of them, his blue eyes snapping and his chubby cheeks flushed with excitement.

Packard heaved a sigh and his shoulders sagged as he preceded Morgan and Corbett out the door. If he was any judge, the telegrapher would have this news all over town in ten minutes, and whatever chance he had of capturing this gang would go spinning away like a trash barrel lid in a Kansas tornado.

Chapter Twenty

"Busted my damned lip." Big Jim Kinealy carefully touched his mouth, spat out the salty taste of blood, and went back into the Hanrahan house. He ignored his wife and McGuinn who were silently gathering in the front parlor with Hughes.

McGuinn picked up the lantern from the floor, turned up the wick, and set it on the marble-top table.

Hughes was sitting on the sofa, handkerchief pressed to the side of his head where Packard's gun barrel had struck him.

"You OK?" Kinealy asked.

"I'm going to kill that son-of-a-bitch!" Hughes hissed in reply.

"Well, you'll have to hurry, then," Kinealy said sarcastically. "Because he's probably halfway to the river road by now."

"Jim, are you hurt?" Janice asked solicitously.

"No, I'm just great," he snorted, laying his pistol on the table and brushing the dirt and grass off his long johns. "Just got run down by a horse, and Packard has taken off to who knows where."

"Let me see that cut on your mouth," Janice said, moving toward him.

But he was feeling mean and brushed past her into the kitchen where he pumped some water onto a towel and wiped his face. His lower lip was split and raw, and one of his teeth was loose. He was barefoot and had stepped on some of the broken glass in the parlor and cut his heel. He sat down on the floor and wiped his feet with the wet towel, using the opportunity to calm himself and to think. He would have to decide, and quickly, what was to be done, and the three in the next room were awaiting his orders. He had been cautious about Packard from the beginning, but it had availed nothing in the end. The man was a puzzle. Whatever, or whoever, he was, Packard was no longer a member of this small group. Kinealy could only assume Packard was a serious threat to the success of the operation, and act accordingly.

He finished wiping the blood and dirt from his feet and stood up, feeling the soreness in the thick pectoral muscles of his chest where the horse had struck him a glancing blow. His short sleep had been interrupted twice this night, and he felt his big body sagging with fatigue. But this was not the time for rest.

He squared his shoulders and strode resolutely back into the lamplit parlor. "OK, let's have your stories about what happened. You first, Janice."

She related briefly the events, mentioning only that she had been talking to Packard when Hughes came out and pulled a gun on them, and then something like smoke appeared in the hallway, and she thought the house had caught fire. She wasn't sure what happened next except that some shooting started, and, when she came to her senses, Packard had run outside.

"Hell, why don't you tell the truth?" Hughes growled, still holding the bloody handkerchief to his scalp wound. "I came out and caught that bastard with his pants down, and pulled a gun to keep him from violating your wife."

"I was just treating his injuries," Janice interrupted, turning on Hughes.

"Yeah, you were getting ready to give him a treat, all right," Hughes sniffed.

"The only way I could keep your hands off me would be to break both your arms," Janice said between clenched teeth, her eyes blazing.

"OK, OK, enough of that," Kinealy broke in, secretly wishing he had left Janice behind in Chicago. Apparently she was up to her old tricks, and two of his own men were competing for her attentions behind his back. He had broken his own long-standing rule of not involving her in his business dealings and was now paying the price for it. Although careful to veil his thoughts behind half-closed eyes, he bitterly blamed her for the troubles that had developed between these two men. "Do you know anything more about Packard?" he asked Janice.

She shook her head. "No. I don't know why he ran off."

"Hell, he was shooting at Lincoln's ghost,"

McGuinn stated. "Then you came down the stairs, boss, and I thought he was shooting at you."

"What the hell are you talking about?" Kinealy asked, with rising irritation. It seemed his little group of conspirators were all going as crazy as Boston Corbett. Maybe their imaginations had been influenced by the creepy atmosphere of this musty old mansion. He probably shouldn't have told them about the Hanrahans.

McGuinn described what he had seen floating in the vapor, and the terrible groaning noise the head had emitted.

Kinealy listened with growing skepticism, then turned to Hughes. "Did you see this ghost, too?"

"Well . . . I saw something, but I don't know what it was," Hughes hedged. "Before I could get a good look, Packard clubbed me from behind."

"Hmm. . . ." McGuinn was the most superstitious of the three, Kinealy thought. Somehow Packard had created some kind of distraction that had allowed him to get away. He took a deep breath and dismissed all this. "OK, as soon as I get dressed, we're moving that coffin."

"What about Packard?" Hughes asked.

"We'll have to figure he's going for the law. If he comes back here with them, we'll just be innocent travelers who stopped here because we couldn't afford a hotel. That's our story for now. But I don't want to have any contact with the law, if we can avoid it."

With that he picked his gun off the table and climbed the stairs.

Fifteen minutes later the three men were carrying the coffin once again. Janice walked along beside them, holding the lantern high enough for Kinealy to see where he was going. She carried a shovel in her other hand. The three men slipped and stumbled on the uneven ground as Kinealy directed their steps north away from the house on a twisting, turning course into the hills. After they had struggled along for nearly twenty minutes, he found what he was looking for — a soft dirt bank about eight feet high that had been undercut by erosion.

"Set 'er down right here," he grunted and the men unburdened themselves. Kinealy was sweating in spite of the chilly night air, but he paid no attention to this as he took the shovel from his wife and began digging at the bank, caving it down over the canvas-covered coffin. Five minutes later, he handed the shovel to McGuinn. Finally Hughes took a turn, grumbling that manual labor was not the cure for a pounding headache.

By the time they had finished, dawn was beginning to soften the darkness around them. Kinealy used the shovel to finish smoothing out the dirt, then directed McGuinn to break off some branches of a nearby bush and begin brushing out the obvious signs of their having been there. It was just light enough for them to see as Kinealy led them back to the house, more than a quarter mile away.

"Stick here for now," Kinealy told them a short time later as he led the other dun up to the front porch. The horse was saddled and bridled with gear he had found in the tack room. "I'm going to town. It's risky, but I've got to get my telegraph message." He swung into the saddle, then paused with a last thought. "If I'm not back by tonight, then something's gone wrong. Don't wait for me. Just walk out of here and get a steamboat or train ticket and scatter." When they only stared at him, he asked: "Understand?"

"Sure, boss," McGuinn finally answered.

Kinealy pulled the horse's head around and kicked him into motion, wondering if he could hold all this together long enough to collect both the ransom and Ben Boyd.

Chapter Twenty-One

Halfway to the jail, Packard thought of something that gave him some reason for hope. During his conversation with Detective Morgan in front of the telegrapher, he had never mentioned the names of any of the gang, or that they were sending and receiving coded messages at that Western Union office. If Kinealy showed up there today to pick up the latest response from his contact in Chicago, the telegrapher would have no way of knowing it was anything other than another customer on routine business. Maybe the police chief would listen to reason and send a few men to the Western Union office to apprehend Kinealy since Packard had no doubt he would be there today.

"You didn't bother to tell that telegrapher to keep his mouth shut about what he just heard," Packard said over his shoulder to Cyrus Morgan who was walking at his back with his gun drawn.

"No need. Those men who operate the key are like lawyers or priests . . . anything they hear or read is kept in confidence."

"I wouldn't bet on it," he muttered.

"It's the next door on your right."

The police station and lock-up was a one-story

red brick building on a corner with no sign to identify it. Packard opened the door and entered. The office smelled like old cigar smoke and coal oil. Just now the indigenous odors were being overridden by the smell of fresh coffee brewing in a black pot on a squat, potbellied stove on one side of the room.

A big man swiveled around in his desk chair as the door opened. He had black hair and eyes and a thick mustache to match. Even his carefully brushed suit was black, relieved only by a white, collarless shirt, and a heavy gold watch chain, one end of which was threaded through a buttonhole of his coat, the other end disappearing into a side pocket. He was about six feet tall when he stood up, but appeared shorter because of his breadth.

"Chief Durkee, I've got somebody here I think you'll want to question," Morgan said as Boston Corbett helped himself to a cup of coffee.

"Oh?" The black brows went up.

"I'm Sterling Packard of the U.S. Secret Service," he said, extending his hand. Durkee took it automatically, throwing a questioning look at the tall detective.

"That's who he claims to be," Morgan replied, holstering his gun, then slipping out Packard's Colt and placing it on the police chief's desk.

Durkee motioned to one of two straight-backed wooden chairs. "Sit down and let's talk. Want some coffee?" he added as an afterthought.

Packard accepted gratefully, sensing that his getting in a frantic rush was not going to help matters. These men represented the law in St. Joe, no matter what he thought, so he gathered himself internally for the ordeal of convincing them.

Corbett was nervously pacing around the office, throwing angry looks at Packard and muttering comments like — "Curse of Satan!" — and — "The Lord reserves hellfire for those who disturb the dead."

"Here. Go down to Missus Mabry's boarding house and bring us some breakfast," Durkee said, flipping him a five-dollar gold piece. "Enough for four."

Once Corbett was gone, Packard relaxed and warmed his hands and his insides with a tin cup of scalding brew. Then he started at the beginning and relayed everything that had happened since he'd infiltrated the gang. Morgan perched on one edge of the chief's desk and listened. Durkee interrupted him only twice with questions that caused him to elaborate on points in his tale. Otherwise, he sat with hands clasped behind his head, leaning back in the swivel chair and regarding Packard with deep black eyes.

When Packard finished, Durkee sat forward in his chair and was silent for several long seconds, absorbing it all. "Damnedest story I ever heard," he finally said.

"I swear to you, Chief Durkee, every word of it's true."

"Maybe. Maybe not." Durkee got up from his chair and turned to the tall detective. "Round up Lawson and Peters. They're on night patrol somewhere in town. Take the paddy wagon out to the old Hanrahan place in the hills. Tell them to be prepared for anything." He took a ring of keys from his desk drawer and went to a gun rack on a side wall. "They better take this besides their side arms." He unlocked the rack and took down a double-barreled shotgun and handed it to Morgan, along with a box of shells from the desk drawer. Pulling a heavy gold watch from his side coat pocket, he popped open the case. "Bender and McNeil will be on duty in a few minutes. I'll send them over to Riley's saloon."

"Right, chief." Morgan took the shotgun and shells and started out the door.

"You better have somebody at the Western Union office to intercept Kinealy when he shows up," Packard said.

"I give the orders around here," Durkee snapped. When the door slammed behind Morgan, Durkee said: "The four men I mentioned are my entire force. We'll get to Western Union, but first things first."

"It may be too late by then."

"When we do go to the telegraph office, it will be to send a wire to the Chicago office of the Secret Service." He dipped a steel-nibbed pen into a brass ink pot on the desk and handed it to Packard. "Write down the name and address of where you want the message sent. We'll not only find out if they have a Sterling Packard working on this case for them, but we'll also get a physical description of that man to see if it fits you."

Packard scratched out the name and address of his boss on a pad of paper. Just as he finished writing, the door opened and Corbett entered, carrying a wicker basket.

"Set it on the desk, and help yourself," Durkee said to the preacher.

"You still don't believe me," Packard said, his stomach rumbling with hunger as Corbett flipped back the red checked napkin covering the basket, releasing a variety of delicious aromas.

"I've got an open mind. When you've been in police work as long as I have, you learn not to jump to any conclusions," Durkee replied evenly. "I'm not charging you with anything at the moment, but I'll have to detain you while we check your story. Hand me that holster rig and then step on back to one of those cells, and I'll bring your breakfast."

Packard complied, knowing there was nothing else he could do at the moment. The tin plate of scrambled eggs, bacon, and toast the chief set on his bunk almost made him ignore the chill, metallic clang of the barred door closing behind him.

"Oh, you got the right man, chief!" Corbett crowed, ripping off a corner of a bacon sandwich with his teeth.

Durkee ignored him and refilled a coffee cup, handing it through the bars.

Packard had several questions of his own whirling around in his head, but hunger came first. He sat down on the board bunk that was suspended from the brick wall by two small chains and did justice to the food.

When he'd finished, he called for Durkee. "I need to talk to you alone," he said, handing him the dishes through the bars. He glanced through the door that led to his office. Corbett was tilted back in the chief's office chair near the stove, sipping coffee and reading what appeared to be a worn, leather-bound testament. Durkee closed the door between the cells and the office.

"What is it?"

"How does Corbett come to be here?"

"He showed up with a lawman on the train the other day."

"Where's the lawman?" Packard asked, hoping it was someone from Springfield who could possibly identify him.

"At his hotel."

"Is he from Springfield?"

"No. A constable named Ed Barksdale from some little town just north of Saint Louis."

Packard's heart sank. Wherever Mullins had turned Corbett loose, it wasn't far enough out in the country to keep him from getting to the nearest law in a hurry.

"Barksdale told me this crazy Boston Corbett came to his office with a tale of being kidnapped by several men who were carrying a coffin," Durkee continued.

"How did Corbett know it was Lincoln's coffin?"

"He didn't. Barksdale could see the man wasn't right in the head, but he knew Corbett by his national reputation. The body-snatching was in all the papers, so Barksdale figured there might be some connection, if there was any truth to Corbett's tale."

Packard nodded. Any policeman worth the name could have sent a wire to the offices of the Toledo, Wabash & Western and the Hannibal & St. Joseph railroads at Hannibal to see what was on their express cars on the dates they'd passed through. Apparently this Ed Barksdale had taken it upon himself to follow up his hunch and track them, bringing Corbett along to identify anyone he found.

"Barksdale's looking to make a reputation for himself," he muttered. "He should have contacted the law in Springfield."

"The trail led to Saint Joe, and they came to me for help in locating the body," Durkee finished.

"I don't care who gets credit for recovering the body or capturing Kinealy's gang of extortionists," Packard said. "But you don't need to be holding me in jail. I'm on your side. I need to be out helping you."

"All in due time, if your story checks out," Durkee replied gruffly. "You look like you could use some rest. I'll let you know what we find out." He went back into his office, leaving the door to the cell block open behind him. "Get out of my chair and go get Barksdale," he told Corbett. "Tell him I need to see him right away."

Packard stepped up onto the bunk and gripped the bars of the single, small window. He had an uninspiring view of the backs of the adjacent buildings and a couple of privies. Somewhere to his left, two or three blocks away, was the Missouri River. The overcast was shredding, and a cold November sun was shining intermittently on the town. He sighed and stepped back down, wondering if Governor Beveridge of Illinois had agreed to pay the ransom. Maybe he would ask Durkee for the latest edition of the *St. Joseph Daily Gazette*. But it probably contained no more than he already knew. By the time the local papers got the national news, it was usually at least a couple of days old. If Kinealy could read the governor's response in the local paper, he would have no need of receiving encoded messages from his contact in Chicago.

Packard was tired. The wear and strain of the past two days was dragging him down, and he slumped on the thin straw mattress of the bunk. Maybe he'd just lie down and rest his eyes for a few minutes. He stretched out with a groan. The cold air seeping in through the barred window was offset somewhat by the warmth of the stove flue that came through the wall from the office before going up through the roof. Even the indifferent comfort of this hard bunk felt as inviting as a feather bed. He stripped off the wool jacket, wrapped it around himself, and lay down. Before he realized it, sleep took him. His exhausted body slumbered the day away, oblivious to all the maneuverings of the law and the lawless. But it wasn't entirely restful. Even in his dreams the struggles didn't cease. He was fearfully trying to protect Janice from Abraham Lincoln who was coming after them, yelling in a deep voice that he wanted an explanation as to why they had killed him. Then McGuinn came out of nowhere and challenged the late President to a boxing match. When McGuinn began flailing, his arms and fists went through the image like so much air. Then Kinealy appeared and announced that he was going to execute Packard for being familiar with his wife. He raised his pistol and took aim. Packard tried to run, but his arms and legs were too tired to move.

"No! No!" He startled himself awake with his yelling. Rolling over, he untangled the jacket from around his neck and sat up on the bunk, sweating, but vastly relieved that it had been just a nightmare. He mopped his brow with a shirt sleeve, then slipped his arms back into the jacket as the cool breeze came through the barred window. His muscles were stiff and sore, so he stood up and had a good stretch, then stepped up onto the bunk and looked out. The sun had set across the river, and a pale blue sky retained the brief light that passed for twilight this time of year. There was nothing to be seen, so he got down. It was then he became aware that it was completely silent, as if the adjacent office were deserted. It was unusual for any lawman to leave his jail unattended, especially when he had a prisoner in the lock-up. He could see nothing through the open door.

"Durkee!" he yelled.

No answer. Maybe the chief had gone to supper, or was at the telegraph office since he had deployed every man of his small force to some other assignment. Or maybe there had been some development in the case. But if Kinealy had been captured or the body recovered, surely Durkee would have awakened him. Then he had a disturbing thought. Durkee had had time enough to wire the Secret Service in Chicago and get a reply — that is, if he had bothered to send the telegram at all. Maybe he'd been too busy with other things, or made a habit of locking the office door and going to supper when he had only rowdy drunks incarcerated. These small towns could get into some sloppy habits when it came to security.

All these thoughts went through his head quickly. He tried the cell door just to make sure it hadn't accidentally been left unlocked. It hadn't. Frustration was beginning to set in. He was rested now and wanted to get out of here and find out what had occurred during the several hours he'd been asleep.

Just then he heard a key in the outer door and someone came in.

"Durkee?"

Someone was shuffling around in the office. Then the chief came through the door, holding a plate of food. "Ah, you're finally awake. I came in here once to make sure you weren't dead." He squatted down with a grunt and slid the tin plate into the cell through a small opening in the bars on the floor.

"What's been going on?" Packard asked, taking the food and digging the spoon into the mashed potatoes as he talked. "Did your men find the body at the Hanrahan place?"

"Nope. They said it looked like somebody'd been there recently. The dust was disturbed, and there were tracks of some horses and a wagon, but it was as vacant as it's been for years."

"They got away again."

"So you say. Sometimes travelers on the river road, who don't know the history of the place, will stop and take shelter there for the night rather than camp out, especially in bad weather. Could have been anybody."

Packard ground his teeth. Apparently it was second nature for this man to play devil's advocate. "What about Riley's saloon?"

"Saloon was open, but the bartender said Riley left town. Said he just saddled up a dun horse and rode out early this morning. Told the bartender to run the place till he got back from taking care of some family business in Virginia."

The horse had apparently found its way home to the stable behind the saloon. Maybe that's what had alerted Riley that something was amiss, and he'd decamped forthwith. "Did you look in the cellar?"

"Yup. There was some loose dirt, like somebody'd been digging around down there, but nothing else."

"I told you that's where Lincoln's body was buried." Packard's voice was rising, in spite of his effort to control it. He had set his plate on the bunk.

"Don't get excited. We also checked the Patee House Hotel, and the desk clerk remembered you and the people you described. I'm inclined to believe you, but I need more than just a hunch."

"Didn't your men try to follow the tracks from the Hanrahan mansion?"

"Of course. They were all up and down that road into the hills. My men couldn't make heads or tails of 'em. There was a buckboard in the barn that didn't appear to have been there very long."

"That was the wagon we hauled Lincoln's body in."

Durkee didn't change expression.

"And I guess there was no one at the Western Union office to intercept Kinealy," Packard said disgustedly, picking up his plate from the bunk and using the handle of the spoon to stab at the tiny piece of tough roast beef.

"Somebody fitting his description had been there and gone by the time I got there. Telegrapher said he picked up a message about a sick uncle, and I got a copy of the reply he sent back to Chicago."

"Where is it? Let me see it."

"It's out on my desk. Just some family stuff about the disbursement of some things from the estate of an aunt who died."

"It's a coded message to be relayed through a contact in Chicago to the governor concerning the demand for ransom," Packard said. "You have anybody on your force who's good at breaking codes?"

"Nope."

"If the message had something to do with disbursement of an aunt's estate, then the code was probably not letter for letter or word for word. Certain phrases mean certain things, and only the two people who made it up could know. Probably instructions to his contact as to how and where the ransom is to be paid."

Packard wondered how Kinealy had gotten to town so quickly and then back to the Hanrahan place and escaped somewhere with the body before the two policeman and the paddy wagon arrived. And how had he transported the body without the buckboard? Yet, Kinealy was no fool, and he could improvise and work under pressure.

"Did you send off to confirm my identity?"

"Sure did. Got a prompt reply, too. Apparently you are who you claim to be, but. . . ."

"Good. Then let me out of here."

He held up his hand. "Not so fast. You didn't let me finish. Your boss, a Mister Elmer

Washburn, says here that I'm to hold you until he can send someone from his office to take you into custody."

"What?" Packard's mind was in a whirl. "What did you say?" He stared at Durkee, open-mouthed. Finally he was able to collect his wits. "Let me see that."

Durkee held out the paper, and he reached between the bars to snatch it. His eyes skipped down the sheet past the brief physical description, apparently taken from his personnel file, to the last section and read:

> **. . . if your Sterling Packard fits this description, hold him for transfer to Chicago via U.S. Marshal. To maintain custody, charge him with suspicion of burglary and kidnapping. Your office will be reimbursed for any expenses incurred.**
>
> **Yours,**
> **Elmer Washburn,**
> **Chief, Midwest Division,**
> **U.S. Secret Service,**
> **Chicago, Illinois.**

Packard couldn't believe what he was reading. He re-read the message carefully this time before numbly handing it back to Durkee who folded and returned it to his coat pocket. He felt as if he'd been kicked in the stomach. As tough as this assignment had been so far, he always felt he had the backing and support of his boss and his agency. This put a whole different light on things. Since they had not heard from him, and he had been seen escaping with the coney men and the coffin, maybe Washburn assumed he was a turncoat. Or maybe he wasn't sure, so this was Washburn's way of being certain he could re-establish contact. Was Washburn planning some disciplinary action? Packard wasn't aware of having violated any regulations. But there was no telling. Government service was riddled with politics. An undercover agent in the field usually had considerable latitude to proceed as he saw fit. If Washburn didn't trust his judgment any more than this, then to hell with him and all his political-appointee bosses.

Somehow Packard had to get out of this jail, preferably before some marshal took him on a train bound for Chicago. If this was not some misunderstanding, Packard vowed to himself that he would capture Kinealy and resolve this case, making Washburn look like a fool in the process for ordering his arrest. Yet, all this was easier decided than accomplished. He had to think and plan very carefully and be ready to change his plans at a moment's notice.

He finished his food. It wasn't tasty, but it was fuel. Durkee waited for him to hand the empty plate and spoon between the bars. "How about a cup of coffee and a blanket? It's getting cold in here."

"Sure."

Durkee went into the office, and Packard sat down on the bunk to think. Much as he wanted to be free of this place, there was nothing he could do for the moment. A feeling of incompleteness, of failure, came over him as he sat there in a cold jail cell while night came down outside. Then he remembered a chance remark Kinealy had made at the Hanrahan house. He had said that he could hide the body and then take a steamboat up the Missouri to Nebraska City or Omaha because he could negotiate with the Illinois governor from anywhere. His heart began beating faster. Kinealy might have just been thinking out loud and exploring alternatives, but it was the only clue he had.

Durkee brought the hot coffee and a blanket, and Packard settled in for the night. Since he had slept most of the day, it promised to be a long, and probably sleepless, night.

About an hour later, after it was completely dark, the door from the office opened, and Durkee stuck his head in. "I'm going home. I'm locking the office door, but one of my men will be on patrol, and he'll check in here every hour or so during the night. See you in the morning."

The man was fair, but very methodical. He'd never get into any trouble by taking too many chances, Packard thought, as the outer door slammed and the key grated in the lock.

The place was as dark as a hogshead of sin. After a time of sitting quietly on the bunk with the blanket wrapped around his shoulders,

Packard could hear the scratchings of what he took to be mice or rats somewhere in the building. Rodents he could deal with, since they generally left humans alone in their hunt for food. Cockroaches and centipedes were another matter. He wondered what manner of insect vermin was living in the cracked mortar between the bricks in the wall, or in the musty straw mattress he had slept on all day. But this place was the Patee House compared to some Mexican *calabozos* he'd heard about.

Sometime later in the night he must have dozed, sitting up with his back to the wall, because suddenly his eyes flew open at a scraping and a metallic clanking sound somewhere above him. Chilled fear prickled up his back, and he leaned to his right and looked up toward the window over his left shoulder. There was a click, then a flash, and a roar, instantly followed by another blast as twin charges of buckshot disintegrated his mattress and bunk. The next thing he knew he was in a corner on his hands and knees, blinded, his ears ringing and his nose full of burnt gunpowder and dust.

How long he remained on the floor, he didn't know. He was aware of being thankful for the total darkness which hid him from his attacker. There were no more shots. Whoever had fired through the window into his bunk must have fled, assuming he was dead. But, with his ears ringing, he could hear neither footsteps nor hoofbeats. Finally he moved, gripped the barred cell front and pulled himself to his feet. Checking gingerly for any wounds or injuries, he found only a few additional sore spots and some stinging abrasions on his hands and knees. Even if there were still someone at the window, he couldn't hold back a reflexive cough as he breathed in the unseen particles still drifting in the dead air.

He stood still, holding onto the bars for a few minutes, letting his heartbeat begin to slow down. Then he heard a scuffing at the front door, and someone came into the outer office. He shrank back against the wall, thinking it might be his would-be assassin, coming to finish the job.

A match scraped, and the flare of a coal-oil lamp swept back the darkness as a man entered the hall in front of his cell. He held up the lamp and peered in. "Packard! Where are you? Are you hurt?"

The voice was strange, and Packard didn't respond.

"It's Deputy McNeil." He set the lamp on the floor. "What happened? Was that a shot I heard?"

Packard feigned a head injury. "Somebody tried to kill me. Shotgunned through the window. Dang near got me. Oh, my head!" Maybe if McNeil thought he'd caught a few buckshot pellets, he'd take him out of this cell and put him somewhere else for the rest of the night.

"Hold on." McNeil went back into the office, and Packard heard keys jangling. He came back into the hall, fumbling with a large ring. "Step back." Unlocking the door, he swung it inward. Then, keeping an eye on Packard, McNeil retrieved his lamp from the floor.

"I'm a lawman like you. You don't have to treat me like a criminal," Packard said. In actuality, the thought of trying to make a break had just crossed his mind. McNeil was lean, about Packard's size, but probably fifteen years younger. Even if Packard managed a successful escape, he'd be making himself a fugitive. But McNeil had not drawn his gun, and Packard was gauging his chances of overpowering the deputy as he held up the lamp.

Chapter Twenty-Two

Janice Kinealy heard the roar of the shotgun a block away and knew she was too late. She staggered to a running stop and leaned against the wall of a building in the darkness, her knees weak. *Oh, no! Oh, my God, please don't let it be so.* She felt as if her heart had exploded.

The gunshot had at last gotten her sense of direction untangled. Now that it didn't matter. Refusing to buckle under to her worst fears, she pushed away from the wall and started on uncertain legs toward the source of the blast. It still took her several minutes to find the jail in the darkness of the unfamiliar streets, but at last she spotted faint lamplight printing the pattern of a barred window on the darkness.

Through the window she saw no one in the office and was surprised to find the door unlocked. With one hand on her Derringer in the pocket of her cloak, she crept quietly inside. The lamplight was coming from the hallway that led to the cells in the rear. She heard the mumble of a man's voice and started toward the sound. But then she paused and proceeded carefully in order to see before being seen.

A man stood in one of the cells with his back to

her, examining the side of Sterling Packard's head. Packard appeared unhurt, and a rush of relief flooded through her. She cocked the .32 Derringer in her pocket and moved silently into the hallway, coming up to the open cell door. She took a deep breath to calm her pounding heart and drew the pistol. "Set that lamp down easy and back away into the corner."

McNeil gave a start and turned around. The nickel-plated Derringer glinted in the lamplight. He gingerly put the lamp on the floor and stepped away to his right, hands at shoulder height.

"Sterling, are you hurt?"

"I'm OK."

"Good. Let's go."

Being careful not to get between them, Packard stepped over to McNeil and lifted his revolver from its holster. "Sorry about this, but tell Durkee I couldn't sit around his jail waiting for someone to kill me."

When McNeil didn't respond, Janice said in her soft dialect: "Don't be embarrassed. You can tell your boss that two or three big men with rifles came up behind you in the dark. You didn't know it was a woman who got the drop on you with a little gun. You never saw me." In truth, her face was still hidden in the shadow of the deep hood.

"I'll leave your gun in the office," Packard told him.

"Over there," Janice said, gesturing with the

shiny Derringer toward the ruined bunk.

McNeil moved obediently to the back of the cell. Packard picked up the lamp, and the two of them backed out. Swinging the cell door shut, Packard turned the key that was still in the lock.

"You'll be all right until morning." Packard started toward the office, then paused. "Oh, I wouldn't do a lot of hollering if I were you. Whoever it was who just tried to kill me might hear you and decide to come back and finish the job." He closed the interconnecting door behind them.

Leaving the ring of keys and McNeil's gun on the desk, Packard retrieved his gun belt that was hanging on a wall peg.

Janice watched him with a great sense of relief. "Let's get out of here in case somebody else might have heard those shots and gets curious." She turned down the wick and snuffed the lamplight, then eased the door open a crack and looked out. "It's clear. Come on," she whispered.

Taking his hand, she led him in a run down the street for a block and then took a right turn and went another block before stopping. They were both panting.

"I've got . . . a horse tied . . . in the alley back here."

"A horse?"

"Let's . . . get off the street and I'll explain."

They walked a few more yards, and she guided him into an alleyway between two brick buildings. She heard the snuffling and the clicking of iron horseshoes on cobblestone and knew her horse was still where she'd left him. "Easy, there," she said, patting the animal's neck, and taking advantage of the pause to allow her breathing to steady down.

A thin wedge of light from a gas street lamp angled a short way into the dark alley, allowing just enough illumination for them to see each other.

"Thank you," Packard said, reaching to pull her into his arms. But she stiffened slightly, so he released her, stepping back. She offered no explanation, so after a moment he said: "I don't know where you came from, but you showed up at the right time."

"No, I showed up just a little late," she replied. "I was trying to get there before Rip Hughes shot you."

"That was Hughes?"

"Thank God he missed."

"If I'd been lying down on the bunk, he wouldn't have. I thought Hughes would've been satisfied just to have me out of the way."

"He has Jim convinced you betrayed us."

"What do you think?" Packard asked.

"Let's not play guessing games," she replied. "I think it's time you told me what you're up to."

"First, tell me what happened after I left," he countered.

She recognized his ploy to force the subject away from himself, but replied: "Jim figured you'd head back to town and maybe bring the law, so the three of them carried the coffin off into the hills and hid it." She chuckled softly. "He had to threaten McGuinn and Hughes before they'd go near the body. Of course, Jim didn't see what we saw. . . ." Her voice trailed off.

"Do you believe that was a supernatural vision?"

"I don't know what it was. We all saw something."

"The ghost of Lincoln," he said.

"I wouldn't go that far," she replied slowly. "But there are things in this world that can't be explained."

"Where did they hide the coffin?"

"Just caved in an undercut dirt bank to cover it up, then scattered a lot of dead leaves around. Scuffed out our tracks. He made me lead the way with the lantern. We did so much twisting and turning in the dark, I doubt I could find the place again in the daylight."

"Where'd you get this horse?" he asked.

"Jim found a saddle and bridle for the other dun and rode into town early yesterday morning. He got his message at Western Union and sent a reply. He rented three saddle horses from a livery and led them back to the house. Also brought us some bread and ham and tinned tomatoes. I was about to starve," she added irrelevantly. "Then Jim said we should leave the buckboard and split up to be less conspicuous.

He sent Hughes and me back to town to see if we could find out anything about you. Then he and McGuinn rode off north to Nebraska City. That's where he's supposed to receive his next message by telegraph. The governor has agreed to pay the ransom, by the way . . . all two hundred thousand dollars of it, and he's releasing Ben Boyd from prison."

"How's the ransom to be paid?"

"I don't know. Jim isn't telling us until it happens."

"He doesn't trust anyone, does he?"

"Hughes and I are supposed to take a riverboat and join him and McGuinn in Nebraska City tomorrow."

"So Big Jim thinks I'm a traitor and sent Hughes to kill me. I'm surprised you came along."

"He didn't send Rip to kill you, but only to find out where you'd gone and to see if he could keep you out of the way. Jim made me go along because he didn't believe what I told him about Hughes. Jim thought I was just trying to protect you." She hesitated, then continued: "As you probably guessed, things aren't going well with us, but Jim's got too much on his mind right now to deal with our personal relationship. Anyway, Hughes and I rented two rooms for the night at the Inter-Ocean Hotel near the dépôt. We found out from the afternoon paper that you were in jail." She pulled a folded newspaper from her deep, side pocket, and it crinkled as she thrust it into his hand. "I suspected Hughes still wanted to hurt you, so I faked a sick spell when he went to supper, then followed and saw him buy a shotgun. I was back in my room by the time he returned."

She stopped suddenly as the sound of voices reached them. She and Packard flattened themselves silently against the wall in the dark as two men, obviously drunk and arguing loudly, shuffled past the opening to the alley and passed on down the street.

Janice realized Packard had a protective arm around her but didn't move away as she continued. "Hughes slipped out in the middle of the night and got his horse. I wasn't sure where he was going, but, by the time I saddled up to follow, he was already out of sight. I guessed he was headed to the jail, so I left my horse here and tried to head him off on foot and stop him. But, somehow, I got all turned around in the dark and couldn't find the jail in time." She paused. "Now you know the whole story. It's time you told me the truth about yourself."

She wasn't ready for what he said next. "Janice, will you come away with me?"

There was a long silence as she wrestled with her emotions. Finally she said: "Wait and ask me that question when all this is over."

As she paused for a reaction, he surprised her again. "I'm a federal agent working for the Secret Service."

The flat statement fell like a lead weight between them. As the silence deepened, she felt she had to force herself to respond. "Ah, I thought it was something like that." Her own voice sounded dull, resigned. "So I guess I should have left you in jail. Are you going to arrest me now?" She felt drained, defeated.

"No, of course not. I may lose my job over it, but I'm going to get you out of this some way."

"What if I don't want out of it?" she asked, a hardness edging into her voice.

"That's up to you, but the others will be caught. I'll do all I can for you, even to letting you get away, or taking you away myself, if you want to come with me."

"I've never been so deceived by anyone before," she replied. "You knew I cared for you, but you lied. You were kissing me, pretending to be someone else, lying about being a grave-robber, and about everything else you told me. You were just using me, stringing me along so you could get at my husband."

The hurt in her voice and the truth of her words apparently stunned him.

She felt her voice almost break into a sob as she said bitterly: "Maybe Hughes should have shot you." She immediately wanted to take the words back, but her throat was closed.

"But I'm telling you the truth now," he said haltingly. "I could have continued to lie and pretend to be a member of this gang, but I really care for you. It's tearing me apart to say this, but you've got to come over to my side now, if you want to keep from spending the next several years of your life in prison."

"Trusting you to save me from the legal system is too much of a gamble," she replied, getting herself under control. "I'm sure you'd try, but it would be mostly out of your hands."

His silence told her she was right. "So, what are you going to do now?" he asked.

"I don't have a lot of choices. I was never a quitter, so I'm going to see this through to the end. No telling where Hughes is. I don't want to risk seeing him again, so I'm not returning to the hotel. I'll just mount up and ride north to Nebraska City and meet Jim. On the way, I'll figure out what to tell him about you and Hughes."

She turned to fumble for the reins that fastened her horse to the downspout.

"So you're going to give me away," he said, almost to himself.

"No. But I think it would be better for all of us if you just got on the next train back to Springfield or Chicago or somewhere. By the time you notify all your bosses about this, maybe Jim and I will have collected the ransom and be beyond reach." She swung her cloak back and mounted.

"Don't our feelings for each other mean anything?" he asked, with what sounded like desperation. "If you ride out of here now, I might never see you again."

She steeled herself against the rush of emotion she felt and replied simply: "They meant a lot to me. But, like I once told you about my becoming a nurse, life often gets in the way of dreams." She pulled her horse's head around. "Good bye, Sterling. You're the best man I've ever really loved."

She galloped her horse out of the alley and up the street, turning left at the next block and heading for the river road, running her horse as if the speed and physical exercise could rid her of all her conflicting feelings.

A few minutes later it began to rain, and Janice was grateful for her horse's instinctive ability to keep to the broad, flat river road, even in darkness with no moon or stars, because her eyes were so brimming with tears that she could not have guided him.

In those blackest hours before dawn the exterior façade she presented to the world seemed to crack, and through that crack she saw nothing ahead but advancing age, lonely self-loathing as she sat in a stone prison cell, hair cut short, dressed in a scratchy woolen shift, hands sore and cracked from work, praying for death to release her. Everything seemed to be slipping away — her husband, Packard, the materially comfortable life she had enjoyed since girlhood. Except for a few isolated attempts at salving her conscience by donating some of her illegal wealth to charitable causes, she had lived mostly for herself, indulging her every whim, from a personal masseuse to the finest jewelry. In retrospect, it had been an essentially dishonest, purposeless, vain existence which had done no one any good, including herself. Nearly every man she met was attracted to her beauty, and she had used this to tease and tempt them — at times, a very dangerous game. It was cold comfort that she had never actually been unfaithful to her husband physically, but in every other way, yes.

Now she had no friends or family left for trust or comfort. In the misery of that wet, lonely night, the piper was about to present his bill, and she found herself spiritually bankrupt. Then the dam broke, and tears came in a flood as great, wrenching sobs racked her body. Her horse slowed and finally stopped altogether in the middle of the road, its head drooping as the rain drummed steadily on beast and rider.

Chapter Twenty-Three

As Janice kicked her mount and went galloping down the street, Packard listened to the drumming of the hoofs, receding into the night. He stood numbly in the dark alley, wondering if he would ever see her again. Nothing can slow time like suffering or fear. The rest of that night dragged like a flat-sided wheel.

When he finally wandered out of the alley and, with a considerable effort, thrust the events of the last hours to the back of his mind, he was able to take stock of his present situation. On the debit side, he was dirty, grubby, unshaven, had only the clothes on his back, and was stiff and sore from head to foot. Adding to that, the pain of rejection and loss was burning a hole in his heart.

On the credit side of the ledger, he had gotten just enough sleep and food in jail to partially refuel his depleted reserves of physical strength and stamina. He had about seventy dollars in greenbacks in his pocket, his gun and a full cartridge belt, and, thanks to Janice, was out of jail and free to do whatever he wanted.

The downtown area was dark and quiet, so he guessed it had to be much later than midnight. If the saloons were still open, they were out of earshot. There was no sign of moon or stars, so he knew the sky was again overcast with the dull pall of November. But, when he came out from behind a warehouse, the breeze was out of the south, and the temperature had actually warmed. Welcoming the change after days of frigid weather, he breathed deeply, smelling rain on the warm, moist air.

He slipped along quietly next to the buildings, moving instinctively toward the river. As he walked, his senses were alert to any sound or movement, but, except for the occasional wharf rat darting across in front of him, the streets were deserted.

What should be his next move? Maybe he'd buy or rent a horse and follow Janice up the river road to Nebraska City, some ninety miles to the north. Because of the jail break, putting St. Joe behind him in a hurry had taken on a great attraction. Durkee and his men would now think he was a criminal for sure. And what about Rip Hughes? Would Packard turn a corner any minute and suddenly come upon him with his shotgun in hand? Did Hughes know his double charge of buckshot had missed? Or had he just fired blindly down into the bunk and then vanished into the dark, assuming Packard could not have survived? What would Hughes do when he returned to his hotel and found Janice gone? But maybe he wouldn't check her room this late at night, thinking she was asleep. Or had he even gone back to his hotel?

Perhaps Packard should rent a horse to ride up into the Loess Hills and search for the hidden lead casket near the Hanrahan mansion. But what good would that do, if the governor was already in the process of paying the ransom? Presumably Kinealy was going to reveal the hiding place of the body to the authorities anyway as soon as he was paid off and his engraver, Ben Boyd, was safely out of Joliet prison. Janice and he had left each other with numerous options.

Then he thought of her suggestion that he just board a train and go home. How simple. But, for some reason he didn't understand, Washburn wanted him arrested. Should he just go back to face whatever awaited him? He could report what he knew, and leave it up to someone else to finish the job of catching and arresting Kinealy and his two men. But, even as the temptation to back off tumbled through his head, he experienced a sense of incompleteness. *I was never a quitter,* Janice had just described herself. Could he be any less?

So, in spite of his logical side urging him to get out of town under cover of darkness and be thankful for surviving intact, he knew the determined, stubborn side of him was going to win out. By the time the lanterns of two moored stern-wheelers came into view along the river, he'd made up his mind to go after Kinealy, McGuinn, and Hughes. There was no logic to the decision; it was based on a gut feeling that he couldn't have defined. Perhaps it had something to do with wanting to get in out of the steady rain that had begun to fall, wetting his hair and soaking through his jacket. And the boats were handy. Not only that, but a riverboat presented the cheapest, quickest, and most comfortable way to reach Nebraska City.

As he stood gazing through the slanting rain at the darkened riverfront, it occurred to him that the affairs of men too often ended in frayed edges. He wanted to trim off the corners of this extortion case and fold it up as neatly as a bogus greenback. Having come so far and endured so much just to leave the ragged edges showing, when he slammed the lid, somehow rankled his sense of order. It would not end like this if he could help it, in spite of what Washburn wanted of him. Janice was not part of this decision in any way. They had apparently come to a parting of the ways. Painful as that was, he had accepted it with his head, if not with his heart.

There was not a soul in sight as he walked down the long, slippery slope of the cobblestone landing and tromped up the springy gangplank of the foremost steamer. Running lanterns hanging along the edge of the pilot house cast a glow on the name plate: **Ella Mai**.

"Hey! Is this boat headed upriver?"

He had to kick the packing box where a half-asleep crewman was perched at the head of the gangway. The man snorted and wiped a hand across his mouth as he tried to blink away the cobwebs. "Yeah."

"I want to buy passage to Nebraska City. How much?"

The crewman spat over the side and wiped his mouth with the back of his hand. "Damn! You're the second jasper in the last hour that's come aboard without a ticket. There's an office just up the street a. . . ."

"No office open at this hour. How much?"

"Ten dollars ought to do it."

"I hope that's for a cabin."

"I think we got just one small stateroom left."

In Packard's experience of Missouri River steamers, all staterooms were small.

"What about that packet tied up behind you?"

"Oh, the *Evening Star*? She's goin' downriver come daylight."

He slid his billfold from an inside pocket and handed over a sawbuck. "When do we get underway?"

The deckhand pulled on a braided rawhide fob, and a worn timepiece appeared out of his jeans pocket. "Comin' up on four. Fires are banked, so it won't take long to get up steam." He pursed his lips as if making some momentous decision. "We'll be underway at first light. Probably five-thirty or six." Shoving the wadded greenback into his pants pocket, he jerked a thumb toward the boiler deck. "Steward's asleep. Your cabin's the last one aft on the port side."

Packard nodded and climbed the steps to the boiler deck. The deserted main cabin was dimly lighted by the glow of a low-burning lamp in a wall sconce. The white painted walls of the narrow salon were lined with a row of seven stateroom doors on each side, and he went directly to his own cabin, lighted the oil lamp attached to the bulkhead, and closed the door. The first thing he noticed was the lower bunk piled full with sacks of flour and corn meal, packs of yeast and tins of biscuits, apparently stowed in this empty cabin to keep these perishable items out of the damp cargo hold below. The crewman who took his money had conveniently forgotten to tell him about all this.

He dried his hair with a towel, hanging on a rack, then stripped off his damp, wool jacket and removed his gun belt. Now that he was in a dry, relatively safe place, he felt himself sagging with fatigue. He had seriously overdrawn his account of physical and nervous energy. All he wanted to do was to climb into the upper bunk and sleep for several hours. But he wouldn't really be safe from pursuit by the law until the boat was well underway. After that, he could relax until he reached Nebraska City.

Then his stomach tensed as he remembered a casual remark by the deckhand below. He'd complained that Packard was the second one in the past hour who'd come aboard without a ticket. Janice mentioned she and Hughes were to take a steamer to Nebraska City today to rendezvous with Kinealy and McGuinn. Was it possible Hughes might be aboard the *Ella Mai*? If he were in Hughes's place and believed he had just gunned down a man in jail, he'd be for ditching the shotgun and getting out of town fast. If he couldn't find Janice, would he make for the first packet that was going upriver? Even if he'd already purchased a ticket on another boat, and had to abandon his rented horse, Packard had a strong feeling that's what Hughes would do.

His hunch was confirmed a few minutes later when he went quietly down to the main deck, reawakened the deckhand, and questioned him about the appearance of the other passenger. There was no doubt it was Hughes.

"I believe that fella's an old friend of mine," Packard said. "Did he give his name as Hughes?"

"Don't recollect that he gave a name a-tall."

"No matter. That's him. What cabin did he take?"

"Number four."

"Thanks. If you happen to see him, don't mention that I was asking. I want to surprise him."

He nodded knowingly, as Packard flipped him a silver dollar.

Then Packard crept back to his cabin, as wide awake and alert as if he had nearly stepped barefoot on a water moccasin. But there was no sign of anyone. Passengers and crew alike were asleep at this deadest hour of the night.

He slid the bolt on his cabin door and sat down in the one small chair, trying to plot his strategy. This time there would be no hesitation. He'd arrest Hughes as soon as he appeared on deck, then get the captain to chain him in the hold until they got to Nebraska City. There was only one problem with this. If the captain demanded some sort of identification, his grubby appearance would be against him, just as it had been earlier when Detective Cyrus Morgan took him in. If the captain wanted Hughes put off his boat and turned over to the local law in St. Joe, Packard was sunk. He decided his best bet was to lie low and make a move when they were several miles upriver. Hughes undoubtedly thought he was dead, so, if Packard could stay out of sight, he'd have the advantage of surprise.

He pulled off his boots, blew out the lamp, and crawled into the upper bunk, stretching his aching frame out on the padded mattress. It was some time after four o'clock, and the drumming of the rain on the roof soothed his tense muscles. Unless he got Hughes, hands down, the man was sure to put up a fight. Packard felt he was more than a match for Hughes physically, if it came to that. But he was dealing with a desperate man. If he didn't take him cleanly, there would be some shooting. With these confined spaces and thin bulkheads, stray bullets could easily wound or kill any of the passengers or crew aboard this vessel. That would never do. He had to arrest Hughes in some professional manner that would ensure no innocent person would be hurt.

The next thing Packard knew, he was awakened as a shudder ran through the boat. Alarmed, his eyes flew open to see that the blackness outside the small window over his head had softened to a dark gray. He heard a faint shout from the main deck below and knew they were getting underway.

He got to his knees in the bunk to peer out the narrow, horizontal window adjacent to the overhead. The rain had apparently stopped, but nothing was visible on this side of the boat except a flat slate of water, ending in a black wall of solid timber bordering the Kansas shore. He rubbed his gritty eyes to clear the film from his vision. But it wasn't his eyes. The coming dawn was muffled by a thick mist rising from the river.

He climbed down. Maybe the early-rising cook would have some food ready so he could grab something and bring it back to his cabin before Hughes made his appearance. Slipping the bolt on the inside door of his cabin, he peered out. No one was in sight. The door to number four cabin was still shut. He slid out quietly in his stocking feet and went forward to the empty salon. The long, narrow table was set for breakfast, and a mouth-watering aroma of frying bacon was drifting back from the kitchen. He stuck his head in the kitchen door.

"Breakfast ready?" he asked.

The cook jumped back from his stove, startled. He was a heavy-set, clean-shaven man in a white coat.

"Won't be long, sir," he responded, recovering himself. "Seat yourself in the dining room, and I'll have it there in a two jerks of a lamb's tail. The early birds will get the first choice."

"I need to get back to some business in my cabin. I'd be obliged if you could wrap a couple of those biscuits around some bacon and let me take it."

He eyed Packard with a twinkle in his eyes. "Ah, some business is it!" he repeated in a slight Irish brogue. "I'd be happy to oblige, sir, but this old cook stove will only work so fast. The biscuits and bacon aren't done yet, unless you want 'em half raw."

Packard glanced back into the salon, and his heart nearly stopped. There, emerging from cabin four, was Rip Hughes. Except for his suitcoat, he was fully dressed, including his gun belt. He was coming straight toward the kitchen where Packard stood in his sock feet, unarmed and with no place to hide.

He turned quickly to the cook. "Give me a scoop of flour."

"What?"

"Some flour. Quick!" The look on Packard's face must have convinced the cook he meant business. He tipped the lid of a barrel in the corner and dug in a wooden scoop as Packard stripped off his shirt and held it out. "Pour it in here."

The cook dumped in the flour, and Packard twisted the shirt around it, then ducked past him through the outside door the cook had left ajar to release some of the smoke. Creeping aft along the deck in the thick fog, he reached the outside door of his cabin and reëntered without being seen.

A sudden idea had occurred to him — if he could make it work. He struck a match to the lamp. Then, wiping some of the wet grime off his boot soles, he smeared it in black circles around and under his eyes. Using the tiny mirror affixed to the bulkhead above the washstand, he cupped handsful of flour and powdered his face a chalky white, including his hair and bare torso. When he had finished putting on the last painstaking touches, the image that stared back at him was still recognizable as Sterling Packard, but was so ghastly that even he shuddered with an involuntary chill.

The deck moved under his feet as the boat swung away from the landing, and he could feel the smooth stroking of the steam engine turning the paddlewheel. They were underway. He wiped the flour from his hands. Then he unloaded his Colt, toweled it off, checked the action, and dried every bit of moisture from the cartridges before reloading it.

The *Ella Mai* was one of the classier river packets whose owners furnished white cotton sheets in addition to blankets for its bunks. He yanked the sheet off the upper bunk and draped it over his head and shoulders. In the thick fog outside, he hoped the specter would be convincingly supernatural. It was something of a crude device, but maybe the disguise would at least make Hughes hesitate long enough to give Packard the edge while he attempted an arrest.

His next problem was how to lure Hughes outside so he could confront him. He tucked the loaded pistol into his belt, far enough to the side so it wouldn't show through the open sheet. He took a quick look outside, but there was no one on the walkway along the port side of the boiler deck. Then he pulled the chair close to the inside door and, by standing on it, was able to see through the glass transom into the salon that was now serving as a dining area. Hughes was filling a thick mug with coffee from a large urn about halfway along the narrow table. Packard watched as he stirred some sugar into it, took a tentative sip, and then began pacing back and forth, glancing toward the kitchen at the forward end. He was in shirt sleeves and vest, but, as he turned, Packard noticed he wore no collar or tie. His hair was neatly parted and slicked down, as usual, but his eyes were puffy. Pulling out a chair, Hughes sat down with his coffee, and then began restlessly picking at his fingernails.

Four other early risers — two men and two women — were standing together and talking a few feet away, two of them munching on apples from a bowl of fruit as they waited for breakfast to be served. Packard stepped down off the chair, wondering how to get Hughes outside on the deck while the light was still uncertain and the gray fog thick. Every minute that passed would make his ruse less effective. He had to do something, and quickly, or the chance would be lost.

Still in his stocking feet, he went through the outside door to the walkway and around the superstructure to where the main cabin opened out onto the back deck. Standing to one side, he opened the door and let it swing slowly outward. Cupping both hands around his mouth, he wailed in a tone just loud enough to be heard inside — "Rip Hughes . . . Riiiip Huuughes." — then paused to listen. He heard a mug hit the table, and all conversation stopped. "You murdered me, Rip Hughes," Packard cried in a thin falsetto. Staying well back in the fog, he and his sheet flowed across the opening.

He heard the crash of a chair overturning and the thump of boots. The other passengers were talking excitedly.

"Rip Hughes . . . murderer," he moaned in his best melodramatic voice.

Hughes rushed, wild-eyed, out of the salon and into the swirling fog. Packard was banking on the ethereal image of Lincoln still being fresh in Hughes's mind, as he glided away to his left, making sure Hughes got a look at his face.

"Rip Hughes . . . you shot me," he groaned, this time in something akin to his natural voice, so Hughes would be sure to recognize it.

Hughes came to a stop, staring at him. "Ahhhh . . . no! No!" came the involuntary cry from his gaping mouth.

As Packard circled farther back into the fog and away from Hughes's gun hand, Hughes pivoted to keep facing the apparition, taking short, nervous steps. It was as if he couldn't control feet that wanted to run and hadn't the strength.

Packard was vaguely aware of the four other people fearfully watching from just inside the salon. "My God, what is it?" Out of the corner of his eye, he saw one of the men pull a pocket pistol, but he didn't aim it.

Packard's powdered face, hands, and chest were beginning to streak with sweat and rivulets of mist. He had to hurry. Holding the sheet with both hands, he swept around past the toilets near the stern. "Rip Hughes . . . you will burn in hell," he wailed, flowing back behind the privy noiselessly in his stocking feet.

As he went out of Hughes's sight, it must have broken the spell, because Packard heard him shout: "You son-of-a-bitch! You'll stay dead this time!"

Breathing heavily, Packard yanked the Colt from his waistband and waited. The steady, heavy swishing of the paddlewheel below masked the sound of Hughes's coming. And suddenly he was there before Packard expected him. Hughes slid to a stop on the wet deck and blasted a shot point-blank. In his haste he must have jerked the trigger and pulled his aim slightly off, or Packard would have been a dead man. Packard whirled the sheet off, trying to fling it at Hughes, but the damp cotton wrapped limply around his gun arm.

"Die, damn you!" Hughes screamed as his pistol exploded again, and something like a red hot poker burned Packard's upper left arm. Packard's gun was tangled in the sheet. In desperation, he threw himself forward and rolled hard into his assailant, kicking at his gun arm with both legs. Another shot blasted wildly as Hughes fell forward. Cursing the sheet that was still between them, Packard lunged for Hughes with his free arm and got the right wrist with his left hand. Hughes was on top of him. Packard cocked his own gun and fired through the sheet. Hughes yelled as the slug took him somewhere in the leg. They were neutralizing each other, when Packard felt the outlaw's teeth sink into his bare right shoulder near the base of his neck. He yelled and gave a mighty heave, throwing Hughes off and losing the grip on his wrist. Hughes staggered back against the wooden wall of the toilets. Then, baring his teeth in a demonic grimace, he brought his gun down at arm's length for a sure shot. In one terrible instant, Packard knew it was over. But he hadn't reckoned on the outlaw's left knee that had been shattered by the slug. As soon as Hughes put weight on it, the leg buckled, and he screamed in agony, the shot just clipping Packard's right ear lobe. Hughes lunged forward on his one good leg, and Packard fired through the sheet again, hitting him somewhere below the belt.

"Aaaahhh!" A yell of rage and pain was torn from Hughes as he fell forward, tripped on Packard, and went headfirst over the rail.

Packard rolled up to his hands and knees, finally throwing off the entangling folds, and looked down through the iron railing. The paddlewheel was steadily churning the dark water as if nothing had happened.

"Man overboard!" he yelled at the top of his voice while scanning the foaming brown track behind the boat to see if a head popped up.

The tall, bewhiskered man who had drawn the pocket pistol came striding up, partially covering Packard with his weapon as he looked over the stern. "I don't know what the hell that was all about, but there's no use yelling man overboard. He's got two slugs in him. He won't be rising out of that cold water until Gabriel blows his horn."

Packard's chest was heaving as he pulled himself to his feet. The man was right. Hughes had been plowed under by the paddlewheel. There was no chance he could live. Packard turned around and saw the crowd that was gathering, gazing at him with horrified fascination. They had good reason; he must have been a sight to behold, wearing only his sodden socks and pants, blood from his right earlobe and the grazing wound of his left shoulder streaking the sticky paste of white flour that remained on his bare torso. He wiped the sweat and condensation from his face, and his hand came away black with the grime that he had rubbed around his eyes.

He stood for a minute, trying to catch his breath and collect his wits. There were ten or twelve people crowding around the two wooden privies on the back deck, staring and murmuring. Most of them hung back, curious but fearful, unwilling witnesses to this violent confrontation.

"I think the captain will want to see you," the tall man with the bushy side-whiskers suggested firmly, pointing the small pocket Smith & Wesson at him. He carefully reached to take the Colt from Packard's unresisting hand.

As if to confirm his statement, a stocky man with a thick mustache and graying blond hair pushed his way through the onlookers.

"I'm Captain Gunderson. What's going on here?"

Packard collected himself with an effort. "Captain, is there some place we can talk?"

Gunderson led the way to his cabin, and they both stood while Packard briefly gave him the story. When Packard finished, the captain grunted and said: "I don't like this sort of thing happening aboard my vessel. Why all this get-up? Why in hell didn't you just arrest the man?"

"I knew he wouldn't come peaceably. I was trying to lure him away from the other passengers. Figured I'd work on his guilty conscience to do it."

"We'll get to Nebraska City about dark. I'll have to report this to the police there."

Packard let out a long breath. At least, this man seemed to believe his story. "Certainly. And I'll notify my bosses in Chicago. By the way, Captain, is there a place I can clean up and shave?"

"Stay here. I'll have some hot water sent up. There's a small tub there in the corner. And there's my razor and a bar of soap. You got any clothes?" he asked, glancing at Packard's half-naked body.

"A dry shirt and jacket in my cabin."

"Well, I can't help you with a pair of pants, since we obviously don't wear the same size."

"That's all right. I'll wear these. I appreciate all this, Captain."

He waved aside Packard's thanks. "I'll be in the pilot house for the next two hours, if you need me. See the steward for some alcohol and bandages for those wounds." He went out and shut the door.

Being able to clean up made Packard feel immeasurably better. But, tired as he was, sleep came only in fitful snatches the rest of the day. It wasn't just the sting of the clipped earlobe and the soreness where the bullet had burned the skin of his upper arm that kept him from relaxing. Every detail of the fatal fight continued to replay itself in his imagination. Except at long musket range during the war he'd never killed a man, and he found the experience very unsettling. It was no matter that he was only defending his life. His conscience clawed at him like an angry bobcat. There was no getting around the fact that he probably could have handled it differently and made a safe arrest. There would be no trial for Rip Hughes. Packard had gotten him so agitated with his ghostly guise, Hughes had begun shooting before he could even attempt an arrest. There was no doubt Packard had carried the ruse too far, underestimating the man's distraught state of mind.

The sun burned off the fog about midmorning, and Packard sought to distract his thoughts by pacing around the perimeter of the hurricane deck, breathing in the fresh air and enjoying the grand scenery sliding by on both banks as the *Ella Mai* churned northward against the swirling, brown Missouri current. He even paused to sit on the deck in the sunshine just below the pilot house steps to read the day-old copy of the *St. Joseph Daily Gazette* Janice had thrust into his hand the night before. He had put it in his coat pocket and forgotten it. A front page article reported that a man named Sterling Packard had been jailed as a suspect in the Lincoln body-snatching case and that further arrests were expected shortly. Another item that caught his eye was a follow-up on the story of the ransom demand. Of course, the reporter indicated that the extortionists' demands came from Chicago and that the Illinois governor was negotiating with a gang of counterfeiters. To his surprise, the national Presidential election between Hayes and Tilden still wasn't decided. The front page story indicated there was some big controversy about the accuracy of the election returns in South Carolina and Florida. Politics as usual. Nearly everything else in this edition, except a few items of local interest, was old news to him.

In spite of feeling rather low, he did find something in the paper to smile about. It seemed two old bachelor brothers who were driving a wagon to their farm late the night before claimed they saw a light and heard strange noises coming from the direction of the old "haunted" Hanrahan mansion in the hills. The author of the article commented that, since the two were well-known gentlemen of the alcoholic persuasion, the reader could make whatever he wished of the veracity of the report.

By the time the sun was slanting down over the rolling country to the west, Packard felt fit again and hungry enough to tackle two large bowls of Irish stew. The other diners at the long table kept to themselves, a few casting furtive glances his way. Even though he had approached Captain Gunderson as he was coming off watch in the pilot house and secured a promise from him that he would keep their conversation confidential, Packard was sure the news of the fight and Hughes's death had spread among passengers and crew within an hour after it happened. Those few who'd actually witnessed it were obliged to tell and retell what they saw in detail.

All day he had noticed clumps of four or five people talking earnestly together. If he happened to approach too close, their animated conversations ceased abruptly.

During the supper hour, the captain did not appear. He might have taken his meal in his quarters to avoid being questioned about the incident. Packard hoped he was in the pilot house because, at the rate the boat was traveling, twisting and turning among the sandbars and shoals, he wanted the most experienced man at the wheel. Gunderson must have had the crew pouring on steam. They had made one wood stop in early afternoon, but the captain's estimate of their arrival time was long by a good hour. The sun was still a hand's breadth above the horizon when Packard stepped out of his cabin on the port side and saw a break in the solid strip of trees that bordered the west bank. The shoreline had gradually risen from water level to a rock bluff higher than the twin smokestacks of their boat. Someone had chosen wisely when they placed Nebraska City on this bluff, far out of reach of the yearly rampages of the river. The steamboat landing was along a solid strip of ground that was usually out of the water at the base of the bluff. But there were no piers.

The steady beat of the paddlewheel slowed, and with a long blast on the steam whistle the helmsman swung the bow in toward the landing. Packard strained to catch a glimpse of the small figures in the distance who were waiting for the arrival of the *Ella Mai*. As they came closer, the paddlewheel stopped, then reversed, lazily slapping the water for several beats as they swung around and nosed in. A deckhand heaved a hawser across to a man waiting ashore.

Then Packard's searching eyes picked up a lone figure, standing by his saddled horse farther up the bank, away from the small cluster of people on the landing. Even though he was standing in the deepening shadows of the bluff and wearing a hat, there was something familiar about the muscular slouch, the slightly thick midsection. Then the man moved, and, with a tightening in his stomach, he recognized Jack McGuinn.

Chapter Twenty-Four

He had been lollygagging and not planning ahead. It was still daylight, but he had to get off this boat without being detained for further questioning by the local law. And this meant getting off without being seen by either the captain or Jack McGuinn. His was the last aft cabin on the port side. Since there was no stairway to the main deck except the one forward, he slipped around to the starboard side and climbed over the rail. He let himself hang by his hands, swung slightly inward, and dropped to the main deck near the steam engine. A couple of the deckhands glanced curiously in his direction, but, when he walked back and stood idly watching the paddlewheel slowly turning, they returned to their work.

As soon as no one was looking, he climbed over the rail and slipped quietly into the river. The shock of the cold water took his breath for a minute, and he had to hold onto the side of the hull as the boat swung slowly his way and nosed in beside another packet. Before the *Ella Mai* butted the landing and dropped her gangplank, Packard had side stroked away, hoping no one on deck would look his way. He was in luck. What few passengers and crew he could see were all intent on docking. Gunderson's head and shoulders were visible in the windows of the pilot house as he gave instructions to the engineer down the speaking tube.

Ignoring the numbing cold, Packard paddled cautiously under the lee of the adjacent boat and then around the stern, pulling himself past the idle wheel to the opposite side. He worked his way along the hull until his feet hit bottom under the forward guards, then stumbled heavily ashore, streaming water. His boots squished water with every step as he walked off down the landing away from the *Ella Mai*.

With another November night coming on, he hated having soaked his clothes in the cold river, knowing he was tempting pneumonia or chilblains, but it had been imperative he get ashore unseen. There were four steamboats angled in side by side, most of them loading or unloading various boxes and barrels of cargo. He stopped behind a stack of wooden crates and looked back. A few passengers were debarking with their dunnage from the *Ella Mai*. There was no outcry, no one rushing around looking for him. He let out a deep breath. The boat would be tied up for the night. Once Gunderson reported to the law, he probably wouldn't care if he ever saw Packard again.

Jack McGuinn was another matter. He was still standing by his horse, watching the debarking passengers from a distance. He'd probably met this boat just on the chance Hughes might have taken it. When Hughes didn't get off, McGuinn would ride away, none the wiser.

After the last passenger had departed, McGuinn waited another minute or two. Then, instead of riding off, presumably to tell Kinealy that neither Janice nor Hughes had been aboard, he walked his horse down the landing, and Packard could see him questioning the blue-jacketed steward near the gangway. A slight wind chilled Packard, and he shivered as he watched the two men talking in the deepening shadows. He knew McGuinn was getting the story of the fight and of Hughes's death. By McGuinn's gestures, Packard could see he wanted to go aboard, but the steward restrained him. Then the steward disappeared and came back a minute later with Captain Gunderson. There was further talk. Apparently the captain told him that Packard was also missing because suddenly McGuinn turned and vaulted into his saddle with an agility Packard had never seen him display. Kicking the animal in the sides, he galloped away from the landing. Shortly after, the tattoo of hoofbeats drifted back as he rode up the steep road that slanted toward the top of the bluff.

Kinealy would know very shortly that Packard had disposed of Hughes and that he was somewhere in the vicinity. So much for the element of surprise. But Packard's immediate problem was to get into some dry clothes. To that end, he noticed several black deckhands unloading cargo from a nearby boat. He approached one of them as he came down the gangplank, balancing a small keg on his shoulder. As he set it on the ground, Packard hailed him.

"I'll give you ten dollars for a spare shirt and a pair of pants," he offered.

The deckhand paused and looked at Packard's sodden appearance.

"I fell in the river," he explained.

"Mistah, I'd sell 'em, but this here's the only clothes I got." He plucked at the sleeve of a heavy canvas jacket he wore. "Dey's a dry goods store up in town. . . ."

"I haven't got time to go up there now," Packard interrupted. "I'm freezing."

"Here, lemme ask Roscoe."

Packard stayed in the shadows, until the Negro returned. "Mah friend's got some extra stuff he'll sell for ten dollars."

The exchange was made, and Packard took the bundle, passing over a wet ten-dollar bill, then walked off into the gathering dusk and changed behind a pile of cordwood. With the exception of his boots and his belt, he left all his clothes where they fell. Now he had no coat, but the cotton shirt was heavy. And just being dry made him much warmer. He sat down out of sight to wait for dark, pulled off his boots, disposed of his wet socks, and rubbed his bare toes to warm them. Afterwards, as he dried his gun and cartridges on his shirt-tail, he thought of Janice and wondered where she was. Traveling on horseback, she would come up the river road about ninety miles and cross here on the ferry. With all the twists and turns, the distance by river was probably at least ten miles farther. She had started about two hours ahead of the boat, but he felt certain he had beaten her here. She and her horse would both need rest and food and water. He doubted that she would arrive before morning.

When lights began to appear in the windows of the few houses he could see on the edge of the bluff among the trees, Packard got up and started on foot toward the rocky road leading upward. A freight wagon passed and offered him a ride, but he shook his head and waved him on. By the time he'd trudged the half mile to the town on the summit, he was thoroughly warmed by the exercise.

He leaned against a hitching rail in front of the drugstore to catch his breath. In the gathering darkness and his second-hand clothes, he blended in well with the men moving up and down the street. Several years had passed since he'd been here. In spite of the commerce and the number of travelers who passed through Nebraska City, it was still a small town. Unlike St. Joe, the houses in this town were mostly white, frame structures with neatly fenced yards. The stores and houses all contributed to a generally prosperous look.

But where to look for Kinealy and McGuinn? Packard's experience in St. Joe had warned him against trying to get the local law on his side. He was completely on his own this time. He would find the Western Union office but would hold off reporting to his bosses until he was able to relay the final details of the capture. Something told him he would have to move fast to avoid the payment of the ransom.

He got up and began to walk the streets, glancing into the stores and saloons. Knowing how Kinealy operated when he was taking care of business, he seriously doubted either of them would be found in a saloon. His hunch was verified after a fairly complete tour of the downtown area. They might be ensconced in one of several small hotels, but there was no way to locate and flush them out. He could spend all night trudging from one hotel to another and probably not find them. Even if they were in a hotel, they were probably registered under assumed names.

Then he thought of Janice. If she planned to meet them here, she would know where they were — unless she was depending on them to meet the steamboat, as originally planned. He decided to see if he could head her off at the ferry landing and get her to lead him, willingly or unwillingly, to her husband and McGuinn. But, first things first. He ducked into the nearest saloon, ordered a beer, and helped himself to the free lunch of crackers and cheese and a couple of boiled eggs. Thus fortified for a long night, he walked back down the steep road and found the ferry landing just to the north of where the boats were tied up for the night. It was near a stand of large cottonwoods. The Missouri was not more than a quarter mile wide at this point. When he saw the yellow square of light illuminating the window of a shack he took to be the ferryman's place, he detoured around it and took a seat on the grass under one of the large cottonwood trees. From this vantage point he could see the current sliding along in the light of the rising moon like a river of shiny quicksilver. The small, steam-powered ferry looked to be just large enough to carry two wagons and teams. Its boiler fires were banked for the night, and it lay along the shore, secured by long, stout ropes to a couple of large trees. Business at Nebraska City was apparently good enough to warrant a similar ferry which he had seen on the opposite shore as the *Ella Mai* pulled in. He leaned back against the tree and wrapped his arms around himself to ward off the creeping chill, then tried to relax to the soft murmur of the nearby river.

Sometime later he dozed, and, when he opened his eyes, the moon was gone and it was very black and very cold. He got up and walked around, flexing his arms and shoulders, trying to work some warmth back into his body. After an eternity of stomping around in his wet boots, the sky began to lighten across the river above the flat Iowa landscape. By the time he could distinguish the uneven horizon, he began to feel a surge of energy to coincide with the rosy glow of the coming sun. It was then he heard the ferry bell clang twice from across the water and could just make out the dark outline of the boat as it detached itself and started his way.

As Janice Kinealy led her horse aboard the ferry, she was still not sure what she was going to tell her husband. She'd had many hours on the road to think about where her life was going and the more immediate problem of what to do about her marriage to the leader of the coney men. She stood by the rail, holding the reins, and felt the cold breath of the river. Instinctively she pulled the cloak about herself, feeling as if she had been in these same clothes for weeks. The insides of her thighs were chafed and sore from many hours in the damp saddle, riding astride in her flannel drawers and petticoat. Her back was tired and sore, and her eyes felt puffy from lack of sleep and from crying.

She looped the reins over the rail, then pulled out a pocket comb from among the few personal items she'd transferred from a handbag to the pockets of her cloak. She ran the comb through her hair, wincing as it caught the tangles. One look at her and Kinealy would know she hadn't come upriver by steamboat. She'd have to tell him something closer to the truth. She'd say that she followed Hughes, suspecting him of wanting to kill Packard in jail. Then she heard a gunshot near the jail and, fearful for her own safety, had just fled to Nebraska City by horseback. She didn't know where Hughes was or if Packard was alive. She reviewed the story again in her mind, examining it for any flaws as the ferry approached the landing on the Nebraska side. It would suffice, because Kinealy knew she disliked Hughes and would not have waited for him.

The paddlewheel stopped, and the ferry nosed in gently. The boatman unhooked the chain, and she led her horse down the ramp to the bank.

"Hello, Janice."

She stopped so suddenly the horse almost knocked her over.

"Sterling," she breathed, glancing around to see if he was alone. "What . . . ?"

"Let's walk and talk." He glanced at the two ferrymen who were securing the boat nearby. They moved off toward the road that ascended the bluff some way ahead. The rented horse stumbled along behind her, its coat streaked with dried sweat.

She eyed him critically from head to foot. "You don't look so good." It was an understatement, she knew, as she noted his ill-fitting clothes, a dirty bandage on one ear, some scratches on his face, his nose red from the cold.

"I reckon not," he replied, raking his fingers through his tangled hair and squinting at her, his eyes bloodshot in the rising sun.

"I thought we said our good byes," she said tiredly.

"Sorry to claw open an unhealed wound," he replied, "but, like it or not, I came after your husband and McGuinn."

"Do you think I'm going to help you?"

"I hope you will," he said simply.

"You put me in a very awkward position. Without my help, I don't know how you can hope to arrest all three of them. . . ."

"There are only two of them now."

"What?"

He briefed her about Hughes's death on the boat.

The information registered in her mind, but she was too dulled with fatigue to feel much emotion. "I didn't hate the man enough to kill him, but I can't shed any tears over his death. Maybe I'm just getting hard-hearted." She was silent for several steps, wondering how Packard's presence and Hughes's death were going to affect the story she had concocted for her husband. Finally she said: "I suppose you don't know where they are, or you wouldn't be here, asking for my help."

"You're not only beautiful, but you're intelligent."

The condescending remark raked her like a claw. She looked sideways at him, trying to read his face.

"I'm sorry," he said, sounding truly contrite. "I meant that as a compliment, but that's not the way it came out." When she didn't reply, he went on. "Yes, I want your help. And, yes, I'm forcing you to make a choice between the life you've led and something better for the future. If you lead me to your husband and McGuinn, there's a good chance you'll get off with a very light sentence or maybe only probation. There, that's as plain as I can make it. Will you do it?"

She considered her options for three or four long minutes. Whatever decision she made now would affect the rest of her life. If she refused to help, he could simply arrest her and go on by himself. She didn't think she could still rely on his affection for her to let her go. Or he might somehow follow her to Kinealy. On the other hand, could she really betray her husband of more than twenty years, then take her chances with him at a trial? The country was so outraged at the theft of Lincoln's body, she hated to think what a jury might do to them. There had to be a third choice, but her tired brain was having trouble finding it.

Packard walked silently beside her, awaiting her answer.

She had a glimmer of an idea. She sighed and squared her sagging shoulders. "This horse is about done in," she said. "Let me get him to a livery with some oats and a rubdown. Then I'll take you to them."

Chapter Twenty-Five

Packard knew he would never have found the place by himself. He tried to think of a way to thank her. He had to show all the support and encouragement possible for her difficult decision to help him.

"There it is." She indicated a white, frame house on the corner. It was at the end of a block and across the street from where they viewed it from behind a tall, board fence. "Jim rented it last year. It's vacant most of the time, but he uses it now and then to meet with coney men from Kansas City and Omaha."

"Thanks. You won't regret it." Packard slipped an arm around her shoulders and gave her a quick hug.

"It's a good place to conduct his business," Janice continued without responding, "because it's out here near the cemetery and away from most of the houses. Another reason Jim likes it is because there's a way out in case of trouble. The place was once used by John Brown when he and his Abolitionists were busy helping runaway slaves escape from Missouri into Kansas and Iowa. There's a tunnel running from the cellar to Table Creek a little ways back there." She gestured vaguely. "Anyway, this is where he told me and Hughes to meet them."

"McGuinn met the boat last night and apparently found out I was aboard with Hughes and killed him."

She nodded. "It wasn't definite which boat we'd be on," she answered, "so it was just chance he was there to meet it."

"Dumb luck. It's about time some of it goes my way."

"I may not be your dumb luck, but I'm your smart fortune," she said, favoring him with a smile that still had the power to devastate his good judgment.

"Do you have your Derringer?"

"Right here."

"Why don't you go on in and pretend nothing's happened. Tell them you just lost track of Hughes, or something. Make sure the door's left unlocked and they're distracted. I'll be in right behind you and get the drop on them. Once they're out of action, and secured, I'll give you a message to send to the Secret Service for me."

She flipped up her hood to hide herself from anyone who might be watching and crossed the street. She went up onto the small porch and rapped on the door.

Packard watched through a crack in the tall, board fence as the door was opened by someone he couldn't see, and she disappeared inside. He waited a count of twenty before moving out from behind the fence. Trusting her to keep them from the windows, he quickly crossed the street, went up onto the porch, and grabbed the doorknob. Throwing the door open so hard it banged back against the wall, he swept the room with his cocked Colt. The startled faces of Kinealy and McGuinn looked up from the far side of the room as Janice stepped back out of the way.

"Ease out those guns and toss 'em on the couch."

McGuinn glared his hatred at Packard. Kinealy only appeared disgusted as he flipped his pistol onto the sofa. It bounced off and clattered onto the wooden floor. "Apparently you were followed, Janice," he said with sarcasm. "You'll have to learn to be more circumspect."

"I'm an agent of the United States Secret Service," Packard said, intoning the words he'd been waiting to say since he'd joined this gang. "You're under arrest for grave-robbing and extortion." He motioned with his gun. "Into the dining room."

All three of them moved, Janice silently acting as if she were also a prisoner.

"Find something to tie them with," Packard ordered Janice.

She came back a few moments later. "There's nothing in the house."

He moved to a back window and looked out. "Go cut down that clothesline."

When she brought in two lengths of line, Packard held the gun while he directed her to tie each of the men. A quarter of an hour later

Kinealy and McGuinn were both hog-tied, each face-down on the floor. Packard made sure the rope was tight, and he retied two of the knots to his satisfaction. Hands and ankles were securely fastened together behind their backs, and the rope was then looped with a slipknot around their necks. Any movement of the hands or feet tended to choke off the breath.

"Aren't you going to tie me?" Janice asked, when he had finished.

"I ran out of rope," he said, still covering for her in front of Kinealy.

"There's probably coffee in the kitchen," she suggested.

"Good. Go make some," he said. "It's been a long night, and I need something to perk me up."

She pretended to be cowed by his threatening attitude and disappeared into the kitchen. He collected the two pistols and cartridge belts and sat down at the small, dining-room table where he could see Janice moving around in the adjacent room.

"So you killed Hughes," Kinealy said, twisting his head so he could see Packard. "I didn't figure you for a killer. Matter of fact, I thought he could probably take you. Must not have been a fair fight."

Packard resisted the urge to explain what had happened; he wouldn't let Kinealy bait him into justifying himself.

"Yeah," McGuinn said, picking up this cue. "I

wish I'd had a go at you. Would've been a different story." Arm and shoulder muscles bulged under his shirt as he strained at the bonds. But Packard had made sure he was securely fastened. McGuinn grew red in the face as his struggles tightened the noose around his neck.

"When and where will the ransom be paid?" Packard asked in a conversational tone, not really expecting an answer. "You'll probably cut a lot off your sentence if you just tell me this was all a lark and you had no intention of really extorting money from the governor. Maybe the jury will believe you."

Neither man replied, so he got up and went to a small writing desk in the front room of the house. Taking a sheet of paper from the drawer, he sat down and dipped the steel-tipped pen into the brass ink pot. He wrote out the name and address of the Secret Service in Chicago and then composed a carefully worded message, giving the essentials of what had happened. With a feeling of satisfaction, he signed his name and flipped the cap shut on the ink well.

Janice was returning with a steaming pot of coffee, as he brought the paper back to the dining room. She set the pot down on a folded towel and then brought a cup and a bowl of sugar. He poured and handed her the cup.

"I don't care for any," she said.

He took it back, stirred some sugar into the brew, had a sip, and then a healthy swallow. It was delicious. Just what he needed to restore his flagging energy after a cold, restless night spent on the riverbank.

"What about them?" She nodded toward the two on the floor.

"They can order their own coffee," he smiled, trying to lighten up her somber mood.

"I mean what are you going to do with them?" She didn't change expression. "They can't stay tied like that for long."

"Come with me." He picked up the paper and took her arm, leading her out to the front porch, closing the door behind them. "Go to the Western Union office and send this," he said, handing her the folded paper and a ten-dollar bill. "Then get back here, and we'll decide what to do with them until they're taken off my hands."

"OK," she replied, sliding the paper and the money into a side pocket of her cloak.

He studied her face but couldn't read her feelings. Then she surprised him by slipping one hand behind his neck and kissing him soundly on the lips. She looked intently into his eyes for several seconds, then turned, and walked down the steps and across the street, the morning sun shining on her soft, brown hair.

He watched her until she turned the corner and was lost to sight, then went back inside and sat down to wait. His message asked for further instructions. If none was forthcoming, he'd see about contacting a federal marshal to help him escort his prisoners to Chicago on a train.

"Hey, Packard, my muscles are cramped. Can you loosen these?" Kinealy asked.

Packard checked their bonds to be sure circulation wasn't being seriously impaired. "No. You'll have to tough it out a little longer."

"Where'd my wife go?"

He didn't answer.

"You trust her out of your sight?" He grunted. "I guess it's true, then, what Hughes said. You've seduced her away from me. You didn't follow her here. She led you here."

Packard drank two more cups of the strong coffee, laced with sugar. This should have given him a good jolt, but he found himself still getting drowsy. Finally, he got up from the table and went to the front room and sat down on the sofa, leaning his head back. He tried to figure out exactly how he'd deal with his two captives when Janice returned, but he was as sleepy as if he'd just eaten a full meal and drunk a glass of wine. His concentration was fading. It was only a natural let-down after the successful conclusion of this long, dangerous case. He'd just close his eyes and rest for a few minutes. He and Janice would discuss it, when she got back.

When his eyes flickered open, he felt as if he'd been deeply asleep for a long time. Beyond the curtains of the front window, the sky had clouded up and a light drizzle was falling. It appeared to be late afternoon or early evening. His arms were heavy and his thinking muzzy.

Forcing himself to a sitting position on the sofa, he began to realize, through the fog in his head, that something was amiss. He staggered to his feet, his legs feeling like posts.

Kinealy and McGuinn were gone! Pieces of the slashed clothesline rope lay scattered on the floor. Blind infatuation had done him in again. It was a bitter draught to swallow.

He staggered to the kitchen, thrust his head under the spout, and pumped until cold water gushed over his hair and face, clearing the cobwebs from his brain. Wiping his face on a sleeve, he returned to the dining room and, when his eyes began to focus properly, saw that the table had been pushed back and the rug under it lay in a pile to one side, revealing a square trap door in the floor. He grabbed the recessed iron ring and jerked it open. A rush of musty, chilled air came up from the dark hole. He lighted the coal-oil lamp on the table, turned up the wick, and went cautiously down the cellar stairs, gun in hand. He found himself in an empty, packed-dirt, windowless room about ten feet by twelve with no outside cellar door. Holding the lamp high and moving around, he discovered a tunnel that opened off into uninviting darkness. He was looking at a portion of John Brown's Underground Railroad. After several cautious steps into the passage he realized a constant stream of fresh air was flowing past him, blowing the tall flame and smoking up the lamp's chimney. Water dripped on his head, and patches of mud here and there revealed only one set of prints — a woman's. He was puzzled, but cocked his Colt and moved forward.

He'd gone fewer than a dozen paces when the tunnel made a slight bend and daylight showed a short distance ahead through a tangle of brush and vines. He carefully pushed his way into the open and stopped short at the steep bank of a creek. The stream, about ten feet below, was flowing toward the Missouri less than a mile away. He had no idea which way she had gone. A canoe to the river? Had she climbed the bank and walked back to town? Why even use this tunnel? She could have just walked out the door with Kinealy and McGuinn. Maybe to lure him into a trap? A cave-in could seal him up so he'd never be found. A cold chill went over him, and he looked quickly around, his ears alert for any unusual sounds. Instinctively he knew she would never do such a thing, and slowly relaxed.

Dusk was coming on and the wind was picking up, blowing big drops of cold rain against his face. As he holstered his gun and turned to go back, he saw a sheet of paper fluttering against the stickers of a rosebush near the entrance. He absently pulled the snagged piece of trash loose and started to crumple it in his hand, when he noticed there was something written on it in a dainty feminine hand. With a sinking feeling in his stomach, he knelt and carefully unfolded the paper on the dirt floor of the tunnel. It was already so blotched by the rain as to make it partially illegible. He read, holding the lamp close:

My Dearest S,

Forgive me, but this was the best way for all of us to get out of this mess. My (your) telegram to your Chicago bosses told — (words blurred) — **could arrest Jim and McGuinn at Omaha where they're headed by steamboat. I told the location of the coffin. Jim thinks I plan to meet him in Omaha — after I drown you while you're unconscious.**

He paused, feeling slightly sick. While he was drugged, all she would've had to do was roll him onto the floor with his face in a pan of water. Did Kinealy really think she was capable of murder? Was this her final test of loyalty to Kinealy and the gang? If so, he breathed a prayer of thanks that she'd failed it. He looked back at the note that was water-splotched even worse in the middle of the page.

The ransom is being carried in greenbacks by Ben Boyd. He's . . . — (words blurred) — **South America to convert . . .** — (words blurred) — **to untraceable gold. I don't know if the law can stop him, and I don't . . .** — (words blurred) —**ght, and I'm through with this life. But I cannot leave my husband for you, or for anybody . . .** — (words blurred) — **I ratted on**

Jim to save . . . — (words blurred) — **heavier penalty later. There's no law against grave-robbing in Illinois . . .** — (words blurred) — **I doubt that . . .** — (words blurred) — **enough evidence . . .** — (word blurred) — **prove extortion . . .** — (words blurred) — **lawyer . . .** — (words blurred) — **get only two or three years . . .** — (words blurred) — **destruction of property at the tomb. As for you and me — well, you know how I feel. If circumstances had only been different . . .**

Love,
J.

P.S. Sorry I had to put laudanum in that pot of coffee, but you'll feel OK in a few hours.

The note had been perfectly placed on the stickers of the rosebush just outside the mouth of the tunnel where its fluttering in the breeze would ensure its being noticed. It had all been neatly done. She'd led him here by way of the obvious trap door. She knew if he didn't see the note, nobody would, because within another hour or two the ink would have been only one big blur or the paper dissolved and fallen to pieces in the rain, her last message to him going forever unread.

He believed her to be correct about the lack of hard evidence. Roundabout coded messages might be linked to Kinealy if his mysterious Chicago contact were ever caught. The telegrams from Kinealy were signed, not with his name, but rather as **The Coney Men**, of which there were many. Even if McGuinn decided to confess and accuse his boss, it wasn't likely the jury would believe a man with his criminal record who was only trying to save himself a heavy sentence. It would probably require testimony from Packard to strengthen the circumstantial case against Kinealy. Considering Janice's wishes, he wasn't inclined to give such testimony.

With one last pull on the oars, Janice Kinealy nosed the leaky skiff into the bank only a few rods from where the clear water of Table Creek flowed into the muddy Missouri. She splashed through the several inches of bilge water, feeling the cold wetness seeping inside her shoes, and tied off the boat to a clump of dead bushes. Climbing out, she started toward the riverboat landing at a fast walk, the hem of her dress dragging in the mud. She felt even dirtier than she had this morning. Finally she stopped and ripped the deep, soggy hem completely off and threw it away in frustration. The dress now ended midway down her calves, revealing the high tops of her muddy shoes. She carried no handbag, but had a total of nearly three hundred dollars in greenbacks she had gotten from Kinealy. Besides the cash, she also had some of her own personal diamond and gold pins and bracelets wrapped in a handkerchief, jewelry she could sell if necessary. And the Derringer was still a reassuring lump in the pocket of her cloak.

The afternoon was gray, and a chilly rain appeared to be settling in for the evening. Would Sterling awaken, find her note, and come after her? She felt she had given herself ample time to escape.

Several packets were lined up at the landing, and, after three inquiries, she found one — the *Vicksburg* — that was bound downriver to St. Louis and from there to New Orleans. Steam was up, and the steward on the foredeck informed her the stern-wheeler would be underway within the hour.

"You're running at night?" she asked.

"Our pilot is an old hand who knows this stretch of the river like his own stateroom. He'd just as soon navigate on a moonless night as the brightest day. Besides, the river's rising, covering some of the shoals."

"Marvelous," she breathed to herself.

"Come aboard, miss, if you're headed downriver. Can I take your luggage?"

"I don't have any."

Janice felt the steward's eyes evaluating her, trying to calculate what manner of woman this might be. She was sure he wasn't admiring her bedraggled beauty.

"What's the fare to New Orleans?"

"One way?"

"Yes." Then she added: "I'll make return arrangements later."

"That would be ninety dollars."

She reached into the pocket of her dress and pulled out the roll of bills, turning away from him to count out the fare.

"There you are."

"Your name?"

"Anna Lee," she lied quickly.

He turned to enter her name on the passenger list.

"Your cabin is the first one on the starboard side. Not many passengers on this leg of the trip."

"Thank you."

As she climbed the stairs to the boiler deck, she repeated her new name — Anna Lee — over and over to herself to ensure it was committed to memory and she would answer to it. Secure in her cabin, she removed her clothes and, using the large pitcher of water and the bowl on the tiny table, took a sponge bath. Not as good as the real thing, but refreshing, nonetheless. While thus engaged, she tried to think of anyone she knew in New Orleans. She had a great aunt who'd lived there before the war, but the old lady was probably long dead. As with most of her family, she'd not kept in touch.

Forty minutes later she stood at the railing outside her stateroom and watched Nebraska City fade into the murky rain. It seemed a great weight had been lifted from her. Kinealy and McGuinn had departed for Omaha shortly before noon, going in the opposite direction. It would be many days before she felt completely safe from pursuit by the law, but she was her own boss now for the first time in her life, and it was a heady feeling. In the tangle of human events, it was difficult to sort out right from wrong, good from bad, while at the same time dealing with personal emotions and weaknesses. She had married James Kinealy for better or for worse, and she'd definitely received some of both, but, given the situation, she felt she had taken the right step for both of them. As long as he lived, there could be no thought of divorcing Kinealy or marrying Packard regardless of how much she cared for him. Her decision was based on a code of conduct instilled in her many years before. Whatever else she might be guilty of, she had made a vow, and she was going to keep it. It was as simple as that. But she was not yet forty. No one knew what the future might bring. And, as she thought of the future, her need for love and caring made her wonder if perhaps Florence Nightingale had established one of her training schools for nurses in New Orleans.

In the gathering dusk, the young steward came along the walkway under the overhang. He nodded, eyeing her with the kind of appreciative look she knew so well. "Dinner will be served at six, Miss Lee."

"Thank you very much."

He paused expectantly, but, when she said nothing further, he moved away down the deck, leaving her alone with her thoughts.

Packard read the note again, almost hearing Janice's voice speak every word, committing her handwriting to memory. Then he twisted the damp paper and held it over the lamp chimney. It dried, began to smoke, and burst into flame. When the blaze reached his fingers, he dropped the end of the paper and watched the dying fire consume the last of his connection with Janice Kinealy. Then, taking a deep breath, he picked up the lamp and started back through the tunnel toward the house, determined to find out if there was a night train with a Pullman going West from here.

He was bone tired, yet knew it was a weariness that sleep couldn't lift. It was caused by the unrelenting press of danger and physical effort and mental strain which had slowly built up a terrible fatigue in him, solidifying like old age. It was a weight he no longer had the strength to carry. He would have to begin relieving himself of this burden before a fresh start could be made. The first step would be to telegraph his resignation to the Chicago office of the U.S. Secret Service, giving poor health as an excuse — and possibly justifying Elmer Washburn's accusations in the process — but somehow that didn't seem to matter. He had always heard that New Mexico boasted a healthy climate. Maybe with time and luck, it could also cure an ailment of the heart.

Epilogue

James Kinealy and Jack McGuinn were apprehended by police detectives at the riverboat landing in Omaha that night and returned to Chicago. Neither man was ever sure if they had been betrayed by Sterling Packard or Janice Kinealy, or both. Twelve days later a grand jury indicted them on a charge of burglary. Insufficient evidence was found to try them for extortion, since no direct link could be found between the ransom demands and the defendants.

Three weeks after these indictments, a suspicious bank president in Río de Janeiro alerted police when an American, identifying himself as Benjamin Boyd, tried to convert two hundred thousand dollars in crisp U.S. currency into gold. He was detained for questioning by Brazilian authorities who later returned him to the United States as an escaped criminal. Based on Janice Kinealy's telegram, a search party was dispatched from Springfield to recover Lincoln's body. The lead coffin was located a few days later under a collapsed dirt bank near the Hanrahan mansion. After verification of its contents, the coffin was crated and shipped, under armed escort back to Springfield for reinterment in its mausoleum.

Kinealy and McGuinn were brought to trial before a jury in May, 1877. Both were found guilty, based mainly on the testimony of Boston Corbett, the revelers at Kinealy's saloon, and Louis Griffin, the Wells Fargo express messenger, all of whom had seen Kinealy and McGuinn in possession of the lead coffin identified as containing the remains of the late President. Additional evidence was the empty cedar casket, found in the back room of Kinealy's saloon. When the issue of their guilt was no longer in doubt, Kinealy, with a touch of professional pride, requested that he be allowed to make a statement for the record so "the newspapers don't get it all screwed up," as he told his attorney. In the process of boasting about how he had planned and pulled off the sensational burglary, he mentioned that he had ordered McGuinn to stay close to Sterling Packard the entire time they were in Oak Ridge Cemetery. Thus it became clear that Packard had had no opportunity to signal the waiting lawmen. Based on this testimony, Elmer Washburn quietly dropped all charges against his former agent.

Kinealy and McGuinn were each sentenced to serve one year at hard labor in the state penitentiary at Joliet. (In 1879, a law was belatedly passed by the Illinois legislature specifically prohibiting the theft of a body from any grave in the state. The penalty for this offense was to be from one to ten years in prison.) Stan Mullins was never heard from again.

Sterling Packard, working in a Santa Fé hotel under an assumed name, followed the trial in a local newspaper. After the verdict, he moved to Las Vegas, New Mexico, resumed using his real name, and took up teaching again, this time as a private tutor. As the months passed, he met and began courting a young widow who lived in the town. Yet, in quiet moments, his thoughts still turned to Janice Kinealy. Where was she? What was she doing?

One hot Sunday in August, 1878 he sat in the shade of his porch, scanning the newspaper. His attention was drawn to a story concerning a severe outbreak of yellow fever that had been raging for several weeks along the lower Mississippi River from New Orleans to Memphis. The more affluent residents were fleeing to cooler, drier areas. But among the more than four thousand who had so far perished in the epidemic were several nurses and doctors. Packard took little notice of their names, but one of the deceased nurses singled out for special heroism in selflessly treating the afflicted was a woman identified as Anna Lee.

About the Author

Tim Champlin, born John Michael Champlin in Fargo, North Dakota, was graduated from Middle Tennessee State University and earned a Master's degree from Peabody College in Nashville, Tennessee. Beginning his career as an author of the Western story with SUMMER OF THE SIOUX in 1982, the American West represents for him "a huge, ever-changing block of space and time in which an individual had more freedom than the average person has today. For those brave, and sometimes desperate souls who ventured West looking for a better life, it must have been an exciting time to be alive." Champlin has achieved a notable stature in being able to capture that time in complex, often exciting, and historically accurate fictional narratives. He is the author of two series of Westerns novels, one concerned with Matt Tierney who comes of age in SUMMER OF THE SIOUX and who begins his professional career as a reporter for the Chicago Times-Herald covering an expeditionary force venturing into the Big Horn country and the Yellowstone, and one with Jay McGraw, a callow youth who is plunged into outlawry at the beginning of COLT LIGHTNING. There are six books in the Matt Tierney series and with DEADLY SEASON a fifth featuring Jay McGraw. In THE LAST CAMPAIGN, Champlin provides a compelling narrative of Geronimo's last days as a renegade leader. SWIFT THUNDER is an exciting and compelling story of the Pony Express. In all of Champlin's stories there are always unconventional plot ingredients, striking historical details, vivid characterizations of the multitude of ethnic and cultural diversity found on the frontier, and narratives rich and original and surprising. His exuberant tapestries include lumber schooners sailing the West Coast, early-day wet-plate photography, daredevils who thrill crowds with gas balloons and the first parachutes, tong wars in San Francisco's Chinatown, Basque sheepherders, and the *Penitentes* of the Southwest, and are always highly entertaining.

The employees of G.K. Hall hope you have enjoyed this Large Print book. All our Large Print titles are designed for easy reading, and all our books are made to last. Other G.K. Hall books are available at your library, through selected bookstores, or directly from us.

For information about titles, please call:

(800) 257-5157

To share your comments, please write:

Publisher
G.K. Hall & Co.
P.O. Box 159
Thorndike, ME 04986